Hannah's Reach

Hannah's Reach

Eileen Snow

in creative collaboration with
Jane Bennion

Bonneville Books
Springville, Utah

Dedicated to, and inspired by

the Dee and Shelie Doman family,
the Wayne and KaLee Harper family,
the Robert and Mary Judd family,
and all the other kind souls who see children
not only as our most important responsibilities
but also as our most precious gifts.

and to Nixzmary.

ISBN 13: 978-1-59955-323-8

Published by Bonneville Books, an imprint of Cedar Fort, Inc., 2373 W. 700 S., Springville, UT, 84663
Distributed by Cedar Fort, Inc., www.cedarfort.com

LIBRARY OF CONGRESS CATALOGING-IN-PUBLICATION DATA

Snow, Eileen.
  Hannah's reach / Eileen H. Snow; in creative collaboration with Jane Bennion.
    p. cm.
  Reprint. Originally published: [New Hope, Ky.] : New Hope Publications, c2007.
  ISBN 978-1-59955-323-8 (alk. paper)
  1. Foster children—Fiction. 2. Executives—Fiction. I. Title.
  PS3619.N675H36 2009
  813'.6--dc22
                              2009015752
Cover design by Jen Boss
Cover design © 2009 by Lyle Mortimer
Edited and typeset by Heidi Doxey

Printed in the United States of America
10 9 8 7 6 5 4 3 2 1
Printed on acid-free paper

Suffer the Children

Eileen Snow (2006)

Suffer the children to come.
Show them all they have inside to give,
That there's a reason why they live
Help them to understand
That they are a part of a plan
Suffer them to come, for of such is the kingdom.

Chorus:
Oh lift them high upon your shoulders
And let them fly on eagle's wings.
Let them soar to get a heavenly view,
For they too are heavenly things.

Suffer the children to stay
Innocent and pure as they come to earth
Untouched and holy as the day of their birth.
With heavenly light in their eyes
Strangers to guile and to lies
Suffer them to stay, for this is their Father's Way

(Repeat chorus)

Take the ragged; make them whole.
Replace the trust that someone stole.
A life that's shattered, love makes new
And lets the face of God shine through.

Suffer the children who hurt.
Bring them to my wounded feet to kneel
And I their wounded hearts will heal.
Give them a place that is safe and warm,
With a loving face and an open arm.
Suffer them to come for of such is my kingdom.
Oh lift them high, let them soar and fly . . .
With you in my kingdom.

Preface

First and foremost, this is a work of fiction, a parable. The characters and events are fictional, maybe even fanciful. And though I don't mean this story to be an example of exactly *how* God works in our lives, it is my statement of faith that He does, in His own time and His own way, despite the detours of agency. He who notices sparrows and clothes all the lilies in gold, knows our heartaches, has shared all the injustices we've endured, and will somehow, through the power of the infinite Atonement, make it right. Somehow, someday, in this life or in the next, He will make it right. Only He can.

Prologue

The twine of highway known as I-95 unwound to the south, warming only slightly with each passing state line. Carlos slept soundly, occasionally snoring and twitching. Patti drove on and on, stopping now and then for gas and some snacks for her *angelita Linda*, the baby in the backseat. Linda means lovely and this little girl certainly was that. Patti could feel herself becoming fonder of her with every passing moment. For most of the last three days, Linda had been very little trouble. Why shouldn't they keep her? Maybe that would be the *right* thing to do. Carlos couldn't be serious about letting that man . . . that beast . . . do anything to her, could he?

With all this cash, Patti thought, *Carlos could stop dealing and they could live decently, downright respectably, like other people. He wouldn't need to do anything else for more money to live on.* In her young mind, she'd already built and moved into the cozy blue house in the quiet suburban neighborhood where they could settle down. They could get married and be a real family.

"We could have another kid or two of our own and one of those big yellow dogs and a yard with a barbecue and everything," she whispered to Carlos as he dreamed. "We could have a life, Carlito, a real life." She was pleading now.

Patti fought with herself for the next several hours. It all played out in vivid scenarios in her mind: her dream of having a family, Margarita's desperate plea, what was best for the baby. And maybe keeping her would make them stop the drugs. Maybe they just needed a good reason to get clean, and maybe this was as good a reason as they would ever find. "We can do this . . . we can," she rationalized.

Suddenly she realized that while she'd been driving and daydreaming,

1

she had been unconsciously smoking a joint.

"Who am I kidding?" she said aloud. As she looked at Carlos, sprawled across the passenger seat, smelling of beer and sleeper's breath, Patti's heart sank. Her eyes then focused on the dried blood smeared on the door handle, and she saw things in the stark light of reality. Carlos was too far gone and too strong for her to fight. Too strong for her to change. She had witnessed a horrible and tragic scene brought on by Carlos and his dealing. Though he'd never hit her, he had threatened her with a beating several times when he was stoned. She could only imagine what an out-of-control, drug-crazed Carlos could do to a helpless little child.

"I can keep Linda safe," Patti had vowed to Margarita. "I promise she'll be okay."

Now it was all clear. Carlos had set a life-altering course that night: this *unwanted* child was going to bring big bucks. He'd break the promise to Margarita. Soon, this money would be gone, up his nose, down his throat, or into his veins. He would be looking for more quick cash and Linda would be the way to get it. When this scam ran dry, he'd sell her to the highest bidder without a thought. Then he would look to Patti. Make her do things for his (or her) next fix. She'd be as expendable as Linda. And just as lost.

Her fragile vision of another kind of future was shattered. The idyllic family portrait dissolved and trickled away as tears ran down her cheek. A thread of smoke from the ashtray caught her eye and tickled her nose with the pungent, magnetic scent of escape. Gulping back a heart-wrenching moan, she reached for the joint and inhaled defeat. She looked back at Linda and heaved a long smoke-filled sigh of genuine sadness and regret.

As the sun slid west, Patti's mood went from hopelessness to despair. Although she had about given up on herself, she searched for a way to save the tiny girl in the backseat. "Please, God," she prayed. "Please help me."

Later, at dusk, somewhere in North Carolina, the sky burned with brilliant color. At that moment, an exit ramp touted a "Scenic Overlook" sign.

With hardly a thought, Patti steered the car onto the turnout and stopped. An awe-inspiring panorama burst into view. The sight was a spectacular, fiery sunset igniting a crimson glow on endless rolling hills of snow-dusted evergreen trees. She reached behind the seat for the well-worn Nikon camera she carried everywhere, put the strap around her neck, and got out to take the shot.

Photography was the one thing that she'd shared with her father; his nickname for her was "shutterbug." Under his guidance she'd learned about cameras and film; he'd even set her up with her own little dark room. As she tried to capture the splendor of the setting sun, her eyes fell upon the answer to her prayers.

There, in the valley below and nestled among the trees, was a beautiful little Catholic church surrounded by a number of tidy buildings Patti recognized as a convent community.

She got back in the car, drove as smoothly and quietly as she could on a dirt road, down to the nearly hidden church below, and then parked behind some trees. Carlos didn't even stir as she slipped out, tiptoed to the doors and peeked inside the vestibule. There seemed to be no one around at all, and Patti wondered if they had run out of people to be nuns and had left the place abandoned. It was so silent that she jumped when the organ sounded and the sisters in the sanctuary began to sing. She stood for a moment and listened to "Angels We Have Heard on High." Patti thought the nuns sounded like the heavenly choir must have when Jesus was born. Beautiful, joyful, and yet peaceful. It was their Christmas mass.

When Patti returned to the car, Linda was playing happily with the stuffed dog that Patti had bought her at a truck stop. Her man was snoring, obviously sound asleep. Patti opened the back door and released the belts that fastened the infant seat to the car. She lifted it, with Linda still strapped in, out onto the trunk lid. She also removed a baby blanket and the diaper bag. From under the front seat, she took some of the rubber-banded bundles of cash. There were stacks of tens, twenties, fifties and hundreds, nearly sixty-five thousand dollars. She quickly counted out $10,000 in one-hundred-dollar bill stacks and tucked them into the Minnie Mouse bag. *This could help care for Linda and other children too. It's her money, really.*

"You deserve more than this, my love, but you understand that this is the best thing, don't you? Carlos and me, we're no good for you. But I wish that I could keep you; I know that I could love you. I wish we could be a family. I'm just afraid of what kind of life you'd have with us. Not good, my darling. But someone will love you and take care of you, and everything will be wonderful real soon. Real soon, sweetie," Patti murmured.

She took some baby wipes from the bag and wiped down the car seat, the bag, and even the money in the small stack.

Inside the bag was a picture of poor, beautiful Margarita. She had given it to Patti a few months before. Patti now wrote on it, "Por mi angelita Linda, con amor, Mami. I will be with you always." Then she took the cross pendant with the daisy on it from her own neck and wrapped the chain around the photo, cleaning it off as best she could. She closed up the bag and put the strap over her other shoulder. With two wipes in her hands, she lifted the car seat from the trunk and crept behind the trees toward the church. She carefully scouted the area but saw no one. From inside, Patti heard the hum of the nuns chanting the Lord's Prayer and recited along from distant childhood memory.

"I'm trying to deliver you from evil, my little love," Patti said.

She placed the child, still strapped in the carrier, along with the diaper bag, just inside the vestibule near the Holy Water. She pulled out her camera, turned on the flash and quickly yet skillfully snapped a couple of photos.

"These are to remember you by."

At the instant that Patti took the photos, Linda raised her little arms, begging to be picked up, to be held, pleading to be loved. The image was stored in the camera and locked in Patti's memory. That perfect milk-chocolate complexion, adorable baby-teeth smile, and the heartbreaking longing in those beautiful eyes were etched in her mind permanently. Linda's chubby little hands held Patti's face as she kissed the child's forehead in farewell.

Patti couldn't stop the tears as she crouched low and crept silently away. She had almost reached the car when she heard the nuns begin to sing "Away in a Manger." The child too began to cry.

She had to flee as far from here as she possibly could. Patti knew that when Carlos finally woke from his long winter's nap, there would be the devil to pay. "She's my blood! I decide what happens to her. I'm the man," he'd holler. He would be furious. Not for leaving the child so much as leaving the money and his easy ticket to so much more. "Adios, mi Linda," she whispered. "God be with you."

Chapter One

The snowflakes floated like lacy fairies in the Manhattan air. The bitter cold was somehow lessened by the warmth of Christmas all around. Strings of white twinkle lights glittered everywhere, and strains of carols and the bells of Salvation Army ringers could be heard floating on the cold but gentle wind. The store windows invited each passerby into a holiday fantasy land, and some stood mesmerized, unable to simply walk on and miss the magic.

Olivia Thomas, an exotic African-American young woman of 29, could easily walk on, and she smiled to herself as she hurried home to her apartment on West 83rd Street. She did not smile in response to the spirit around her; instead, hers was an almost mocking smile. Livy was an executive in a toy company, and the Christmas season always represented the culmination of months and months of work and preparation that usually paid off handsomely in a large fourth-quarter bonus. Many of these haggard shoppers were helping to swell that bonus, and she knew that she should really be thanking them, not judging them.

But she really didn't get it. Every year she would see the quarterly reports and the actual numbers of dollars spent on the toys and games for her company and other gift companies and was amazed. She observed all the foods and wines and holiday apparel and all the useless gifts of every variety. Who in the world would really want a fruitcake—or worse, a Chia Pet? Heaven forbid. It was as if there was some kind of Yuletide gas in the air, and Livy was the only one with a protective mask. On they went—these robots of Christmas—must buy, must give, must spend, must eat, and must rush. *On and on it goes, and how my bonus grows.* And so, shaking her head, Livy smiled to herself.

Earlier in the season—the day after Thanksgiving, to be exact—she had felt just a touch of what she thought Christmas spirit might feel like. Her boss had given her the dreaded PR assignment of delivering some of the company toys to kids in some kind of interim care shelter. A couple of photographers and an in-house reporter had tagged along. It felt less than genuine, very contrived. *JOY'S TOYS cares and we have pictures to prove it.* Photos of the event were immediately published in the *New York Post* in what looked like an article but was really paid advertising.

The shelter was for kids between foster situations or those recently removed from their homes and waiting to be assigned to foster families for the first time. A few teens were there on their way to juvenile detention. What did Christmas mean to all of them? Wasn't it just another occasion to keenly feel unwanted, forgotten, unloved, and so different from other "regular" kids? It was uncomfortable, even painful for Livy to be there.

But she played her role and did this part of her job as superbly as she handled the rest of her duties. Dressed in her finest green and red, she sat in an overstuffed chair surrounded by beautifully wrapped packages. Taking a deep breath, she picked up the first one, and read the name on the tag. "This is for Sasha, straight from Santa's workshop! Where is Sasha?"

A little brown-skinned girl who looked barely three shyly came forward. She had wild hair and wore a tattered little romper. She reached for the package and shook it. She wasn't sure what to do with it. Livy realized that she had possibly never received a pretty, wrapped present before.

A young man with Down syndrome, dressed as an elf, appeared from the crowd to help her open it. He seemed a bit too old to be in the shelter, so Livy guessed that he must be a volunteer. She *hoped* he was a volunteer and not just some unfortunate soul who'd wandered in off the street.

The gift was a teddy bear dressed for ballet.

"A dancing bear for a dancing girl!" the elf said.

He lifted Sasha high in the air and made a clumsy little twirl. She gleefully clutched the toy tightly and gave the young man a hug too. He then helped Livy pass out the gifts to the rest of the younger children.

The little ones were completely oblivious to his handicap. Some of the young teens headed for juvenile detention made cracks, but he didn't seem to hear or pay them any attention. His entire focus was on bringing joy to those little ones. They readily climbed onto his lap, gobbling up his affection and friendly laugh like a starving stray devours scraps from anyone who will offer. He was so excited for them, so delighted to help open each package and see what magical item lay waiting inside.

The children got more of their joy and thrill from this elf and the happiness he showed for them, than from the gifts themselves. Livy felt warm inside, like she had just sipped a soothing cup of peppermint tea. There was just the slightest tingle of gooseflesh down her arms, and she felt a lump in her throat.

The handicapped volunteer looked up and caught Livy watching him. He smiled a loving smile and said, "Thank you, toy lady." He walked over and sweetly wrapped his arms around her. She winced and stiffened. Then the young man drew back and looked intensely into her eyes. Suddenly, his expression brightened, and he raised his eyebrows as if he recognized her. "It *is* you. I knew it was you. You're here!"

"You know me?" Livy asked, pulling away. "I don't think so."

He still held onto her hand. "I can *see* you now. You're my friend and Jesus knew you'd come."

"Oh, he did, huh?" she said as she recoiled.

"He loves you. You don't think he does. But he does; I can *see* it. Thank you for everything. Thank you for coming."

He hugged her again, for a long time, and then he happily went back to working his magic with the children and their gifts. Every once in a while, he glanced up and something in his smile stirred a hidden place within her . . . like a distant memory or some vaguely familiar feeling.

It was strange. As a rule, she was not comfortable with children and even less so with the mentally impaired talking about Jesus, but there, on that day, she had felt something warm and sweet and wonderful. *Is this what Christmas is supposed to feel like?* she had wondered. Suddenly, fleetingly, a Christmas that was "strictly business" hadn't been enough, and an old familiar longing for love, for a place at the Christmas table, returned. And one more desperate prayer had escaped her heart without permission.

But that was weeks ago and now, on December 21, that feeling was gone. Thankfully. She was almost home and the holiday season was nearly behind her.

She pulled her coat tighter around her tall, thin frame as the damp

December air chilled her to the very bone. At last she reached the steps of her apartment building. As with most evenings recently, it was the new late-shift doorman, Bryan Kimball, who was on duty.

"Hello, Ms. Thomas," Bryan called out in greeting. "Another late night? I guess this is the season when you'll work the hardest and the latest. You work for a toy company, right?"

"Well, this season is pretty much done as far as my part is concerned. Has been for a long time. We just watch and see how successful we've been about forecasting what kids will want. It looks good so far," Livy explained.

Livy liked Bryan but she wasn't sure why. He didn't fit into the Manhattan scene any more than Dolly Parton belonged at the "Met." He was young, too young for her, but quite tall, blonde, and very nice looking. He had big blue eyes that were childlike and bright, and in them, Livy could see the innocence and trust that she was sure this town would quickly cure him of. He was a nosy little imp, though, and usually she just wanted to avoid him. He always stopped her, wanting to chat and get to know her, always cheerful, but a bit too talkative. And there was something else Livy couldn't put her finger on. She didn't encourage him, but he persisted. Although he was the hick right off the turnip truck, somehow she could not find it in her heart to dismiss him as she did the Christmas shoppers.

"So why so late? It's nearly ten, and if this Christmas is done, then why—?" Bryan began, partly blocking the door.

"Because I'm working hard to come up with some great idea for next year's hit toy or game or collectible—something that will really take hold. These things take months of planning and designing and marketing. So, Bryan, what are you doing for the holidays? Are you going home to . . . Wyoming, was it?" She kicked the snow off her boots.

"It's Idaho, actually. Blackfoot, Idaho, the potato capital of the world!" He said it with such pride.

"Wow!" Livy inadvertently rolled her eyes and made a move toward the entry.

"I don't know if I'll get the chance to go look in on the folks this year. I have so many things that I'm working on. It would be great though, if I could. How about you? Are you going to visit family for Christmas?"

"I don't have . . . plans. I don't have time for vacation right now." Livy shivered and reached for the door. "But if I did, I think I'd find someone to visit in Florida or Aruba where it's warm!"

"Yeah, Idaho is pretty cold, but I sure would like to see my new little sister. She just . . . Oh duh! It's freezing out here. I'm sorry. You don't want to stand here freezing while I go into my whole family history, do you?"

"Sure I do, Bryan," Livy lied. "It's just that tonight I'm so burned out and exhausted, I just want to go upstairs and crash. You know what I mean? Sometime, though, I want to see the family photos and everything, all right?"

Inside, though, she hoped she would never really have to go through the scrapbooks or the family trip to Disneyland, which she was sure he'd be happy to share. Again she reached for the door, and this time Bryan caught on and opened it for her, as a good doorman should. He even bowed a little.

"Oh! Speaking of photos," he said as he ushered her inside, "you got some mail." He fished the card from his inside coat pocket. "It got put in someone else's box by mistake, so they asked me to get it to you. Here."

He gave her a holiday postcard with a picture of an attractive young couple in a Christmas setting. The pretty wife was obviously pregnant, and from the expressions on their faces, one could see they were very pleased about it. Livy wasn't so pleased.

"Thanks," Livy said, a little annoyed that Bryan was looking over her shoulder trying to read the card.

"Who are they?" he asked.

"It's from Julie, my college roommate, and her husband, Kevin. They got married last year and against their better judgment, and mine, I might add, they went ahead and got going on a family. They could at least let the dust settle and the wedding cake get stale before they decided to have a baby."

The card read,

> There once was a family called Keatings
> Who loved sending holiday greetings.
> Hope your Christmas is swell . . .
> Ours is, can you tell?
> You can tell just how much I've been eating!

Underneath was a handwritten note.

Hey Liv!

What are you up to? I haven't heard from you in about a year and I miss you. I want your opinion. Do I have that beautiful motherly glow, or am I just a fat and ugly whale? Kevin gave the right answer when I asked him, if only to keep his happy home. What do you say? Baby is coming in March and we're so excited! They think it's a boy. What's new with you, power-lunch woman? Call me, okay?

Love,

Julie

"Good ol' Julie. That'll be a lucky kid who gets you for a Mom. Though you are a ditz sometimes."

Bryan cleared his throat. She got his signal.

"Well, she is. But I like her, and she is probably my best friend. I guess I *am* happy for her. But what is it with babies?" she asked, shaking her head.

"What do you mean? What about babies?" Bryan asked.

"I mean they poop, they cry, they smell, they soon get into everything, they are very expensive and very time consuming. Who wants to mess with all that? What do the parents get out of the deal? They are so much work and yet some people are crazy about them."

"That's *why* people are crazy about them. You have to invest so much time and love and effort and, yes, money into them, and you can't expect anything in return."

"Sounds great so far," Livy said.

"But people *want to be needed,* and that's what being a parent is about, being needed and being able to give," Bryan said.

He sounded a little canned and probably had no idea what he was talking about. Surely, he wasn't speaking from experience as a father. So he obviously came from a pie-in-the sky, small-town family.

"It's like this Christmas nonsense. It seems like the more work and money and time that go into it, the more people like it. I don't get it. Seems like a lot more stress than fun!" Livy said.

"Christmas is like that to some degree, sure. But sometimes people just get caught up in the wrong things, and they stress out. Don't you like Christmas either?"

"It's not that I don't like it. I've just never understood what all the fuss was about. I don't have a lot of good Christmasy Santa Claus memories and I'm not religious—" She shrugged.

"You believe in God, don't you?"

Livy sighed in exasperation and replied, "Sometimes I do, sometimes I don't know. We have this works-both-ways relationship, God and I. He doesn't seem to know that I'm alive, and I don't know if He's alive. That's fair, isn't it?"

"He knows."

"Oh boy. Not another one. Let's not talk about it, okay?" She definitely did not want to be up half the night listening to the Gospel according to Bryan. "Listen, I really am beat. I need to get to bed. So . . . uh . . . good night, Bryan." She was already at the elevator.

"Okay. Good night, Ms. Thomas," he called out.

"Good night, Bryan, and stop calling me Ms. Thomas. It makes me feel like your crabby old third grade teacher. Call me Livy. We see each other practically every night. Call me Livy, okay?

"Great! Good night, Livy."

"Good night!"

Chapter Two

There was no escaping it. Christmas arrived a few days later. Livy lay in bed, watching the dirty scarlet sun squeeze its way into the sky between the buildings of the Manhattan skyline. She imagined all the hyper kids in those high-rise apartment buildings, waking long before dawn, anxiously cajoling their parents into getting up and getting the Christmas mayhem started. She remembered mornings like that . . . well, sort of. She tried to go back to sleep but couldn't. She was looking at the clock when someone knocked at her door. Who would be knocking on her door at dawn on Christmas morning, for Pete's sake?

She threw on her ratty robe and went to the door. The knocking was insistent and incessant—maybe there was a fire. She looked through the peephole and saw that it was Bryan. It took a moment to recognize the face since he was out of uniform and dressed for an arctic climate. Suddenly his giant eye met hers at the tiny window.

"I see you in there. Open up! It's Christmas morning! 'Jolly old St. Nicholas, lean your ear this way. . . .' " He had started singing loudly and continued the tune with his own words, "Open up and let me in, don't say 'go away.' "

Livy quickly threw open the door, pulled him inside, and slammed it behind him. "Stop that! The neighbors will complain and you'll get fired. Maybe they'll throw me out with you too."

"They have kids next door; they're up laughing and playing. So, Merry Christmas, Ms. Thomas! Oops! I mean Livy!" He surveyed the room. "Nice! But I knew you wouldn't have one."

He pulled a tiny Christmas tree from behind his back and ran over to set it up in front of the nine-foot-tall window overlooking the city. After plugging it in, he stepped back and admired it. All of eighteen inches high, the tree was totally dwarfed by the majesty of the view. Still, he smiled and said, "Perfect!"

He ran out the door and came back with a loaded black trash bag in his arms.

Livy stood there in shock.

"There are probably three hundred apartments in this building. Why me? I don't know what to say."

"I'll tell you what to say," he said as he took off his coat. "You say, 'Merry Christmas, Bryan.' It's just that I'm homesick and I wanted to spend Christmas with someone. And you said you didn't have plans, so. . . ."

"All right, Merry Christmas, Bryan. This is all so sweet, but I don't have anything for you, and it's embarrassing."

"Yes, you do have something for me. Just let me come and have Christmas morning with you, okay? That's all I need. I don't like the thought of being alone on Christmas, do you?"

"It must be déjà vu. I think I spent Christmas morning with Mr. Potato Head when I was about eight."

"Now, no Idaho jokes. Are we going to have Christmas or not?" He whined like a little kid begging for a new toy.

"Bryan, I don't know you that well, and honestly, I feel a little awkward."

"I'm sorry. I should have warned you. But let's just have Christmas morning. No strings attached. I have gifts and food. Please?"

She sighed in defeat. "Okay. Show me how it's done."

And he did. He excitedly opened his Santa sack and laid out four presents around the tree in order of largest to smallest. Then he stood back and waited for her to go for one of them. As she reached for the biggest one, he stopped her.

"Nope, not yet. Mom says everybody has to have a cup of cocoa and a cinnamon roll before we open anything. It keeps us from getting light-headed from all the excitement and not having anything in our stomachs."

With a gleeful grin, Bryan ran out into the hall and produced a cardboard box containing cocoa and cinnamon rolls he had purchased from a vendor down the block. "Here you are, my dear. It'll warm the cockles of your . . . wherever your cockles are."

Livy took a sip of the cocoa and a bite of the delicious cinnamon Danish. "Mmm. This is just what I need." She gobbled down several morsels. The treat was a guilty pleasure she had not allowed herself in some time.

"Okay. Now that I have my strength for the day, can I open one?"

Bryan shook his head teasingly. "Nope, not yet. This is when Dad would always stop us and say, 'You can't open anything until I get the video camera set up. Just hold your horses, kids.' And the anticipation was terrible! But it was awesome too. It made the moment last a little longer! I don't actually have a video camera with me, but I wanted you to feel that heightened anticipation. Did it work? Are you excited yet?"

"Yes, I'm excited. Can I open it now?" Livy laughed.

"Nope, not yet. You have to sit down and I have to play Santa Claus and bring it to you." He sat her down on the couch. "Now, which one?"

"The big one, of course."

"Are you sure?"

"Yes." Livy laughed. "I'm sure. And if you make me wait again I'm going to throw you out of here!"

She had picked the box that was about the size of a one foot cube. She was starting to tear away the wrapping when she noticed that he was glaring at her.

"What? What now?"

He shrugged and said, "Oh, nothing. It's just that it's customary to shake it first. And then you have to sort of guess what it is."

She shook it, and it rattled and thudded like there were rocks in it, hitting something.

"It's a box of rocks. No—I know; it's lumps of coal because I have been very naughty. I know about these things. I'm practically an elf in Santa's workshop, you know."

She had to admit to herself she was enjoying this. She looked at him as if to say "Now?" and he nodded.

She opened it to find a worn box that said, "Deluxe Deep Fryer." She assumed that it had to be just a box he found to put something else in but upon further investigation she found that it really was a used deep-fryer. Surrounding it in the box were about six large potatoes. Livy rarely ate anything fried, let alone deep-fried, and she didn't quite know what to say. Finally, she offered, "Hey. Wow, a deep fryer and some potatoes! Great!"

She was thinking she must have been *really* naughty.

But Bryan was thrilled and exclaimed, "We can make hash browns! Mom always makes deep-fried hash browns on Christmas. Those are real Idaho potatoes, I'll have you know. This is just like home! Thanks, Livy."

"What for?"

"For letting me come and do this with you, of course."

"Well, thank *you*, Bryan. Where did you find this?"

"At the Salvation Army Thrift Store. I hope you don't mind that it's used. But that's what us kids usually do for our Christmas shopping. Only in Blackfoot we have the Deseret Industries and the Idaho Youth Ranch Store. You can always find something for not too much money there, and well, New York is pretty expensive and—"

"No, this is great, really. And very resourceful of you. You'll have to give me your mom's recipe for hash browns. Thank you so much. Do I have to do something now: jump through any hoops or anything before I open another one? Do we need to make the hash browns first?"

"Nope. Just go for it." He was tapping his feet in eagerness.

She started to go for the second gift and then remembered the protocol. After letting him hand it to her very ceremoniously, she shook it and something shifted quietly inside. It wasn't heavy and it wasn't too big.

"It's a stuffed animal?"

"Nope."

She pulled off the paper, and inside the box were a multi-colored, but mostly blue, knitted hat, a scarf, and matching mittens. At first she thought maybe his mother had made them. But no, they had tags on them.

"Thank you, Bryan. I can really use these. You know how cold it can get around here. But I feel so bad about not having anything for you. These are kind of unisex. Maybe you should have these for yourself."

"No, I have some that my mom made and they always do the job. I just haven't noticed you wearing a hat or mittens, and I thought that you needed them. They're still from the thrift store but they aren't used . . . unless someone used them with the tags on them. You'll need them today. It's really cold."

Great. He's watching what I'm wearing and whether I'm cold or not, Livy thought.

"Well, I will use them and will always think of you when I do. Thank you again."

He brought her the third gift, and she could tell by the size and shape that it was obviously a book.

"I don't have to shake this one. I know it's a book."

"Nope."

She tore away the paper and found not one but two books. One was a copy of the New Testament and the other was *The Best Christmas Pageant Ever,* by Barbara Robinson. They were definitely well worn, thrift store merchandise.

"I saw this," he said, holding up the New Testament, "and thought it would be perfect for working on that two-way relationship of yours. And the other was just me being sentimental again. We always do a Christmas pageant at home, and sometimes the church or even the whole town does one. I missed that this year," he said with a sigh.

He got lost in a silent smile for a moment, as if savoring a memory.

"I believe I was in one once, when I was really little. I played some kind of stable animal, I think," Livy recalled. "I remember now. I was a lamb. I messed up my part and spent a good portion of the evening crying about it."

He picked up the little paperback. "Then you'll love this story. It's a hoot. But it has a message too."

"It's a hoot, huh?" she asked with a slightly mocking tone. "I'll read it next Christmas and try to get more in the mood than I was this year."

"And the other book, will you read that too?"

"I'll think about it." Livy took a long sip of her cocoa, hoping he would change the subject.

When she was done, Bryan took the cup, carried it to the kitchen counter, and instructed, "Okay, there's only one gift left, but we have to save it for later. That makes the fun last longer. So, is it all right if I make hash browns and you can make something like eggs to go with them?"

It had been quite a while since Livy had cooked for anyone but herself, and she thought it might be fun. He seemed safe enough for her to let him stay for breakfast.

"Sure, I can make a mean ham, cheese, and onion omelet. How does that sound?"

"It sounds delicious."

Bryan set about grating potatoes and heating up the oil in the deep fryer.

"Here's the super secret recipe: potatoes, oil, salt, and pepper. And then of course, fry sauce." He sang Christmas songs as he worked.

His voice isn't half bad, Livy thought.

She didn't inquire about the fry sauce, as she was sure she'd find out soon enough. For now, she would just go with the flow. The omelet turned out beautifully and she was even able to flip it over without breaking it, a feat she seldom accomplished. Strawberry banana yogurt and orange juice were added to the menu and breakfast was ready, just as Bryan finished a chorus of "Joy to the World." He had set the table nicely and even lit a candle. When she was ready, he walked her around to the far side and pulled out her chair.

Sitting down at his place, Bryan reached for Livy's hand and said, "Do you mind if I say grace?"

She gave him her hand. What was going on here? Was this guy trying to preach to her or flirt with her or what? He was nice, but what was he up to?

"Dear precious Father," Bryan began, "we come before you on this Christmas morning and thank you for all your blessings and wonders. Especially, we thank you for the birth of your Son that we celebrate today. I thank you that Livy and I could spend this Christmas morning together. Please bless her, Dear Lord, with all the good desires of her heart. Thank you for this food and bless it to our good. In Jesus' name we pray, amen."

"Does that mean that those boiled-in-oil potatoes are good for me now?"

"Better than protein shakes and wheat germ," he said, taking the catsup bottle and emptying a good portion of it onto a saucer. Bryan then stirred in a tablespoon or two of mayonnaise. "Hark! We have fry sauce."

He smeared it all over his potatoes and on her precious omelet and looked up just in time to see her grimace. "It's a western thing, I guess."

After finishing breakfast, Bryan went over to the little pile of presents, picked up the small remaining box, and put it in his pocket. He got the scarf set and brought it to Livy.

"You're going to need these. Where's your coat?"

For the first time since she had opened the door, Livy realized that she hadn't even dressed or combed her hair. *I must look like the bride of Frankenstein.* "I think I need a lot more than my coat. Give me twenty minutes to shower and get presentable before we talk about going out."

She caught a glimpse of herself in the chrome toaster. Her hair was standing out like a true 70's Afro. She was suddenly filled with tremendous gratitude that Bryan had not brought his video camera.

"Why didn't you tell me that I looked like something off a landscape truck? You could have put lights and ornaments on my head!"

Livy quickly started working on a French braid.

"You know, I hardly noticed," Bryan said, laughing. "But that's not a bad idea . . . a little tinsel here, some spray-on snow there. . . . But you can't get dressed. Against the rules. You have to come in your P.J.'s and your robe. And a coat. It's way cold out there."

"No way! Besides, you got dressed. That's not fair."

"Yeah, but I'm the dad here. Mom and Dad go fully dressed, but the kids wear their jammies."

"You're my dad? I'm almost thirty, and you're what, fourteen?"

"Ha ha. It's a Christmas miracle. Don't ask questions."

"And where are we going? Does Christmas morning last all day?"

Bryan's countenance fell and his blue eyes lost their sparkle.

"Do you want me to just go and leave you alone? Aren't you having a good time?"

She considered it for just an instant. It was a little epiphany. "I'm having a wonderful time. This is the best Christmas I've had in years. Of course that's not saying much. I didn't mean I wanted to get rid of you. But what about calling home or other plans you might have? I don't want to keep you. You know what I mean."

"Don't worry, I'll check up on the folks a little later. It just isn't Christmas if we don't do the *widow run*."

Excitement oozed from him again; he sounded like a four-year-old trying to say, "Little one."

"If we don't do the what?"

"The widow run," Bryan said, pronouncing it slowly and clearly.

Livy was imagining a relay you do with elderly people and their walkers or something.

Excitement danced in Bryan's eyes as he explained, "We have several widows near us back home, and on Christmas, after the presents, of course, we take out Great-Grandpa's big old horse-drawn sleigh and go get Mrs. Johnson and Mrs. Webb and Mrs. Bennion, and some others if they aren't with their children, and give them sleigh rides all over the hills between our farm and the Indian Reservation. It's just about the best part of the day. Dad lets them drive the horses sometimes. That Mrs. Johnson is a corker! You should hear her singing carols, if you can call it singing, at the bonfire at Jensen Grove."

The next thing Livy knew, she was stepping out of a cab at Central Park. She wore a parka over her bathrobe as Bryan had insisted. Her quick attempt at a braid had long since fallen out and she felt ridiculous but resigned. Taking her by the elbow, Bryan led her over to a path under a little brick bridge. Underneath was a tiny, elderly woman covered in layers of tattered clothes, happily feeding pigeons. She was cooing at them cheerfully.

"Merry Christmas, Martha," Bryan said.

"Merry Christmas, Bryan." She seemed happy and not at all surprised to see him.

"Did you get to that shelter last night like I told you to?" Bryan asked.

"I did. I'm not stupid, you know. But I'm back here to spend Christmas with my little friends." She gestured at the birds all around her fighting for the crumbs she threw them. Then she nodded at a woman sitting at her right. "And this is Lucille. I've met her at the shelter a few times. Can she come too?"

"Certainly she can come. How do you do, Lucille? I'm Bryan and this is Olivia," Bryan said, extending his hand to the hefty redheaded woman.

She gave Livy the once-over. "Which shelter did you stay at last night, young woman?" She shook her finger in Livy's face. "I hope you had the sense God gave a goose and got into a shelter! You haven't got enough meat on yer bones to keep a cricket warm."

"Oh, I did. Uh . . . thank you," Livy stammered and then turned and gave Bryan a look that could've maimed him for life. He didn't even crack a smile.

"Well ladies, let's go. Are you ready? Oh yeah. I brought you something. Do you like cinnamon rolls?"

"Howard loves them."

"Howard? Is he coming too?" Bryan asked.

Martha grabbed a roll and broke it into little pieces and threw them across the ground for the pigeons.

"Howard's the big bluish one over there. See how he dove for it?"

Soon they were climbing into one of the horse-drawn carriages that paraded around the park. Livy was afraid the driver might complain, but she found out later that Bryan had paid him extra to be accommodating.

It took both men, grunting and holding their breath, to get Lucille up in the cab.

Martha bounded right up with vigor and shouted a hearty "Well, giddy-up!" when she saw everyone was situated.

The driver repeated the command and off they trotted. They sang "Jingle Bells" at the top of their lungs. Martha knew all the words to "Sleigh Ride" and "Winter Wonderland." The rest of them faked their way through, following her lead.

Martha told stories about growing up in a flat above a bakery in New Jersey and how her father's Christmas Stollen Bread was the best in the world. Lucille reminisced about her days as a department store model. She demonstrated how she would strut around the store in the outfits for sale in the Ladies' Better Dresses section.

"I was quite the looker in my day! And in those fancy Christmas gowns? I was a knockout. I had meat on my bones and in all the right places too," she assured them as she winked at Livy.

Bryan told stories of his childhood exploits with his brothers, like how he and Jackson were supposed to hunt down a wild turkey for Christmas dinner. Naming the bird Ralphie was his big mistake. When it came down to the kill, Bryan ran home with Jackson's pellet gun and wouldn't let him shoot the thing. He couldn't kill something that he'd named. Jackson finally caught the poor fowl, knocked him out with a rock and then cut the head off. Bryan refused to eat dinner that day. After that, whenever Jackson wanted more than his share of some meat, he always gave it a name and sure enough, Bryan wouldn't touch it.

"Howard would like you," Martha observed.

The ride lasted about thirty minutes, and Livy was surprised when she found she was sad it was over. Bryan kissed each of the women on the cheek as he said good-bye, and Lucille pulled close to his ear and whispered something. He nodded and replied, "Thank you, Lucille. I sure will do that. Bye now."

On the cab ride home, Livy asked, "What was that about, Bryan? What did Lucille say?"

"She was worried about you. She said, 'Tell her to come find me in the park anytime, I'll make sure she gets plenty to eat and some better clothes. I bet she'd clean up real good looking.' "

"She *obviously* knows where all the best dumpsters are," Livy mumbled under her breath. "Well Bryan, you've taken me from riches to rags today and I hope you're happy. Actually, that was fun."

When the cab stopped, Livy rushed up the stairs to the door of the apartment building, trying to hide her face from anyone passing by. Bryan had to skip steps to keep up with her. "How do you know Martha, anyway?" she asked.

"I met her at the park one day last week and we got to talking. She's been a widow since she was thirty-six. She had one child, a son, and she's lost track of him. I just thought she was a perfect candidate for the widow run and she was open to the idea, so there you are. I don't know Lucille's story. But when you really look at them, they're just people like everyone else." Bryan reached for Livy's hand. "Well, tell me your story, Livy."

She awkwardly dropped his hand and began twisting a lock of her hair. "I told you, I don't have any good Christmas memories to tell. But maybe I do now; I have today. Thank you, Bryan. It's been a wonderful morning. But I still feel bad that I don't have anything for you. It's all been about me. Is there something that you need that I could buy you?"

"I got more than I bargained for already. Just spending Christmas morning with you has meant more to me than you can imagine. I wanted to taste a little bit of home. Like that baby thing again, I guess. I just wanted to be able to give."

"What about Martha and her son? She probably gave and gave and where is he now? Or maybe she threw him out, and he never came back."

"I don't know, but I do know one thing, she still loves him. She was positively radiant when she talked about him as a baby—how smart he was, how cute he was, and how she liked to dress him like the little Dutch Boy. The more she did for him, the more I'm sure she loved him. That's the way it works, and your friend, Julie, will find that out. The more you love and sacrifice, the more you want to give, and the more you give, the more you love."

"Oh Bryan, what do *you* know? I think maybe I could love a cat. But a baby? I have plans for my life and kids aren't in it. Wait a minute. . . . wait a minute! That's it! Bryan, you are brilliant."

"I am? What did I say? How was I so smart?" he replied, genuinely flattered. He pretended to spit on his fingers and proudly brushed back each side of his blonde wavy hair. She grabbed his arm and squeezed it.

"You've given me an idea. A toy that needs you! A toy that demands some work, just like you said. The more they have to do with it and for it, the more they love it. Thank you, Bryan."

She nearly ran to the elevator to get up to her apartment to work on her idea. Then she stopped and turned back to Bryan, who had stayed at the door.

"I'm sorry. I should go while the idea is in my head."

"I really should get going too. I'm supposed to spend the afternoon working with some troubled kids. You know, my internship and all. This is a hard day for them, and that's why I'm here, so . . . thanks again for this morning, Livy. Oh! I almost forgot. I still have your last present." He pulled the small square box from his pocket.

She reluctantly walked back to where he stood. "You've already given me so much. I'm still trying to figure out why you singled me out. You really are too young for me and we don't have much in common. We're not dating. You realize that, don't you? That's not what this is about, right?"

"No, it's you that's way too old for me. But then you saw how I have this thing for old ladies and all. . . ."

She was about to smack him when he handed her the box. Inside, she found a delicate little Nativity set. It was beautiful in its fine detail. Livy studied each piece. Mary's face was especially lovely, though to appreciate it fully, she knew she would need a magnifying glass. A beautiful Baby Jesus was cradled in Mary's arms instead of sleeping in the manger as Livy usually had seen him.

"I've never seen one like it before. It really is beautiful, Bryan. Thank you."

"Will you display it?" he asked hopefully.

"I'm not sure what it will mean, but I'll put it out."

She replaced it in the box, smiled at him and moved toward the elevator. He stopped her and tried to give her a hug, but she pulled away slightly and so instead he took her hand.

"Merry Christmas, Livy."

"Merry Christmas. Thank you. For everything. That was one of the nicest Christmas mornings I ever had. See you later, Bryan."

As the elevator doors closed on his still smiling face, she again felt just the slightest tingle of goose bumps. She also felt a twinge of guilt. *Maybe I should at least invite him up to brainstorm with me or for lunch.* She hit the open button, but when the doors parted he was gone.

Chapter Three

The weeks went by, and Livy worked tirelessly on her new idea, gathering little bits of unsolicited inspiration from Bryan along the way. The more she worked on the project, the more she liked it. What Bryan said was true. The more she gave this baby her all, the more she was hooked. It was a very special doll she had christened Hold-Me-Hannah, and it would have that same effect on the children who would receive one. Hannah would need them, and they would give her all they had. They (or their parents) would buy all the gear, the outfits, strollers, bottles, blankets, and any number of Hannah accessories. It was marketing genius, a gold mine.

By late January she had presented the idea to Mel Jameson, the CEO of JTC. More than a little intrigued, he immediately could see the potential there, but worried about the technology necessary to bring about the prototype. A doll that could actually make facial expressions would indeed be a coup, if it could be done, and Mel pledged his support to get it moving. Existing technologies needed only to be modified slightly to fit the concept. As he promised, he personally took the idea to the engineers in the technology department to see if the thing was possible and used his clout as CEO to give them incentive to *make* it possible.

Livy enjoyed the company of Mr. Jameson. He was an impressive man. He stood about six feet four inches, had gracefully graying dark hair and a strong handsome face, and he wore his authority well. And he, in turn, was impressed with Livy and was approachable to her. She could tell he liked her drive and her no-nonsense approach to business. Plus, in a business setting, she felt attractive and confident, which made a good impression for the company when he sent her on various marketing assignments and conferences. No question, she was valuable to him.

The fact that she was of mixed race showed the company was fair and progressive. Sometimes, she wondered if race might have been a factor in her obtaining promotions and climbing the success ladder faster than others. Some co-workers in her department seemed to resent her, but so what? She worked hard and deserved everything she got.

There was a vice president position opening up that Livy and several colleagues had their eyes on. She felt she was one success away from having that prize within her grasp. In the end, business was politics and as much about appearance as about competence; Livy knew she scored well in both. In the three years she had been with Joy's Toys, Mel Jameson had schooled her in the ways of the company and the business world. He was the key to her overall plan, and with his help, she would go far. With Livy's contributions, Jameson's company would do well too.

Mrs. Joy Jameson was another matter. Joy belied her name. A generally unhappy person, the missus was a bit too thin, in her mid-fifties but looking a bit older, and she dressed in styles more appropriate for women half her age. She was fastidious to the point of obsessive about her spiky red hair, dramatic make-up, and those nails. Livy knew Joy felt threatened by her. In spite of being the namesake of the company, she had earned a college degree in English literature and had wanted nothing to do with the family business that carried her name. It wasn't until after she married Mel, the company's rising star and her father's protégé, that Joy took an interest in the company at all. In the last few years she had insisted on taking a major part in things, and since her father practically left her the position of chairman of the board in his will, she could do just that. Making arbitrary decisions based on emotion and not on business savvy, Joy was out to prove to Mel and the rest of the employees that she was, indeed, in charge. Mel cleaned up after her mistakes and kept the business afloat.

Perhaps she felt Livy was second-guessing some of those decisions, and if the truth were known, she was. Joy terminated some of Livy's projects that had great potential simply out of spite or a need to feel superior. And Livy resented her because of it. Other times, Joy seemed to push some idea that nearly all the executives dismissed as doomed to fail. Last year, it was "Nail Biters—edible fingernails for those who chew." Joy promised they would really take off with kids. She said that if they bit their nails anyway they could at least buy some press-on candy nails that tasted good. Joy pushed the idea as inspiration, while everyone else, including the buying public, thought it was gross. Why didn't she stay home, read stuffy literature and her *Cosmo,* and just get out of the way?

Livy looked around her office and spied a framed blown-up photo of Livy shaking hands with Martha Harrington, senator from New York, and one day, everyone thought, a serious contender for either slot on a national ticket. On display were Livy's diplomas—a BS in marketing from the University of South Florida and an MBA from Wharton School of Business. She leaned back in her large custom-made ergonomically designed chair and imagined herself someday as chair of the board or perhaps, founder of her own international company or, she chuckled at her thought, even part of a national ticket herself. She only half-laughed at her delusions of grandeur because her other half was very serious about her ambition. She studied the framed photo of herself receiving the "Rookie of the Year" award from Mel, a few years back.

I've done everything I've done so far on my own. And with the help and support of someone like Melvin Jameson, there isn't anything that I can't do.

Now mid-February, it was time to present Hold-Me-Hannah to the rest of the executives. Mel had promised to be there to support her and cheer on her project.

"Well, Ms. Olivia, are you ready?" Mel asked as he entered her office just before the presentation. He looked especially excited for the occasion—his hair perfectly in place, his shirt extra crisp, and his smile eager. She was honored by his enthusiasm.

"I think I'm ready. I hope so," Livy replied with a deep breath.

"I've lined up all the gizmo nerds, and they have the technical mockups ready and say the thing is definitely do-able . . . and they'll be there to back you up at the meeting," Mel assured her. "But now the question is, can you sell it? There are some pretty hard cases in there."

"You're the one making me nervous. You're on board with it, aren't you?" Livy asked.

"Absolutely. You know that." Mel smiled and put his arm around her. "I saw genius in you from the start."

Livy gave a nervous glance at the arm on her shoulder, and he removed it casually. "Were they able to work up an approximate price?" she asked.

That was always a sticking point with the profit-margin-minded accountants.

"That is the one thing that concerns me just a little. Without knowing all the details, and I don't even know if they're close, but their rough estimates put it at $250 to $300. It might be a bit pricey for a toy," Mel said.

Livy gathered her large portfolio under her arm, and Mel picked up the rest of her presentation materials. They continued their conversation as they headed for the conference room.

"Well, those video systems are more than that, and do they sell? They do, indeed. And what about the motorized Barbie car? That's in about the same range, I think, and it certainly sells. But that's what we've got these great minds gathered here for. They'll work out all the bugs and make it happen for the right price and the right profit. Right?"

They were at the door, and Livy was suddenly uncharacteristically anxious. She felt as if she were on trial.

"Take a another deep breath. It'll be fine. You'll do great," Mel reassured her.

Most of the executives were already seated, but a few more were still arriving. Marcie Jones was wrapping up a conversation on her cell phone, saving the chair next to her for Bob Farrell and slyly pulling her neckline lower for his benefit. Bob was the top-dog in his division, and Marcie, here just longer than Livy, had hitched her caboose to Bob's accelerating success train. Now both of them felt the pressure of Livy's growing momentum. The two of them worked with Livy in the new products marketing division but usually on different projects.

Bob moved his large frame around the table and sat down in his reserved spot. Marcie filled his ear with some tidbit as she pointed at Livy and Mel entering the room together. Joy was just behind Livy and Mel. Mel let Livy pass through the doorway and waited for his wife. He leaned over to whisper something as she passed, but she avoided it and kept her stare on Livy.

"This had better be good, Mel," Joy warned him.

"It is. You'll see."

Joy walked to her seat at the end of the table, sat down, and folded her arms.

Mel placed the materials in front of the screen and walked up the small podium. He instructed everyone to take a seat and began the meeting.

"This past Christmas season was one of our best in recent years and you are all to be congratulated—especially you, Farrell, with the "Beat Box Boogie" project. The success of that product took us all by surprise. Thank you for all your hard work on that. And to all of you, thank you. The fourth quarter reports have come in, and our shareholders are very happy, and so are we, right, Joy? I know this is corny, but give yourselves a hand."

Marcie commented, "I'd rather just have the bonus."

"Well," Mel responded as he cleared his throat, "the proverbial check is in the mail. Honest. It is."

Then they did break out in applause.

"Everyone's except Jones's, that is. Just kidding. I think you will all be pleased," Mel laughed.

There was a lot of chatter around the room and Mel looked at Livy as if to say, *Here we go!* He held his hands up to signal that he again needed their attention and began his introduction.

"Well, maybe next year your bonuses will be even bigger if your departments can help us make the magic happen again. As you all know, we are in production for the new action figures for that blockbuster coming out near Memorial Day weekend. What's the movie called again?"

"It's *Peter Powerful and the Forces of Oberon*," Matheson offered. He had been heavily involved in landing the movie tie-in. Bob and Marcie would be heading up the project.

The company CFO, Kyle Fitzgerald, who looked more like a balding, freckled, Irish leprechaun than an accountant, piped in, "It's a slam dunk winner. All the kids are reading the book; I know mine are, and I liked it too. Anything derived from it will do very, very well."

"We can always trust Kyle to give us the inside scoop on the childish mind," said Bob, keeping his voice low. Marcie smiled in derisive agreement.

"These action figures will be the most animatronic released so far by us or anyone else. It's a bit of a risk, but we want to be the company that's cutting edge, leading the industry in the technological arena."

"And, continuing along those lines and coming in on the heels of that success will be something we think will be our secret weapon in the toy wars next Christmas season. This little number just might give us our biggest holiday numbers ever. Move over, Hasbro and Mattel! This idea is really the 'brainchild' of Olivia Thomas from the new products marketing division. I'll let her introduce 'Hannah' to you."

Marcie slipped a note covered in doodled hearts and flowers to Bob that read, "Teacher's pet."

Livy stood up and placed her closed portfolio on the easel positioned next to the podium. She smiled and confidently began the most important pitch of her career.

"Thank you, Mr. Jameson. And also, thank you to all the members of the techno team who have joined us today. They have really knocked themselves out to assure us that this little 'baby' is possible.

"You know, just before Christmas I got the news from a friend that she was expecting. She was so excited and you know me, I just kind of wondered, *What's the big deal?* Really, I mean babies require so much of their mothers and others; they exhaust me just thinking about it. But then I thought, maybe that's it! That's why people love them. Babies ask something from them; they make them give, they make the parent indispensable. Everyone needs to feel that way to one degree or another, even little kids. I've also heard it said, on occasion, that babies are cute. Hence . . .

"Ladies and Gentlemen, I give you Hold-Me-Hannah."

The lights went down and the PowerPoint presentation began. A picture of a faceless baby doll appeared on the screen, and a few of those present gasped and some even laughed.

"Hold on, people, don't despair. We will not introduce Hannah to the public quite like this. We'll discuss the little detail of a face later in the presentation. It will be an exciting component, I assure you. But for now, let's talk about what makes Hannah the next Furbee, Tickle-me-Elmo, Playstation 3, or other such Christmas must-have bank-busters.

"She is not like any baby doll we've seen before, although she may incorporate many features seen in various places and products. She may be described as a composite of Betsy Wetsy of decades past, the Disney animatronic figures, and the virtual pets that were so popular in the late nineties." Slides of these items appeared on the screen.

"She is irresistible precisely because she is interactive and requires attention from the child. She pays back big time, too. Her facial expressions will actually change, eliciting certain actions from the child, and the doll will react in turn with more expressions and actions of her own.

The expressions will change according to a pre-programmed cycle but will seem random to the child. This virtual baby will have several modes such as Babble mode, Hungry-and-Feed-Me mode, the Tired-and-Fussy mode, and Sleeping mode. For example, she could be in Fussy mode and cry some 'real' tears, but when the child rocks and comforts her with a lullaby, the doll falls into Sleep mode, triggered by sensors to either motion and/or sound. The baby can be awakened or would eventually wake on her own cycle, sometimes cheerful and babbling, and at other times cranky and hungry. The little mother, or little dad, only has to do what comes naturally to be the perfect parent."

Livy opened her portfolio and displayed some artist conceptions of the different moods and modes of Hannah.

"The feature that I think will be, I don't know, let's say the most popular, will be the Pick-Me-Up feature. Hannah will be in her glory! She'll respond to Mommy by raising her arms, kicking her feet, and giving an expression of eager expectation. When the child picks her up, Hannah breaks forth in giggles of pure delight. In this mode, when little Mommy squeezes her, Hannah's arms squeeze back in a hug, but with more leg kicking. I see her represented as just barely pre-walking age where babies still want to be picked up. She may say a few words and could be taught to say some more, perhaps, something along the lines of the Furbee.

"And Hannah will have a feature that most parents will wish their real child had: an *Off* switch so baby won't bother everyone at the dinner party or in the middle of the night."

Some executives nodded and smiled in agreement.

"So now, we get to the face. As you have seen, the facial expressions of this doll are key and so it has to be just the *right* face, one that with just small adjustments can be an 'everychild,' as it were. It can be changed slightly to be Asian, Black, Hispanic, or White, and yes, of course, a male version of any of the above. So we need the right face and where will we find that perfect face?"

Kyle Fitzgerald immediately jumped up, pulled out his wallet, and let the whole photo album unfold showing his wife and seven children.

"Here," he said. "Take your pick. I have all the fabulous and irresistible faces you'll ever need to choose from."

Livy laughed. "You have stepped right into my trap, Kyle. You exemplify exactly what I have in mind. Most every parent thinks they have the most beautiful kid in the world. Don't they?"

Fitzgerald remained standing, smiling and still exhibiting the photos. "Yes, but the rest of the world is wrong!"

"So, we have a contest. I'm sorry Fitz, you cannot enter your kids—you are an employee. You may want to sit down now."

Disappointed, Fitzgerald sat back down.

"We will ask families all over America, and everywhere else for that matter, to send in photos of their children to be considered for the face of Hannah and her boy counterpart. This will pique their interest in the doll long before it is released and give them a reason to stay tuned for that big day when Hannah takes the stage. The winning family will get some great prizes, and we will take computer images of the child in various expressions to use as models for the doll. All the entries will receive some kind of coupon for a discount on the doll or for a free accessory so their interest remains high.

"We'll hype it up big and before Hannah is even unveiled, she will be a household name and a *given* as far as purchasing is concerned. We will also get a nice big list of families with children to work with in future marketing efforts. Even though it's only February now, all of this needs to happen immediately so everything can be ready for an October or maybe even September release. I want my girls sold out by Thanksgiving! And then we'll unveil the boy."

Bob's hand rose up in a sarcastic gesture. " 'Hold-me-Hannah?' What about the boys? What are you going to call the little wonder, 'Beam-Me-Up-Scotty'?"

Some in the group chuckled.

Marcie said, "Not bad!" and gave Bob a high five. Then she added, "We could always name it in honor of you and your kid, Bob. How about 'Sit-Down-and-Shut-up-Sammy'?" She looked around at the others. "I'm sorry, I couldn't resist."

"How about we name it in honor of your kid and just call it 'Chucky'!" Bob snapped back.

At company get-togethers, Bob's boy had distinguished himself as the hyper-nuisance while Marcie's son was obviously spoiled beyond belief.

"See? I told you," Livy said. "Somebody needs that *Off* switch. But this is no Chucky, I assure you. She's just a sweet, needy baby."

"Needy? Is that what we want?" Jameson asked.

"Oh yes, definitely. She needs a new outfit, she needs a stroller . . . she needs lots of things. See what I—?"

Bob cut her off, loosening his tie and releasing the top button that struggled to contain his sizable neck. "Now I know why you were saying that we have to make the magic happen. This is fantasy land. First of all, can we really do this? *And* can we do it in the time that we have? I doubt it."

Matheson from procurement jumped in with, "I agree with Mr. Jameson. If this is done well and with the contest and everything, we could have a real winner on our hands. But Farrell does have a point. Is this too complicated, too technical, and too expensive? I want it to work and be ready by the Christmas buying season with no delays. We'll have to keep the momentum we build with the contest."

"The gizmo-nerds," Livy started to say, and then cleared her throat, "excuse me, our techno-geniuses say they *can* do it, and they have some prototypes to show you in just a few moments. Patents are being applied for as we speak, and, as you can see, we've already invested some in R&D. It's coming along, but before we go any further, we want to know that all of you, the backbone of this company, are behind the project 100 percent. After you see what they have to show you, I'll need to know we have the full go-ahead and what your different divisions will need to make this happen. Thank you and I'll give the floor to technology. Mr. Howard?"

Before Livy could sit down and Mr. Howard could begin speaking, Mr. Jameson stood up and said, "I think when you have heard what Jeff Howard has to say you will be believers as I have become. I hope you will get on board and support this wholeheartedly. Let's have a round of applause for all the hard work that Olivia has put into this presentation."

The room broke into applause except for Bob, Marcie, and Joy, who all sat with their arms folded.

Howard began his impressive demonstration of Hannah in action and why he thought she would be a major step forward for Joy's Toys. The prototype was already moving, making lifelike giggles and cries, and astounding most of the doubters.

If Livy read things right, she and Hannah were both on their way.

Chapter Four

Who is it this time? Sister Bernadette wondered when she heard the completely out of pitch wail during the singing. *Someone should make decent singing a prerequisite for becoming a nun.*

The elderly woman's hearing wasn't the best, but even she knew something was out of kilter in the sound. After a moment, she realized it wasn't an errant soprano—it was a baby's cry.

She grabbed the sleeve of the also elderly Reverend Mother sitting beside her and whispered, "Do you hear that?"

"Hear what, the singing? I'm not deaf yet, Sister."

"Listen, I think I hear a baby crying."

"A baby?" She listened intently, smiled and said, "I think you're right. We must have company!"

"Another poor unfortunate girl!" Sister Bernadette cried.

"We can't feed the children we have now over at St. Anthony's. We fast and pray for funding, and we get another mouth to feed," the Reverend Mother said.

Searching the hallway for the baby or the poor girl who must have brought it, the sisters found no one. The sound was coming from the vestibule. There, just inside the door and bathed in colorful light from the stained glass window, was a beautiful, but very unhappy baby. Seeing no mother and hoping to find a note, Sister Bernadette searched the diaper bag and nearly fainted when she found $10,000 in crisp one-hundred-dollar bills.

This convent was affiliated with one of the last religious orphanages on the East Coast. State funding was drying up quickly, and this little godsend of cash would see them through the present crisis. The nuns had just finished a three-day period of fasting and prayer.

The baby was assigned to the care of Sister Marian Margaret, a loving nun and teacher, in her mid forties. It was love at first sight for both of them.

The two became quite a pair of M&M's—Marian Margaret and Little Miss Minnie Mouse. According to information also gleaned from the bag left with the little one, her name *might* be Linda. Someone, probably her mother, had written *Angelita Linda* on a photo. It could mean pretty little angel or little angel Linda. They went with the name but the nun always called her Minnie. When Linda learned to talk, she called her nun, Sister M&M, and eventually just Sister M.

She got along well with the other children there and was quick to learn. She learned to read, to run, to dance, and to sing. All in all, she was a happy child. Now and again, a child would be adopted from the orphanage. And sometimes Linda began to wonder when her mom and dad would come and take her home. She wasn't anxious about it because she was happy with Sister M and the world she had come to know. She just wondered.

"Sister M, what does *eligible* mean?" she would ask.

It was just after Christmas of her sixth year when Linda's life abruptly changed again. Her deeply loving bond with Sister M was broken.

A judge somewhere, who had never met Linda, decided that although she had been abandoned at a religious institution, there was no proof that a parent was voicing a desire for her to be raised in any particular religious setting. She was now to be taken into state-run foster care. The same applied to several other children at St. Anthony's Orphanage and School for Needy Children. Though no one said anything, everyone at St. Anthony's knew that the orphanage would not survive this change.

In Linda's case, there was also the matter of her father's rights. It had been assumed when she was abandoned, since the child had a picture of someone who was most likely her mother, that the mother had given up all rights. There was no indication of the father's wishes or whereabouts and, therefore, the child was determined not to be free for adoption until at least a token search for the identity of the father had been conducted. After six years, that detail still had not been completely settled.

Sister M tried to remain cheerful as she helped little Linda pack her Minnie Mouse bag. She checked her neck. "Do you still have your little daisy-cross on? Okay, don't ever lose that." She took an undershirt and gently wrapped Linda's now framed picture of Mommy in it and tucked it inside the bag. "Don't worry. It will be like having a real family, my little darling. You'll have a mommy and a daddy and maybe brothers and sisters too."

"But I won't have you. I want to be with you. I don't want somebody else's mommy and daddy. I want you."

Linda buried herself into the folds of the sister's habit.

"I know, Minnie Linda. I know. I want to be with you too."

She held her close and then gently pushed away to memorize her face. The nun smoothed her curls from her forehead and said, "There are just some things that happen that we can't help. You can send me pictures that you draw and write me letters. Will you do that?"

Sister M could hardly finish the question for the lump in her throat. She couldn't love Linda more if she were her own.

A stern looking woman in gray hair and a gray suit had appeared in the dormitory doorway, watching the farewell scene unfold.

"We don't encourage that type of thing, Sister. It just hampers the child's ability to make new connections. It's better if she just makes a clean break. What's the child's name? This is Linda, am I right?"

The child answered, "I am Minnie, and I don't want to go." She turned back to Sister M. "Why do I have to go?"

"Promise me you'll try your best to be happy," Sister M said, blowing a kiss.

She gulped down the knot in her throat and nodded. Her eyes were wet and solemn.

The woman took Linda's bag and her hand and, without another word to the nun, she marched Linda down the hall. Linda turned to see Sister Marian crying and waving good-bye.

"We have a great big van downstairs. It will take you and the other children to the city. Have you been to the city before?" the woman asked her.

Remembering her promise, Linda took a deep breath and tried to answer cheerfully. "Once I went to the zoo. Is that the city? It didn't smell so good in the zoo."

"I promise the whole city does not smell like the zoo. You will get to meet your new family this afternoon. How does that sound?"

Her first family was really just a temporary waystation while the children's welfare people looked for a more permanent placement. She went to three such families, for just days at a time, and spent two nights in a respite care facility.

Then she went to the Sheila and Eric Jones household in Raleigh for about six months. Mrs. Jones was nice and Mr. Jones was almost never home. When Mrs. Jones found out that she was pregnant, she decided that she had better put her time and attention toward preparing for the birth of her own child.

Tina Winston took her in for about seven weeks. Ms. Winston was a single mother of five children and shortly found out that six was indeed beyond her limit, emotionally and financially. She called the children's services department to come and pick Linda up . . . two days before Christmas. Even though she kept Linda's state money, she said there was not enough to go around.

"I'm sure you can find some nice place for her for the holidays," the woman said.

The stay in the interim home did little in the way of celebration, and nothing for Linda's lonely little heart.

After the New Year, Linda was assigned a new caseworker, Stephanie Clancy. New to the system, Mrs. Clancy took Linda's case to heart and found her a home that looked very promising. She said that she was going to a couple's home where she might very likely be adopted, when the state was able to make her eligible. The young foster mom had found out from her doctor that she wouldn't be able to have children of her own, and she was interested in adoption. They were a mixed-race couple, and it would seem natural for them to have a brown child like Linda.

Already, Linda was learning to be careful about trusting people, especially those who seemed overly kind to begin with, and she held back quite a while before letting herself hope that she had found a real home with these people—Karena and Rick Marshall.

Over time, Linda couldn't help herself. She was bonding with Karena in ways that she hadn't with the other short-term "moms." Karena and Linda seemed to have similar senses of humor and laughed at things Rick just didn't find amusing at all. Because he was a marine, and had that "inspection mentality," Karena kept a house that was immaculate. Linda learned that she, herself, was tending to be somewhat of a neatnik and she felt at home in the orderly environment. Some of her previous homes were less than tidy and that added to her discomfort in those situations. When she and Karena went into town to go shopping, sometimes Linda felt like she was Karena's doll and that Karena was playing dress-up with her. When Rick was away, they'd indulge themselves in girls' nights out, going shopping or to a chick-flick, followed by doing each other's hair and nails.

Karena watched as Linda grew more confident and more comfortable. Looking better made her feel better, and she grew more outgoing socially. A girl from her second-grade music class, Daphne, was becoming Linda's new best friend. They shared whispered secrets and laughed at all the boys in class. The two girls were inseparable at school. At the Marshall home, they made up dances and sang into hairbrushes and made their own music video with Daddy Rick acting as cameraman. For her three-month anniversary of being in this home, Linda had a sleepover with Daphne. They ate pizza and watched a scary movie on TV and then could hardly go to sleep because of it.

Karena had read the file and knew that Linda had had a difficult time adjusting at her last two temporary homes. She was pleased that Linda seemed to be becoming a real kid, a normal kid. Most everything seemed to be going so well until lately, when she had begun to withdraw from Rick and Karena just a little. Karena wondered if it was because she was thinking that at any time she might be sent away. That was the last thing that Karena wanted. She had found a match—a little girl made just for them. She called Mrs. Clancy, the social worker, to come over and discuss the future of their arrangement.

Karena was told that Linda was now free to be adopted and that only some last legal hurdles needed to be cleared, and of course a final home inspection would have to take place in order to make them a *real* family.

Gleaming and inviting, like something out of *Better Homes and Gardens,* the house awaited final approval. Karena and Linda had scrubbed and straightened, polished and primped. Ready or not, the appointed time was here, and Linda was sure that at last she had found a place to belong.

Sending Linda upstairs to dress in her new outfit, bought especially for this occasion, Karena thought of one more detail that she had better see to. Mr. Marine was a gun buff and had a chest where he kept some of his prized weapons. If the social workers were to find those weapons unsecured, it would probably ruin any chances for approval. She knew she had better make sure the chest was safely locked.

It must have been inspiration. As she was digging in the back of the closet of Rick's den, she found the chest open, with the lock lying on the floor beside it. She was so glad she had thought to check it . . . so glad until she looked inside. She didn't just find three German pistols and a semi-automatic rifle—she found stacks and stacks of pornography.

She tried to put her best spin on the situation by rationalizing, *Well, he's a Marine, and a macho kind of guy; you have to expect a certain amount of—*

Then her world and her dreams of a family with little Linda came to a screeching halt. It was child porn. She rummaged through piles of horrific pictures. There were movies, magazines, and loose photos. Under several magazines lay the most damning evidence of all. Some of the pictures were of neighborhood children that she recognized as being shot literally in her own backyard. Obviously, Rick had to have taken the pictures. Who knew what else he had planned or what else he had done? She could only pray that Linda had not been part of this. *Not my Linda! Not my Rick! This cannot be happening!*

Karena couldn't breathe. She couldn't think. How could she breathe or think or go on when her heart had been so thoroughly broken? Suddenly the doorbell was ringing, and she heard Linda's happy greeting.

"Mrs. Clancy, we're all ready! Do you like my new capris? Mommy Karena bought them for me."

Karena knew she couldn't let her stay and be part of this hideousness. But she had not yet come to the point where she was ready to turn Rick over to authorities, either. He would go to jail. If she confronted him, perhaps she could help him turn away from this evil addiction. Losing them both would be more than she could handle. But one thing was sure: Linda, darling Linda, could not stay in that house. The worst of it was that Karena couldn't tell her why. Naturally, Linda would tell one of the counselors and they would come and take not just Linda away, but Rick too. Linda would never understand that this heartbreaking disappointment was for her own good.

Despite her weak knees and brimming eyes, Karena made it down the stairs and into the living room. "Linda, honey, run to the kitchen and get the pitcher of lemonade I made and a glass for Mrs. Clancy."

She skipped cheerfully to the kitchen. Karena knew she wouldn't be able to bear the hurt in Linda's face when she told the social worker they couldn't adopt Linda after all.

"What's wrong, Mrs. Marshall? Are you quite well?" Mrs. Clancy asked, noticing her troubled state.

Karena's voice shook. "You know, Mrs. Clancy, I'm so sorry to tell you this, but I don't think we are ready to go ahead with the adoption after all."

She was twisting her skirt into a knot.

"What? After everything we did to expedite it? I thought it was all settled." Mrs. Clancy was clearly angered and baffled by this turn of events.

"As you can probably tell, I'm very upset about coming to this realization right now, of all times, but Linda needs to find another family to adopt her. It's just not the right move for us at this point."

She heard a crash and turned to find Linda standing in the doorway over the broken pitcher she had just dropped. She had heard.

She ran over and fell at Karena's feet. "Why, Mommy Karena? Why? I want to stay with you!" Karena just stared painfully at the ceiling, the tears now flowing. She did all she could to avoid looking at Linda's face, unable to bear seeing the hurt she was causing.

"Has she done something to make you abruptly change your mind like this?" Mrs. Clancy asked.

"No, no. It isn't her. She's been an angel, and I would love to keep her, but I realize that Rick is not ready, and our marriage is in serious trouble. I can't force this on him if he's not ready."

She finally turned to face her would-be daughter.

"Linda, please understand that I wanted more than anything to be your mommy, but I just can't. We just can't."

"Why, Mommy Karena? Why? Did I do something bad? Please tell me, and I won't do it ever again. Please tell me, what did I do?" Linda pleaded, clutching Karena's knee.

She dropped down to Linda's eye level and embraced her fiercely. "You didn't do anything wrong, I want you to know that. I love you and want to have you here with us, but I can't. I just can't."

Once again, Linda packed up her Minnie Mouse bag, her doll, her picture, and her cross pendant, and set out to face the world alone. Quietly sitting in the backseat of Mrs. Clancy's car, she felt a jumble of emotions: overwhelming sadness, confusion, and fear of what would happen to her next.

She made me go away. I must be very, very bad.

Chapter Five

Mel and Livy waited in his office until after quitting time on the day that each department was supposed to give its verdict, yea or nay, on the Hold-Me-Hannah project. By about 5:40, the results started coming in. By 6:30, it was a done deal. Most of the emails were overwhelmingly positive, and there were just a couple who weren't enthusiastic, but wouldn't stand in the way. Joy didn't weigh in. She and her husband had held their debate at home, and he had won, at least *this* round.

After they had read all the emails from the different departments, Mel exclaimed, "Congratulations, Livy! You did it!"

"Yes!" Livy threw both fists into the air in a gesture of victory. "Yes! Yes! Oh Yes! Houston, we have ignition!"

"This is going to be great! But don't use that space analogy; it makes me nervous. This better not crash and burn on liftoff. It's a lot of responsibility on your shoulders, you know. But whatever you need to make it happen, you just let me know."

"This will make it and make it big! Thank you, Mr. Jameson. Thank you for everything!"

She almost lost it. She wanted so badly to just hug him! But he was the boss, so she restrained herself.

"Please call me Mel. And thank you! You did it and deserve the credit. Go home and celebrate with your boyfriend. Open some champagne! Tomorrow's Valentine's Day, you know. Make it special."

She wondered if he was floating a trial balloon to get her to confirm or deny that she had a boyfriend. She wasn't biting.

"Thanks, Mel, that's good advice. I hope your Valentine is okay with all this."

"Don't worry about Joy. She'll be on board as soon as the money starts rolling in. I've assured her that it will."

"All right, the Hannah train has left the station, and I am outta here!"

Livy gathered her purse, her coat, and her briefcase and fairly floated to the elevator. She didn't know she could feel so good.

She got on the subway at her usual station but after only two stops she decided to get off. *I feel like walking. I feel like the queen of the city, and I want to be out about among my subjects!*

She laughed at her ridiculous thought. *I am really getting full of myself, aren't I?*

She got off at a stop that left her about twenty blocks of walking. And it was still winter. However, she was feeling warm from the inside out. She strode unafraid through the partially-lit park. Nothing could touch her tonight. It was her night. Although caught up in her own euphoric feelings, she was more aware of the people around her than usual.

She noticed the lovers snuggling in the cold. She observed the families with children returning from some outing or another. One father carried a sleeping little toddler in his arms, and he kept looking at his daughter like she was the most amazing thing the world had ever known.

She heard that disgusted, angry voice again, echoing from distant memory and spitting out the words, *I'm not your Dad; not anymore. You have no home here!*

She shook it off and reminded herself that tonight she would celebrate—tonight she was queen.

It was after nine when she finally reached the 83rd block. Bryan would be on duty again. He was always the one there after 8 PM. Did she feel like dealing with him right now? He'd want to know all the details and would keep her talking. She just wanted to go upstairs and take a victory bubble bath. Maybe he'd trap someone else into a conversation tonight, and she could sneak by unnoticed. Not likely. He never seemed to even notice the other residents. She still thought maybe he had a crush on her. *He's just too much of a goody-two-shoes country boy for me.*

His radar was on tonight. He spotted her way down the block, and he lit up like a Christmas tree. When she got a little closer, he bounded to the bottom of the stairs and took off his hat. He waved it across his middle as he bowed and said, "Good evening, Ms. Thomas!"

"Hello, Bryan. You haven't called me Ms. Thomas since Christmas, remember?"

"Oh yeah, third grade teacher and all that. I was just trying to be very official. You don't look like my scary old schoolteacher at all, so don't you worry about that. She was no fun and not too attractive because she didn't care to be. That's not you at all."

"Thank you—I think, although I'm often mistaken for a homeless person."

"You are beautiful and you don't even have to try. And I think that you work too much. Here it is after 9 PM, and you are just coming home from the office? Again?"

"Yeah, but tonight I don't mind so much."

"Why is that? You do act like the cougar that ate the cat that ate the canary."

"Well, my Christmas roll-out idea was accepted and is on the fast track for the coming season. It's kind of exciting." She was trying to keep her exhilaration inside, but despite her efforts, it was leaking out.

"Kind of? It's really exciting! What are you going to do to celebrate? Party time? Go out on the town?" Bryan said, caught up in her exciting news while she only shook her head. "Hey! So this has to do with when I was brilliant? The baby doll idea?" he asked.

"That's the one. It was approved!"

"So I'll celebrate with you! I get off in twenty minutes. What do you say?"

Oh boy! Here he goes. "Hey! You're not supposed to hit on the residents. And besides, you are way too young for me," Livy said chidingly.

Actually, she could have entertained the idea of a good-looking younger guy, but she hoped he'd be a little more sophisticated than Bryan.

"I'm not hitting on you . . . just thought that you might like some of my brilliant company."

"Don't think there's anywhere to go cow tipping around here, do ya think?"

"I'll ignore that. You have to celebrate something this good, and I happen to be the only one standing here, so let's go do it."

"You're right. We should do something. But I don't know . . . now don't go getting ideas about you and me. But oh . . . Why not? You did help inspire the idea. Want to go get a burger or something?"

"Burgers? You call that celebrating?"

"You're right again. How about steak? And yes, I'm buying. What do you say?" She knew he would agree so she opened the door and entered the building. She turned and said, "I'll change and be back here in twenty minutes."

"You're buying? Then I know just the place," he called after her. "Now you just remember that you're too old for me."

Livy laughed in spite of herself and called back, "We've established that, now don't push it!"

In twenty-five minutes she was back. She was wearing jeans, a big oversized sweater, and the hat he had given her. He had changed as well. He was in jeans, a sweater, and a large plaid wool coat. Livy thought it looked like a horse blanket and almost snickered when she saw it.

"So, where are we going?" Livy asked as they began walking.

"It's called *Phantasm*, and it's considered very cool."

"And so why would *you* know about it?" she teased.

"I've heard some of the residents talk about it, and they all really liked the food and say it's got a fun atmosphere. You don't think I can be cool, do you?"

"Not really, no. And, if anyone asks, I'm your old maiden aunt, okay?"

"You've got no coat, Livy."

"Strike that. If anyone asks, *you* are *my* mother," Livy jabbed at him.

"Please. Let's just say I'm your little brother who doesn't want you to catch pneumonia. Do you want to wear my coat?"

"That coat? Not even if you had a gun to my head. So I'm your big sister, huh? Tell me about our family, bro."

"Well, there's you and me and Mom and Dad, and our fifteen brothers and sisters."

Livy nearly choked. "What? You're kidding me, right?"

"No, I'm not." Bryan laughed, raised an eyebrow in a mock-sexy way, and said, "Well, you know, there's not much to do in Idaho, and it's cold and one can always use more help on the farm. I told you that I recently got a new little sister."

"You are *how* old?" Livy asked, still in shock.

"Let's see . . . I'm twenty-two in April."

"And your mom, excuse me, *our* mom is still poppin' out kids?"

"More like pickin' up kids. Eight are their natural children and the rest are adopted or fostered. My new little sister is seven and she's from Ethiopia."

Livy was astonished. She knew he was a farm boy but didn't know they raised kids like cattle. *Maybe they'll get thirty head 'afore they're done.* "Wow! How big is your house?"

"Not that big, really," he explained. "The four older boys, we had a heated room over the barn, and Mom and Dad made a bedroom for themselves out of the garage. You could say it's a bit too cozy, I guess, but it works. Oh . . . and one brother and one sister are married now, so there's plenty of room for you."

"Oh good. I don't want to put anyone out or anything. How was it growing up like that? Were you starving for attention?"

"No, I was just starving. You really had to jump for the food because if you hesitated, it was all gone. But really, it was a great way to grow up. We had our huge farm to romp around on and animals, and there was always someone to play with. And, oh yeah, lots of work to keep us busy." He made a nerdy face and said, "You see? I'm very well adjusted!"

"I'm glad to hear it because I just now realize that outside of your yuletide traditions, I really don't know anything about you. For all I know, you could be a serial killer."

Bryan took on an ominous expression and tone. "I am. It's true. I kill cereal. I finished off Tony the Tiger and the Frosted Flakes this morning. And tomorrow? Little Miss Fruity Pebbles is history. So now that you know, do you still want to be part of the family?"

"I'll have to give it some serious thought."

"So, tell me about your side of the family, sis."

"My family? Well, like I told you, that isn't a subject that I like to discuss much."

"Can I ask why?" Bryan queried carefully.

"There's nothing to tell. It's not much of a family story. It certainly isn't interesting like yours must be."

"Your family must be proud of all your accomplishments. You know, your degrees and your executive job and all that. And when they hear about this—wow! They must think that you're pretty great. I'm sure they are very pleased that you are doing so well."

"Let's just say that I don't know what they think, and I don't care. We're not in touch."

Her tone of voice pretty much said, *Drop it!* Bryan got the message.

"I'm sorry. Well, you are part of our family now and *we* think you are *awesome!*"

"Thank you. You are pretty . . . well, you are really something . . . yourself."

It didn't take long to reach the *Phantasm Café*. It was now after 10 PM and there were still plenty of people waiting for tables. It was lively and raucous; all around were the sounds of people having a good time. Bryan put the name Kimball on the waiting list and told Livy the wait was likely more than half an hour.

There was a group of people at a nearby table who had just received their entrees, and oohs and aahs were heard as each plate was delivered. Bryan and Livy looked on hungrily, and then one attractive young black man in the group glanced up and made eye contact with Livy. A look of total surprise and recognition lit up his face. He got up, excused himself from the group, and made his way through the crowd to where Livy was standing. She figured Bryan saw him coming because he'd apparently decided it was a good time to hang up his coat and give them some space. He blended into the crowd as he wandered back.

"Livy? Is that you?" The big handsome man opened his arms.

"Garrett!" She gave him an uncomfortable embrace. He had another five or six inches over her six-foot frame. "What are you doing in the Big Apple?"

"Being a worm and eating my way out. I just got the most enormous meal served to me. Sooner or later everyone ends up here in New York, don't they? It's like an American pilgrimage. Do you want to come join us? Please? It's so good to see you."

Livy nonchalantly reached over and grabbed Bryan's arm and pulled him from the crowd.

Garrett took the hint. "Oh, I'm sorry. I'm interrupting."

Bryan smiled and insisted, "No, no, you're not. I'm like her squirrelly little brother, and it's probably well past my bedtime, so why don't you two just visit?"

"Bryan! We're supposed to be celebrating! Garrett Garner, I'd like you to meet my friend Bryan Kimball. Bryan, this is Garrett. He's an old friend from college."

Garrett extended his hand to shake Bryan's. "It's nice to meet you. I'm sorry. You two go ahead and celebrate. It is so great to see you again. Can we talk while I'm here? How can I reach you? Then you can tell me all about what you're celebrating. We can catch up."

Obviously, he was sincerely happy to run into her.

"Okay, I might as well tell you," Livy said as she wrapped her arm around Bryan's. "Bryan and I are having a baby."

Bryan and Garrett looked at each other with equal shock. Bryan was beet red and shaking his head.

Livy continued, "I will have to tell you all about it. Here's a napkin and I'll put my cell on it. I'd love to hear how you and Shelly are doing. Really, Garrett, call me, okay?"

"I will. I'll call you tomorrow sometime, is that all right?"

He still looked somewhat stunned.

"That will be great. Call me around lunchtime."

"I'll plan on it. I can't believe you're here."

"I'll talk to you tomorrow, then." Livy said as Garrett made his way back to his table and waved good-bye.

"Why did you say that?" Bryan asked, still shocked and embarrassed.

"Say what?"

"The baby?"

"I said it because it's true. Because of your inspiration, at least partly, my new baby-doll will be the next toy sensation. That's what we're celebrating. I wasn't going to leave our party and go join his. That would be rude."

"But what must he think? First I say I'm your little brother, and then you say we're having a baby. Sheesh! Who is he anyway? Were you glad to see him or trying to scare him away?"

Livy thought for a second.

"That seems to be one of the major questions hanging over my life," she said, finally. "The answer is both, I guess. At one time we were thinking of getting married."

"And?"

"And we didn't."

"Because . . . ?"

Livy heaved an exasperated sigh and answered, "Because I wasn't ready, I suppose. And he *was* ready. And so rather than wait forever for me to *get* ready, he married someone else."

"I'm sorry. How did you feel about that?"

"What was I supposed to feel? I was the one who broke it off. I told him he was free to move on with his life."

"But did you love him?"

"I *think* I did. Especially now looking back at it." Livy sighed again.

"You *think* you did? Why couldn't you marry him?"

"I just couldn't believe that if he really knew me he would love me, or even if he did that he would keep loving me . . . just like . . . . I couldn't trust the idea of commitment."

She abruptly stopped talking and asked, "Why am I telling you all this? I don't do that. I don't air this stuff to anyone." She was sounding almost angry. "Um . . . suddenly, I'm not hungry and I don't feel like celebrating anymore. Do you mind if we just go home?"

"Maybe it's time you did air it to someone. We don't have to stay if you don't want to. I can walk you home, and you can just talk. I'll be quiet and let you say whatever you want. Deal?" Bryan suggested gently.

"Oh, that's right. You're here doing some kind of social work internship or something. Well, I've had enough of shrinks, and I don't want you to practice on me." She could feel her walls coming up, shutting her off from anyone trying to get close.

"I'm going to get my coat," Bryan said.

"Oh, must you?"

"Very funny. Livy, I'm just trying to be a friend. And I do think you need one."

"A shrink or a friend?"

"A coat! And a friend."

"Well, I don't need anyone. In the end, I take care of myself. It's easier that way. And I don't want to talk about it, okay?"

And they didn't. He walked her back to the apartment building in strained silence.

Chapter Six

K yle Fitzgerald, the CFO and holiday fanatic, had done it again. His office was decked out in all new Valentine style. There were paper hearts on the door and candy dishes full of conversation hearts. Cupid was hanging from the ceiling light fixture. When the door opened, a sensor would activate cupid to shoot a plastic arrow at the person entering. There were pictures of Kyle's wife, Debbie, and all the children displayed all around the room. Livy ducked the arrow when she entered.

"Kyle, you never cease to amaze me. Every holiday you manage to come up with something new and cute and annoying. I can't believe someone like you is an accountant."

Kyle didn't bother to take offense. He cheerfully told her, "I'm one of those people whose mother forced them to eat with their right hand and play the right-handed guitar even when she knew I was left-handed. It made me both right and left brained, I guess."

"Or maybe just harebrained," she teased.

"Is that where my hair went?" He laughed, playing with the remaining five red hairs on the top of his head. "Is there something I can do for you, Olivia?"

"I'm sorry. Do you have the estimated numbers on the contest costs?"

"I don't have enough details to go on yet. You have to let me know exactly what it is you want. How much TV do you want? How much print? Which networks? Then I can work it up."

"Marketing hasn't got all that to you yet? I thought that would be done by today."

"Olivia, the project was only officially approved yesterday. Give them a little time."

Kyle always tried to be the peacemaker in the office.

"I still say that you could save money and cut to the chase just by using one of these little darlings. Look at those faces," he said as he gestured at the pictures around the room. "It'd be so easy, you know."

"Call me crazy, but I really do want the whole entire country to choose from—not that your kids aren't spectacular. Let me know when you've got the projections. This has to happen fast. All right?"

She turned to go and bumped into her secretary, Barbara, in the doorway. This time she got hit by the arrow. Barbara retrieved it and playfully chucked it back at Kyle.

"Excuse me, Olivia. You have a phone call on your cell in your office. I answered it for you," Barbara said.

"Who is it?"

"He said his name is Garrett something. He didn't say what company he was with."

"Tell him to hold, please. I'll be right there." She turned to Kyle. "How do you do it, Kyle?"

"Do what? The decorations? The projections?"

"No, the family. That's a whole lot of responsibility, isn't it? But do you know what? I found someone who's got you beat. They have fifteen or sixteen kids."

"Sixteen? That's why it's good that I'm an accountant. I can add, and I can stop adding at seven."

"Anyway, see you later, Kyle."

Garrett did as she'd asked, called around noon, and invited her to join him for lunch. She suggested the park near her office as it was an unseasonably beautiful day for February. She was to meet him at the hot dog vendor just inside. She caught sight of him from the street and literally had to compose herself. She felt that familiar tingle rush through her that she had always experienced when he was near. It was a wonderful and yet annoying tingle. Like a drug, it had side effects; it made her say and do stupid things and feel extra self-conscious.

He's a married man now. Why can't I just relax?

He spotted her and walked toward her, smiling that devastating dimpled smile of his. He was decked out in an expensive gray suit and burgundy tie and was still gorgeous, even more gorgeous than when they parted six and a half years ago. Marriage definitely agreed with him.

"Livy! You came!" He gave her another hug. He lingered there a moment, arms wrapped around her.

She breathed in the familiar smell of his aftershave and broke away. "Of course I did. How are you, Garrett? Are you enjoying your visit to New York?"

"I'm okay, I guess. And yes, I'm enjoying New York. I haven't had time to see much of it though. I'm in seminars and meetings most of the time. They want all of us to get ready to take the New York Bar. And I leave tomorrow. I'm glad I get the chance to see you today. It's amazing that I ran into you like that." He spotted the vendor. "Can I buy you a Polish dog?"

"By all means, thank you." He seemed very glad to see her. Maybe too glad.

"Where did you go last night?" he asked. "I looked for you to say good-bye but you had disappeared."

"We decided it was too late to wait a half hour for a table so we just went somewhere else."

"You weren't trying to avoid me, were you?"

"No, of course not," Livy lied. "I'm sorry if I was weird at the restaurant last night. It was just such a surprise to see you. I think Bryan was uncomfortable."

"And you're not really having a baby with him are you?"

"Who me? You know me better than that. I'm not sure that I ever want to do that. Who has the time?" *I might have felt differently if I'd married you, Garrett.*

"And Brandon, was that his name? He's not your brother either, is he? You never told me anything about having a brother."

"Yeah, sure he is. I just came out all dark meat and he came out all white," Livy teased.

"Are you seeing him?" Garrett asked as he paid the vendor and took the hot dogs. He dressed hers just as she had always liked them. Catsup, no mustard, and lots of relish. He gave it to her.

"You remembered. Thank you. His name is Bryan and he's not my brother or my boyfriend. He's just a nice, young—"

"Safe." Garrett supplied, taking the first bite of his loaded hot dog.

"He's just a guy. I have a baby-doll project at work and it . . . he sort of inspired the idea . . . and we were celebrating that. Anyway, he's *like* a little brother to me in a way."

"So . . . where do you work?"

"I'm at Joy's Toys. I'm in the new products marketing division."

"That's great but it's kind of ironic. Someone who doesn't think she wants kids is coming up with the latest and greatest toys."

Livy was wishing she hadn't made that comment about not wanting kids. *Why?*

"So what's with this doll? What makes it special?"

"It's going to be very interactive. The child does something, and the doll will react and do something. Along the virtual pet lines except in human form. It's complicated. But the kicker is, and you might be interested in this, we're having a contest to find the best baby face in all of America. You must have some kids by now. Am I right? Don't tell me. You have . . . uh . . . four."

"What? I only got married five years ago; I have two. I have a boy, Mark, who is two, and a girl, Staci, who is four and looks just like her mother." Garrett's eyes conveyed affection and something else, something deeper.

"So you are a proud papa."

"They are my life." Garrett brightened just talking about them.

"*Two* kids, huh? Well, good. Everyone I meet lately seems to be over-populating. So how are you doing? Are you still with the big old law firm in Pittsburgh?"

"Still there. Shelly's parents are there, and they want to be very involved with the kids, so it's a good place to be for now. Is this a good place for you? Are you happy here, Livy?"

"I am. Where better to challenge myself than here in the hub of everything? These are the big leagues. There's energy and an excitement in this town. So I'm good, I guess. I'm moving up the ladder in the company, and my boss seems to appreciate me."

Garrett got a suspicious look on his face. "I'm sure he does."

"No, not that. At least I don't think so. I sure hope not. He's just mentoring me and grooming me for bigger things."

"Uh-huh. What kind of things?"

"Really, he is not like that. Besides, his wife is his boss."

It was flattering that Garrett was concerned about her honor. He looked down at his food and seemed to gather his courage.

He finally asked, "But are you happy, Livy? Are there some real live people in your life? Not just co-workers or the latest toy or promotion or whatever?"

"Of course there are."

"Like Brandon—Bryan, I mean? Someone safe you don't have to worry about getting hurt by? He's not going to demand anything from you, no commitment, and no ties. You're older and you have all the control and none of the risks."

"Garrett, you're making something out of nothing. I was taking him out to dinner. Big whopping deal. He's my doorman, for crying out loud. Why do you care who I have dinner with?"

She was doing it again. She knew she was going to do or say something stupid.

"Liv, you're right. This is none of my business. I just want you to be happy. I just want you to belong to someone."

"Oh, so now I'm like a lost dog?"

"Being married and having kids has just opened my eyes to so much and I want you to . . . it's just that I still care about you."

"You do? Thank you. I care about you too. But you've moved on and are living happily ever after with Shelly and the kids and that's your life. This is mine, and I like it this way. I'm okay with it. Really I am."

"Have you *ever* needed someone? Have you ever let someone really need you? Do you want to go through life alone with no one to witness how wonderful you are?"

"What's so *wonderful*? Why are you doing this?"

"I just care. That's all." Garrett shook his head and asked, "You haven't changed at all, have you? You've got to look for some dark, secret motive, some reason not to trust that somebody just plain cares about you. You have to shut everyone out."

"Did you want to start something up again? Is that why you seem to object to Bryan or my boss? You want to start some kind of fling while you're away from the wife and kids?"

Garrett's face froze in a mask of pain. "Shelly's gone, Livy," he said quietly.

For the first time Livy glanced at his left hand. "You're not even wearing your wedding ring . . . and yet you're lecturing me about belonging and commitment? You're not even married anymore?"

Garrett looked fiercely into her eyes and in a flash of anger barked, "Nope, I'm not. That's right, she had no staying power. She just up and left me with two kids! Is that what you want to hear? Do you want to say 'See, I told you so'?"

"So you're divorced? Who are you to tell me about—? Aren't you a bit of a hypocrite!" She hated herself as soon as she'd said it.

"She died, Livy. Shelly died last fall."

He threw the rest of his food in a nearby trash barrel and stormed away.

Livy felt like she had been slapped.

"What?" she asked as she trailed after him. "Oh, Garrett. I'm so sorry. I feel terrible. Why didn't you tell me? Why did you let me make such a fool of myself?"

She chased after him and laid her hand on his arm, she tried to make peace. "How did she die?"

Garrett kept walking but slowed down. After a moment he turned to her and spoke slowly and painfully. "It was a brain tumor, a damn vicious one. It tore her apart in a matter of months. There was nothing they could do—it was inoperable. There was nothing that *I* could do except to stay at her side and helplessly watch her be eaten away by it. Week after week, she was just. . . . They found it in August, and by November she was gone." Tears were gliding down his cheeks, and he sat down on a bench, emotionally spent.

"How do you handle it?"

He licked a tear from the corner of his mouth and said, "Obviously, sometimes I don't. But mostly, I have to. I have to keep going for the kids. I'm so afraid that they will forget their mommy, and I just can't let that happen. She hated leaving them so much . . . and just one month before Christmas."

Livy sat down on the bench next to him. She stared at her feet and kicked a rock across the cement.

She was mostly talking to herself when she said, "But everyone does. Everyone leaves. They die or maybe they walk away; they grow apart; they move on. Or they don't want you anymore. Garrett, you bought into forever, but it never works out that way, does it?"

"I didn't leave you, Livy. You sent me away. You pushed me away," he said gently.

"I know I did. I was afraid."

"Maybe I should have been afraid that something like this tragedy would happen, but you know what? I thank God for those five years with Shelly even as I curse the next fifty years without her. I'll miss her terribly, but there's something much sadder, Livy, and that's having no one to miss. I'm grateful that I got to be there at her bedside, to hold her hand and tell her how happy she had made me. I got to thank her for giving me those sweet, wonderful kids and for loving me and letting me love her so completely that it would hurt this much to lose her. It was a privilege, Livy, a privilege to be there when she passed on. And I knew that I *knew* what love really, really was and that I had walked in its sunshine—and in its shadow. We had five years, wonderful years that I will treasure forever. You see?"

He lifted Livy's chin and looked her right in the eye. "In a way, I do get forever after all. And I have Mark and Staci and—" His voice broke off.

"I'm so glad that you have them. I'm sorry that I was such a jerk. I wish you had told me before I made an idiot of myself."

"I'm sorry. I should have said something."

"I need to be getting back to the office," she said. "Walk with me and tell me about those kids on the way, would you?"

Garrett was happy to oblige. He described how beautiful they were, the funny things they said, and how he loved to peek in and watch them sleep. He made it sound . . . fulfilling. Maybe it was.

All too soon they had walked the seven blocks to her office.

Livy said, "This is my building. You're leaving tomorrow then?"

"Yeah, 8 AM. So . . . uh, take care of yourself, Liv."

"I always do. Garrett, I'm so glad that we got to see each other. I don't know what to say except I hope you will forgive me. Keep my number. Maybe give me a call and let me know how you're doing and all about the kids. And don't forget to enter our contest." She took his hand. "I'm sure they're beautiful children. Shelly was, wasn't she?"

"Yes, she *was* beautiful . . . inside and out. Well, good-bye, Livy."

He dropped her hand and gave her another hug. She kissed him lightly on the cheek.

"Bye, Garrett."

He turned and started down the street. She could still smell his lingering aftershave as she opened the door and walked inside. She stopped, opened the door again, and watched him walk away . . . probably for the last time.

Chapter Seven

After the encounter at lunch, Livy had a hard time getting herself back into working mode. There wasn't a lot she could do about her project while she waited for initial department reports, so she decided for once she'd go home early—five o'clock—like a normal person.

She had just come out of the building when she met Bryan coming toward her. He was carrying the telltale white bags of take-out.

"Since you deprived me of my celebration dinner last night, I brought one for tonight, thoughtfully delivering it in person to your office. Instinctively I knew there's nowhere else you'd rather spend Valentine's evening than behind your desk.

He looked very proud of himself until he noticed Livy's coat and briefcase.

"I guess I was wrong. Hot date?"

"No hot date. Just don't feel like working."

"Great!" Bryan grinned and said, "You get me, dinner, *and* the dining location of your choice! But it better be close because dinner will be getting cold in a second."

Livy paused, considering whether she wanted to hurt Bryan's feelings and just make a beeline for home, or eat in the park for the second time in one day. Looking into Bryan's cheerful, affectionate face, she realized she had no choice.

"Follow me, Boy Scout. I have the perfect spot," she said. She steered Bryan to the same park and the same bench she had recently shared with Garrett.

"So, did he call you?" Bryan asked, seeming to read her thoughts.

"Who?"

"Don't act dumb. Him . . . what's his name . . . Garrett?"

"Yes he did, and we had lunch today."

"Well, how was it? I mean I know you said he's married and every-thing but—"

"Oh, I don't know. Why did you have to pick *that* restaurant last night? I made a total jackass of myself."

"You did not. Look, I see no ears, no tail . . . no evidence of donkey whatsoever. What happened? Here, eat your double cheeseburger and tell me what happened."

"Cheeseburger? What happened to steak?"

"You weren't buying so . . ."

"Give me that. It'll probably kill me, and right now I hope it does."

Livy took a big, fat, angry bite and said while still chewing, "He was giving me this big spiel about commitment and belonging, and I flat-out called him a hypocrite."

"What? Where did that come from? You must have had a reason."

"Well, when I looked at his hand and didn't see a wedding ring, I thought he was talking about commitment while dumping his wife and hitting on me or something. So, I'm in the middle of yelling at him and he just mentions that, oh, by the way, she died. He's still mourning her, and I'm screaming at him. I'm such a creep."

Bryan made a face. "Eeeeoooh, that sounds awkward." He put down his burger, dug out a napkin, and wiped a smear of mustard from her cheek. "So what happened? Did you leave it like that? Did he stomp away all mad and insulted and everything?"

"He started to, but I sort of smoothed things over . . . I hope. I'm not sure, but I bet he thinks I'm the biggest jerk. I hope he . . . well, I think he was hoping we could be friends again. Maybe something more. But I sufficiently erased that idea from his mind, didn't I?"

"Did you clear up the you-and-I-having-a-baby thing?" Bryan mum-bled while his mouth was working on his second burger.

"Oh yeah. I blew that part too. I pretty much convinced him that I don't ever want kids, and then he tells me that he has two."

"Hmm . . . Well, Livy, he's not ready for anything yet if his wife just died. He was unavailable before and nothing's really changed. Just give him a few months and then call him, you know, just to see how he's doing. Show him that you care, that's all."

"Thank you, Dr. Laura. Any other advice you'd like to pass along from your vast experience as an Idaho tractor jockey? What do you know about *love?* Do you even have a girlfriend?"

"Not right now. I have someone in mind, but I have to give her some more time. Timing is everything, you know."

"Yeah, like today, my timing was fabulous." She taunted in a sing-song voice, "Bryan's got a girlfriend. What's her name?"

"Uh-uh." Bryan shook his head. "You'd go look her up and tell her I'm a loser and that I dress funny. Uh-uh, not gonna tell ya."

Livy grimaced and was starting to think to herself, *Yeah, because it's me,* when he said, "And no, it isn't you. Her first name is Lou Ann, and that's all I'm going to say."

Deciding to change the subject, Livy stared at his well-used bowling shoes. "Okay, I never said you were a loser, but . . ." She trailed off, wadded up the trash, and stuffed it back in the bag.

He took it from her and shot it like a basketball into a nearby trash can. "Yeah, but you thought it. And what's wrong with my shoes? They were fifty cents. And now for the second part of our activity," he said.

"What? What now?"

"If you are going to go around creating toys, then you have to remember what it was like to be a kid." He stood up, turned his back to her, and squatted down. "Get on."

"What are you doing?"

"I'm giving you a piggyback ride."

"No, you're not. I'll break your back."

She kept licking the catsup from the French fries she was eating.

"You won't break my back," he said as she shook her head. "I'm superman. I double-dog dare you. Just get on."

She put her food on the bench and looked around. There were a few little children on playground equipment across the park, but other than their mothers, there was no one else around. So Livy climbed on Bryan's back, all six feet of her. She couldn't remember ever having a piggyback ride before. He trotted around the park to the laughter and amazement of the children on the bars and swings.

"Is this what they do in Idaho for excitement?" Livy gasped in a bouncing voice.

"Oh yes. We've elevated it to an art form in my—*our* family. The bottom guy is the horse and the top one is the knight. We get those long foam pool poles and we joust. It's a blast."

"You sound like you still do it, not like it was years ago when you were little."

"We *do* still do it and even my Dad does and sometimes Mom joins in. We all speak in these really bad British accents and chase each other all over the potato fields. The last knight standing wins," Bryan said in just such an accent. "Grab that broken branch up there in that tree; there's your lance, Sir Livilot."

"You're crazy, and this is embarrassing!"

She was laughing almost uncontrollably.

He made a loop and ended up once again approaching the tree.

"Come on. Just try it! You'll get this amazing sense of power!"

Bryan wrapped his hands around Livy's feet and she was now standing on his forearms. He didn't slow down as she made a desperate grab for the branch. She missed it and ended up swinging wildly from a lower attached limb as Bryan kept on trotting with only her shoes in hand, pretending that he still carried her. By now he had the attention of the kids, and they were delighted, chasing him and laughing at his ruse.

"Well, m'lady. How light you are! You're like a feather."

"Bryan! You come back here! It's too far to drop! Come get me down!"

"You lost your lady! She's yelling for help," the children said, giggling. "She's over there hanging from the tree."

Bryan looked in the wrong direction.

"Where? I don't see her."

"*Bryan!*" Livy called, no longer amused. "Get me down from here! And I need my shoes!"

"What's that I hear? My lady is in trouble. I must save her at once!" He and his little army hustled to the rescue and assembled under the tree.

"This is an expensive designer pantsuit and if you make me ruin—"

"No need to fear, my beautiful damsel. We've got it under control, right, guys?" He raised his arms up and instructed his little friends to hold him up from the sides. "I am ready, fair maid. Release the branch. I'll catch you."

"Are you sure?"

"Trust me. Let go."

She did, and he caught her safely but then made staggering steps as if losing his balance and then purposely falling backwards with Livy on top of him.

Bryan said, "Dog pile!" and suddenly there were kids crawling all over them both.

Livy jumped up like she had discovered she'd sat in a nest of spiders. She dusted herself off, quickly slipped on her shoes, and explained, "It's February, for Pete's sake. The ground is all wet and muddy."

But Bryan sensed it was the kids more than the fairly dry ground that made her uncomfortable.

The mothers had gradually wandered over to watch their children in this momentary drama and now gathered them up and led them away. As Livy watched, one curly-headed little boy of about four suddenly stopped, bent down to the ground, and then ran back to Livy and held out a little purple crocus.

"This is for you, my lady. It's the first flower," he said.

She bent down to take it, and the little fellow rose up on his toes and kissed her cheek. Livy started to thank him, but he'd already run back to take his mother's hand.

Out of necessity, the marketing team worked up the contest campaign in record time. After consultation with the legal department, a double blind receiving system was created to insure impartiality. Each entry form was dated and filed in a cryptographically monitored database, leaving each picture identified only by number. The family of the winning photo would receive $50,000 cash and a Fantasy Line cruise for up to eight family members and friends.

Ten finalists would win a cruise for four and receive a limited edition Hannah doll of their choice, sure to be valuable collectibles in the future. Entries were available Wendy's restaurants nationwide or online at the Hold-Me-Hannah website sponsored by Joy's Toys. Applications were to be submitted online and all photos electronically scanned. Entries needed to be received by midnight April 1, and the winner would be announced April 30 on live national television.

The country was bombarded with ads in print, television, and radio, and in Wendy's restaurants there were huge displays with application instructions. The advertising department invested in pop-ups on every imaginable website regarding parents and children. Everywhere in the country, ads reached out and tapped limitless proud parents. Ads like:

It happens all the time, doesn't it? People constantly telling you that your child is "just a doll!" C'mon, admit it. They're right! And now you can prove it! Mom, take that picture off the wall! Grandparents, get out that brag book and show us that special face—the one no one can resist, the face that melts every heart.

Livy's instincts had been right. The hype worked even better than predicted. Grandparents raided stacks of photo albums and scanned in shots of their gaggle of grandchildren. Parents of every race sent in baby pictures and school photos. Glamour and kiddie photography shops were booked solid for weeks in advance. People everywhere were sure their children were the best, the brightest and, of course, the most beautiful. Entries poured in by the thousands. Some vain adults even sent in their own baby pictures. Why not? Soon the computer techs couldn't keep up with the submissions. Fifty temps were hired to organize the vast quantities of data and help the judges to select the finalists.

Although she would never have admitted it, even Livy was amazed at the response. Former skeptics like Bob Farrell and Marcie Jones reluctantly congratulated her on her success. Even Kyle had become a genuine supporter of the company's choosing a wonderful mystery child instead of one of his own, and Mel was thrilled to refute his wife's prediction that the whole idea would bomb. Hannah was becoming exactly what Livy had predicted: a household name.

Several states to the South, Carlos Sotomayor couldn't believe his eyes. He had spent most of the last few years in the Florida State Penitentiary and had been released only weeks before he saw the commercial announcing the Joy's Toys baby contest.

How fabulous! How convenient! Just when I need a little funding. This is way too easy! I am back, ladies and gentlemen—back in business.

Pulling out the wallet graciously stored at government expense for such a long time, he let out a wicked chortle. Yes, the picture was still there.

Oh, Patti, my dear, I know you gave me this photo to make me feel ashamed, but once again, I have no shame. Sin verguenza! My little gold mine just might pan out after all.

He knew she was exactly what they were looking for. She was perfect. Her little arms reaching up, her lovely longing little face just epitomizing the name of the doll: *Hold-Me-Hannah.* He knew that entering the photo would shake things up a bit for that New York witch.

But oh, Patti, you must admit, she deserves it!

How he would take pleasure in at last squeezing every possible dime out of her!

She's practically leaving the door to the chicken coop wide open for the wolf. Hmm . . . Let's see, where will I find the offices of Joy's Toys Corporation? It's so simple. Our little darling wins the contest, and the witch pays through the nose. It's as easy as child's play!

Chapter Eight

It was a spring Saturday, about 7 AM, and Livy was in the midst of a delicious dream about the horse property she was hoping to buy in upstate New York. If the doll were the kind of success she hoped it would be, then the rural estate near the Finger Lakes would be well within her financial reach. The listing photos on the Internet displayed rolling green pastures lined with trees captured in a time of autumn splendor. In her dream, she now wandered happily along a leafy trail leading to a large barn. As settings in dreams often do, the scene morphed from colorful fall glory to winter fairyland in an instant. Suddenly the grounds were covered in newly-fallen snow, sparkling like diamond dust under a December moon. The path was now marked with glowing lanterns, and Livy felt drawn toward the barn as if something wonderful awaited her inside. Abruptly, the peaceful setting was shattered by the sound of her dream horses kicking at their stalls. She was startled but pushed on. The pounding continued, and she then reluctantly realized it wasn't the horses. The scene melted away as someone continued banging on her apartment door.

Why don't they go bother someone else?

When the knocking didn't stop, she finally donned a robe, pulled her voluminous hair up in a twist, and answered the door. No surprise. It was Bryan in sweats. In the past few months, Livy and Bryan had truly become the brother and sister team that they had at first only joked about. It was almost frightening. They spent much of their free time together, and Livy had to admit that she was becoming as close to Bryan as anyone she could remember throughout her life—despite her original resistance.

"Hey! Did I wake you?" he asked with a laugh. "Nah, couldn't have. You're a workaholic and you don't know how to sleep in."

"Wrong! I was just having the best dream, and you were not in it. No, on second thought, you *were* in it at the end. You were the back end of a horse. What are you doing here?"

"I'm taking you on an outing, dear sister."

"What if I told you that I have plans, pesky brother?"

"What plans?"

"I was going to go to the gym, and then I thought I would rent a car and go for a ride out in the country."

She thought she might just go hunting for that country estate.

"Well, this outing will accomplish the same ends, so get dressed in your gym clothes and let's go."

He was jumping around the apartment like a kitten on catnip.

"Go where? What are you so excited about?"

"You'll see. You've wanted to know a little about what I'm doing, so I'm taking you along on some fieldwork. You'll like it. Don't worry. Get yourself some good sports shoes on."

"Does this mean I'm supposed to roll in the mud with some kid again or something? Thanks anyway, but I'm not in the mood."

"No mud, I promise. But I really want you to come."

She looked at those big blue pleading eyes of his and relented with a sigh. "You know you really are a little on the pushy side." Livy managed to round up some gym clothes and shoes, and when she was all ready, she asked, "Do I need a jacket?"

"Nah, it's an absolutely gorgeous spring day."

Fifteen minutes later, they were on the subway platform waiting for the train. Forty-five minutes later, they were in South Bronx approaching a public housing neighborhood. Many of the windows in the dilapidated buildings were shattered, and some were boarded up. Poverty and hopelessness seemed to hang over the apartments like a brooding cloud. Most of the walls sported graffiti in vivid color and artistic style. Only trash wandered through the streets, blown by the April morning breeze. People were strangely absent. There were no trees in blossom, and no grass was visible anywhere. It was a typical Saturday in the projects.

"What are you up to, Bryan? Why are we here? Is it safe?" Livy asked, sizing up her surroundings.

"Just thought you needed a little exercise, and I want you to meet some friends of mine. We've been hangin' out for a while."

"You're hanging out here? I don't think that's too wise. You tend to stand out with your blond hair and skin roughly the color of a vanilla shake." She was half teasing and half seriously concerned. "Really, Bryan. You should be careful."

"That's why I brought you—protection."

"What? You're using me for cover? I have a bad feeling about this place, Bryan. Let's go back."

"It's okay, Livy. Trust me. I've been over here lots of times, and they don't seem to mind so far."

"Who are *they*, exactly?"

"My young basketball buddies. They wanted nothing to do with me at first, but I warmed them up a bit."

"How did you do that? What could you possibly have that they'd want?"

"Thanks a lot, Livy. I thought you liked me now," Bryan said, sounding just a little offended.

"I'm sorry. You know I like you, it's just that . . . well . . ."

"You're right, I can't be cool even if I try. But if you must know, I told them I was going to write about them, and they liked the idea. Doesn't everyone want to be noticed?"

"So now they are part of your case studies?"

"Yup. Here they are, my loyal 'subjects,' so to speak."

He guided her toward the public housing playground.

Six boys between the ages of eleven and thirteen were playing basketball on the fenced-in court. The painted lines on the pavement were nearly all worn away, and the basket was merely a bent piece of metal. Any semblance of a net was gone ages ago. The boys didn't care. They were having a marvelous time and were really quite skilled. On a makeshift bench, fashioned out of two two-by-fours suspended between two large paint buckets, sat a pretty little girl who appeared to be about five years old. It had been a while since her hair had been combed, and her tattered brown hoodie showed signs of last night's dinner. Her little lips moved slightly as she hummed a happy tune. She was intensely studying a bug on the pavement under her swinging feet.

When one of the boys noticed them approaching, he grabbed the ball and tossed it out the gate at Bryan.

One of the other boys protested, "What you doin', Bozo?"

"It's Bryan! I just thought I'd wake him up, see if he payin' attention," the first boy replied.

"Hey, white boy! You ready for your lesson?" asked a tall, older black boy. "You gon' get schooled today!"

"How do you know that I'm not just holding out on ya? How do you know that I'm not a Larry Bird kinda white boy just waiting for the right moment to go in for the kill?" Bryan sauntered around the court, dribbling now and then.

"Who's Larry Bird?" one boy asked.

"Nobody!" the other boys replied in unison.

At that, Bryan made a power run at the hoop and leapt up for a dunk. The power behind his vertical jump was impressive but his aim was lacking. The ball slipped from his hands, hit the rim, and sailed across the court to where the little girl was sitting. She jumped up after it, as if it were always her assigned duty. She held it up, ready to toss it back to them, but then changed her mind. Instead, she threw it to Livy.

Taken off guard, Livy didn't quite react fast enough to snare it. It bounced off her hands, and she made a few sad attempts to capture it. Finally, it came rolling back on to the court.

"Who da sista?" one of the boys asked.

"She's my sister," Bryan answered with a totally straight face.

Another boy laughed and slapped Bryan on the back. "Your sister is a *sista?*"

"Yeah, so how cool is that?" Bryan stepped over to Livy's side to introduce her.

"It's cool for you, but I feel sorry for her, having you for a sorry a—" Bryan glared at him, and he didn't finish the word, adding only, "brother."

"Don't mind Jimmy, Olivia. He loves me. He really does. Boys, I'd like you to meet my sister, Livy Thomas. I thought maybe she could show us a few moves, but after that sad display we just witnessed, maybe not."

She took the bait. "Excuuuuse me! You big . . ." She couldn't think of the appropriate name so she grabbed the ball away and dashed in for an impressive lay up of her own. She easily made it and came back and handed the ball to Bryan. She faced the boys and said, "University of South Florida Women's Basketball team. Full scholarship. Now, can I have a little respect?" She turned back to Bryan. "Please?"

The boys were laughing their heads off. "She nailed you, brother white boy!" said the smallest and youngest of the group. He looked eleven or maybe younger.

"And she older than you, too. She yo' old lady?"

They laughed louder.

"Well, so much for respect!" Livy said in mock sadness. "Who's our little friend over there?"

"That's Josie, short for Josette," the smallest boy replied. "She *my* sister. I'm always stuck with her on Saturdays 'cuz our mom gotta work."

"And he's Frankie, short for *Francois*," another boy said with a very exaggerated French accent. "Their mother's from Haiti."

"You got a problem wid 'at?" Frankie said in a mock accent of his own. "Yo mutha's from Hades," he retorted.

Bryan stepped between them. "Boys! Let's play some hoops, okay? My dad's from Paris . . . Idaho, so who cares? Why don't you show me that pick n' roll you've been working on?"

Livy was amazed at how Bryan got them back into friendly game-mode. They happily got to work on the fundamentals of basketball. Bryan motioned to Livy, and she reluctantly joined in and demonstrated some defense strategies. She was able to coach much-needed follow-through into Jamal's suffering foul shots, and strutted her stuff over and over at the hoop. The boys were impressed, but she sensed they were a little deflated by her prowess.

Fine. I don't really want to be here anyway.

Faking an ankle twist, she limped over to sit with Josette.

How did I let Bryan drag me into this?

"Hi, Josie. I'm Livy. Do you want to take that jacket off? It's getting kind of warm." She put her arms out towards the child to help her remove the little hoodie.

Pulling away, she looked at Livy with suspicious eyes. "Mommy says I can't take it off and 'sides, I don' have no shirt." She pulled her ragged little warm-up jacket around her protectively.

"Okay. Do the boys ever let you play?"

"No, 'dey say my job in the game be to chase da' ball."

"I noticed that. You throw it really well, though. Have you ever tried to make a basket?"

"I'm too little. I can't throw it dat high."

After a few uncomfortably quiet moments, Livy finally asked, "How old are you, Josie?"

"I's seven but I's little for my age, my mama says. Dat's why da boys never let me play . . . and 'cuz I's a girl." She returned her gaze to the bug on the asphalt.

"Yeah, they don't get it," Livy added in commiseration. "Boys da fool and girls *rule!*" Josie looked up and beamed a smile.

Livy squatted down in front of her and whispered conspiratorially, "When I was a kid, I was always taller than everyone else and wanted to try being little for awhile. Why don't you get on my shoulders and try out what it's like to be big, okay?"

Josie studied her for a moment, as if trying to decide if she could trust this tall stranger to not only touch her, but also to pick her up. She chose to risk it; she put her arms up toward Livy and climbed aboard. She was nearly weightless on Livy's shoulders and gripped Livy's ponytail for dear life.

"Josie, wrap your feet under my arms and around the back, so you can use your hands too," Livy instructed as she ran onto the court. "Hey, watch out, guys! Here we come!" she taunted. "Together we make a center that can look Shaquille in the eye, and he'd feel the heat!"

Livy motioned to Bryan to pass the ball. She caught it, driving in toward the basket. She handed it up to Josie as they reached the bottom of the key. Josie shot with ease, and the ball swished through the invisible net as Josie giggled with delight.

Something deep inside Livy was touched by this little waif, but she didn't want to be touched. What had Bryan gotten her into?

Chapter Nine

He loved it. He could see that everything about him unnerved the secretary. Carlos, alias Charlie Majors, sat waiting in the office. The prison-gifted suit gave the appropriate impression and so did the scar on his dark cheek . . . also acquired in prison. He had assured the secretary that he indeed had an appointment and that his business with her boss was urgent for both him and her. She probably had just been detained.

The secretary's hand shook slightly as she handed Charlie the cup of coffee he had demanded with off-hand assurance. "Cream," he suggested as he caressed her trembling wrist. "And three sugars . . . and a donut or something if you've got it."

It was unlikely that her boss would have forgotten an appointment with a man like him, but he made sure she didn't dare cross him.

"There are some muffins and Danish on the credenza," she said slyly, but not slyly enough, setting the phone to intercom while pretending to straighten items on her boss's desk. He knew she wanted to hear if he started rummaging around the desk or opening files.

"Thank you," he said, getting up to check out the food choices. "I left my hotel without breakfast and—"

"Sure, help yourself."

He oozed bad vibes; he excelled at it. He knew she couldn't throw him out. She could call security, but fearing he was the important big shot he claimed to be, she wouldn't risk being fired for that. What to do . . . what to do . . . . Obviously, she was both reluctant and relieved to leave him alone in the office.

When the "New York witch," as Patti had dubbed her, appeared moments later, Carlos went for her like the easy mark she had been before.

She extended her hand to him. He took it and held on to it menacingly.

"I'm sorry," she said, trying to appear calm, "but I'm quite sure there's been a miscommunication here. You say we had an appointment, and yet I don't have anything here in my planner." She pulled her hand away to open the PDA that she carried in her other hand. "Charlie Majors, is it?" She finally looked him squarely in the face. "I'm . . . uh . . . have we met?"

"Oh yes. We've had a pending appointment to clear up some unfinished business for a long time now. It's about time we kept it," Carlos said with a wicked grin and then waited patiently for recognition.

The touch of Spanish accent, his eerily familiar face, his manner, it would all click soon enough. Then suddenly he could see her heart nearly stop when she put it together. He was back, that Christmas nightmare she had tried so hard to erase from her mind.

"I see that you remember me now. I'd be so hurt if you didn't. We meant so much to each other. How could you forget that one night we shared together?"

"What do you want?" She tried to sound firm, but he could feel that she was terrified. He liked that.

"Before we talk business, I think maybe you should turn off the intercom." He watched her hastily do it and added, "Good. I think your secretary thinks I'm a little bit dangerous. And our business is very personal; I'm sure you agree. No need to concern anyone else . . . yet. It seems we have some new business to discuss."

"What business? I gave you everything you asked for. That was supposed to be the end of it."

"Of course, I wouldn't hold our . . . previous arrangement . . . over your head. It's just that your little contest reminded me of something. Or should I say someone? And naturally I thought of you and how much I've missed you."

"Why didn't you get put away for good? Or end up dead in the street?"

"They tried . . . on both counts." He moved around the desk toward her and produced a photo from his pocket. "Let me refresh your memory. Isn't she sweet? Isn't she just a beautiful child? What a shame you didn't keep her."

She stared at it in disbelief. He waved it close enough for her to get a good look and pulled it quickly away when she tried to grab it. He made a clicking sound with his tongue and said, "No, no, no. We mustn't touch."

"What do you want?"

"I'm sure that you're starting to understand that it is very important that our little beauty wins the contest. You just make sure that the winner is kept anonymous and the prize money goes to charity when she wins—very specific charities—that will be eternally grateful for your kind donations. Here are the names and accounts. You'll all look so generous and socially responsible. Everybody wins."

"But you can't get away with this. Don't you see how much attention this contest is drawing? Someone is bound to scrutinize everything we do and then you will go to jail."

"Been there already—the food's not bad—no good lookin' woman like you around to keep me warm at night but . . ." He was running his hand up her arm.

She shook herself free of him. "Stop it! Shut up! Just shut up. You're making me sick!"

He cackled at her fear and repulsion. "Now, I may go to jail, but let's look at what happens to you if something goes wrong and all this gets out. You may also go to jail, maybe not. But even more interesting is all you have to lose. It must be so nice to have the kind of life you live, the money you make, the nice place you live in, the clothes . . . all yours because of children. You just *love* those little children. Ha! They would be so crushed to find out the history behind this little one, don't you think?"

He reached out and grabbed her again. "And you've got even more to lose now than just the man you loved. There's so much more riding on this little girl. You don't want to lose it all now, do you? Not to mention the company here. You'd take *it* down with you. Like you said, this contest is drawing a lot of attention. A little DNA is all I need to prove everything."

"Where is she? What did you do with her?" There was panic in her voice.

"You didn't care what happened to her then, so why now? You said to get rid of her, and we did. It wasn't pretty but that didn't matter, did it? Not to you. All it would take would be one phone call to tell her and the world would know the whole disgusting story. She'll be so touched to know that you've changed your mind . . . to know you're looking forward to a nice family reunion," he said. "But let's not talk about that for now. I happen to have a lock of her hair that Patti saved. She was so sentimental that way. You remember Patti, don't you? That's all I need. Science is so amazing! The things we can do with just a piece of hair!"

"So now what? You seem to have thought of everything."

He produced a sweat-soaked piece of paper from his pocket. "Here is the information about the charities. If you stick to the script, then we'll be just fine. You'll be fine. I'll be finer." He laughed.

"But I have other people involved in this project, you know. I don't have total control."

"No, *I* do." He cranked up his voice a few decibels. "Just make it happen or it will not be a pretty day for you and that baby doll. I'm sure the company has sunk millions into it already. There's no going back now." He gave her a pre-paid cell phone with a direct connection feature and instructed her to only contact him through the phone. "You can be sure that I will be watching your every move. I'll be in *touch*," he said as he ran his hand slowly and sinisterly across her.

She was shaking and backed herself into the bookcase. He pinned her there and, breathing his cigar stench into her face, whispered, "Now, if *you* can't handle it, there's someone else I can think of who might just love to help. You know who I mean. Should we ask for some help?"

"No, please! I'll do what you ask."

"Good girl! Here's a chance for you to show just how capable and strong you really are." He gestured at a diploma on the wall. "All that college education made you so smart. You can do it." He pressed his lips to her ear and hissed, "And if you don't . . . well, that's not an option."

He was having more fun than he'd had in years. As he left the office, he spied the Danish and muffins remaining on the credenza and took them all. "Don't mind if I do."

On the way down the hall to the elevator, he bit ferociously into a cheese roll as he realized that he would have to find and silence Patti once and for all. The last thing he needed was for her to show herself and mess things up. *I tried to kill you once, baby; don't make me have to try again. This time I won't fail.*

Chapter Ten

T he very next Saturday would be the day before Easter, and once again Livy had to learn the appropriate Kimball family customs. Soon, she would be an expert on what it was like to be a child during any season on the Kimball family farm. She could already name all the Kimball siblings and all their ages. She learned about the hunt at Jensen's Grove for the notorious missing basket, the bunny they had dyed green, and all about the store-bought eggs that an eight-year-old Bryan had tried to incubate in his closet with the use of a string of blue Christmas lights (and the horrible smell that ensued). And she learned all about sunrise services on Easter morn, the private Kimball ones. Easter was a very special holiday for the Kimball family; they seemed to embody the very meaning of Easter. When each new child came into the Kimball home, his or her life began anew, just like it had for Jesus on that glorious Resurrection morning. This year, a new life had begun for Sarah, Bryan's recently adopted little sister from Ethiopia.

So naturally, for Bryan, Easter anywhere meant that an Easter-egg-hunt would be involved. Bryan roped Livy into helping him put together such an event for the kids he was working with from the projects. City Square Park would be the site, and he figured they could get away with a mere one hundred fifty colored eggs.

"One hundred fifty? I'm supposed to boil or blow one hundred fifty eggs?"

"Nah. You're not supposed to use real eggs anymore. They're afraid they'll go bad and all the kids will get bird flu or 'Sal Minelli' or something. We have to stuff plastic eggs with candy and hide them around the park at about dawn. If we do it the night before, animals or some home-less guys might find them first, and then we'll have a bunch of unhappy kids. You don't want to be around a horde of angry kids, believe me."

"I'm not thrilled to be around any unhappy kids. One's more than enough if he's like the one I sat next to on the plane to Toronto last month. Drove me nuts! Bryan, why do I let you talk me into this stuff? People at the office would freak if they knew half the things you dragged me into. And why an Easter egg hunt? With the possible exception of Josie, these kids are too old for that, aren't they? They're not little tiny children, you know."

"That's just it. For the most part, they never got to be little kids. They were practically born with adult-sized problems. I'd like them to have a day away from all that—away from the concrete and broken glass and the discarded needles—a day just to be children . . . out in the fresh air, roll-ing in the grass, having fun. I really want them away from there, just for the day. I don't have anyone else to help me, so are you in?"

She failed to come up with a good excuse. She scowled at him and said, "You are not getting me into a bunny suit and that is non-nego-tiable."

"How else are we going to manage to hide your identity? Those people at the office are sure to find out all your dirty secrets if we aren't careful." Bryan laughed.

She teasingly grabbed him by the shirt collar and made herself clear. "I'm not kidding . . . non-negotiable!"

So Livy was out hiding eggs in the park on that Saturday morning. By 10 AM she was deep into the hunt, pointing their young friends in all the right directions. This time there were no pictures to prove it, no Joy's Toys PR paparazzi, but Livy *was* starting to enjoy the company of these kids and was amused to see how much they seemed to like her. Livy and Josie grew closer that day. When she had first started helping Bryan, Livy had kept her distance with the kids and almost resented Bryan for having involved her with them. Josie sensed it and was a little slow to warm up to Livy too. Gradually though, especially today, true and sweet affection grew between them.

At one point, Livy spied Josie sitting dejected in the grass. "Aren't you finding the candy, Josie?"

"I just sees one and then da boys come and steal it," she said almost in tears.

"Come with me. I know where all the best stuff is hidden!" She carried Josie piggyback to the best remaining hidden treasures but left the actual discovery of the candy for her to make. The child's infectious laugh and huge smile as she grabbed up her basketful of goodies made a great reward.

After the hunt, Bryan taught them all his favorite Easter game, "Colored Eggs." Each child had to pick a color. Bryan would be the wicked wolf who would come knocking at the door asking for colored eggs. They would ask, "What color?" and he would reply, "Blue" or whatever color came to mind, and the kid with that color had to run around a mini-obstacle course with the wolf chasing them and then back to home base. If one was caught, he had to join the band of wicked wolves until they had caught all but one. That one was declared winner and became the head wolf for the next round. And on and on it went. They had a blast acting like a bunch of six-year-olds.

Interestingly, it was Jimmy who got into the action the most enthusiastically. He was the oldest and tallest and could outrun them all. But he liked to draw it out and tease and trap, making the fun last longer for the smaller kids.

"Nobody eva' call out my color!" Terrence complained. "I don' never get to run!"

"What's yo color, dummy?" Jamal asked.

"Magenta. You know dat my favorite color!"

Bryan said, "Yeah, when I was little, I always picked *metallic gold* and wondered why I never got a turn. I finally figured it out . . . last week. Don't be so creative."

Livy was amazed that the boys were bonding with Bryan in a way that no one would have expected. There was always plenty of teasing and pretended hostility but nothing of substance. Behind all the "white boy" talk was a genuine respect and gratitude for someone who had taken an interest in them and really cared. Livy knew when they got back to the neighborhood, the boys would never brag to their friends that they had spent the morning with a white nerd and the wicked wolf. But she also knew that they'd never forget that day.

Bryan told Livy how he'd learned and documented a great deal about the lives of these boys by now. Some had opened up more than others, but they had all experienced more horror and disappointment in their short years than he would ever have experienced in Idaho in a lifetime. Between the six of them, they had three family members serving time, two siblings who had dropped out of school, five running and using drugs, and Jamal's sister had been raped. Jimmy's older brother, Aaron, was a leading member of the *Jex Jax,* a local gang. Only one of the kids, Leroy, had a relationship with his father.

Today, Josie looked so frail and undernourished that it bothered Livy. She was glad when Bryan suggested they hit Burger King before accompanying them home.

Knowing Bryan's part-time job as doorman wouldn't pay much, and wanting to avoid the discussion, Livy walked up to the restaurant counter and announced, "I'm buying! Get whatever you want but please try to find a food group in there somewhere!"

One would think they hadn't eaten in weeks. They ordered Double Whoppers, super-sized fries, desserts, and gallons of sodas.

Frankie and Josie hung back from the group. Frankie shook his head at Livy. "I got it," he said determinedly.

"It's my treat, okay Frankie?" Livy insisted.

"I take care of Josie and I take care a' me. I got it." He pulled a fifty-dollar bill out of his pants pocket.

She gasped. "Where did you get that?"

"My mom gave it to me. She said don' owe nobody nothin'. They be your boss forever dat way." He pushed his way to the next cashier and ordered kids' meals.

Bryan, who had been watching, just shrugged his shoulders and changed the subject. "Let's take that corner over there by the jungle gym. You can play while we wait. I know. You're too big and too old. But not today, guys, not today. Just play."

They ate like NFL jocks; they played like toddlers. After a while Livy was more than ready to call it a day.

"Bryan, let's pack it in. I've got other things on my agenda today that I'd like to get to. Let's get these kids back home."

Bryan glanced at his watch. "Just ten more minutes . . . then we can go."

"Why ten more—?"

Bryan cut her off. "It's important. They need just a few more minutes. Let 'em play."

Soon enough, they put their shoes back on and headed for the subway to go home. When the little crowd of friends got off the train with Livy and Bryan near their neighborhood, they laughed and reminisced about the day they had enjoyed.

Over the scream of sirens, Leroy elbowed Jimmy and taunted, "Dog, Jimmy, you run like a girl! You couldn't catch me no way."

"Oh yeah? I'll catch you now!" Jimmy barked back and chased after his friend.

The boys rounded the corner at Rhoades and Walker Street and stopped cold. Up ahead was the playground where they usually spent their Saturdays with Bryan. Cop cars surrounded it with lights flashing. EMTs loaded injured teens into ambulances, and a few frightened neighborhood residents began to emerge from the nearby apartments to comfort each other and to see what had happened. A young, tough-acting, shaved-bald kid was handcuffed and stuffed into the backseat of one of the police vehicles. He didn't look much older than Frankie. One tattoo-covered gangbanger, knife still in hand, lay in a pool of red up against the chain link fence. Over the next few minutes it became clear what had happened. A rival gang had challenged the Jex Jax for the playground turf. The Jax had retained control but had lost Jimmy's brother, Aaron, in the process. The whole event had lasted no more than a few minutes.

Terrified, little Josie climbed Livy like a tree and clung to her desperately, burying her face in her protector's shoulder. Livy held her tightly and stroked her back. Livy just wanted to be out of there. She carried Josie to Frankie and left her in his care. "Take her home, Frankie. Go home and lock the door and . . ." She wasn't sure there was any safety there either. "Just take her, okay, Frankie?" She brushed a tear from Josie's cheek and sent them home.

Livy was suddenly hit with a startling realization: If the kids had stayed and played basketball at their usual time, they would have been caught in the crossfire. Or perhaps, if they hadn't stayed to play on the jungle gym for just those extra few minutes . . . God only knew what might have happened.

She wanted all of them to be away from there. She turned to talk to Bryan, but he had gone over to comfort Jimmy who was kneeling next to the lifeless body of his brother.

The boy wasn't crying; he was just rocking back and forth repeating, "Aaron? Not Aaron, man." He sensed Bryan's presence and said without turning, "You gotta write about Aaron. Please, Bryan. You gotta tell about my brother."

Bryan knelt beside him and, laying his arm around his shoulder, said, "I will, Jimmy, I will. I'm so sorry, friend." Bryan glanced up. "Look, your mother's coming. You'd better go help her. You need to be with her. She looks like she can barely stand up."

Jimmy got to his mother just in time for her to collapse like a sobbing rag doll in his arms. Bryan reached out and touched the mother's trembling hand and murmured a quiet prayer. "I'm so sorry."

Bryan shuffled slowly and sadly back to where the other boys were, and Livy pulled Bryan aside. "We are getting out of here. Maybe you can't see it right now, but the tensions have to be rising. I don't think we should hang around waiting for more trouble. Let's go."

"You don't have to get mad. It's okay." Bryan said.

Now she *was* angry. "Its not okay! Do realize that if we had come back here just a little earlier . . . or if you and the kids had been on that playground what would have happened?"

"But it didn't. Not to us." He looked back at Jimmy and his mom. "We're all right. I wish I could say as much for Jimmy's brother. I'm just going to say good-bye to the guys and then we can go."

Their good-byes consisted of silent expressions, waves, and touches. Livy stood apart.

Chapter Eleven

The time for the judging had arrived, and it had become quite the anticipated event. Livy was in a panic. What if something went wrong and the whole thing blew up in her face? She was a professional, possibly the next executive VP of New Products Marketing, and she could handle it. She had to handle it. All eyes were upon her and upon Hannah. Joy's Toys had extended the invitation to all to send in their best and most beautiful children's faces, and the nation had responded in record fashion. "America's baby icon" was the vernacular for the Hannah phenomenon. The pre-orders for the doll and her gear were already pouring in. It was only April, but already it would be just a matter of a few weeks until Hannah would recoup the investment. Livy wondered what kind of money they were likely to see come October and November.

Inside the office, she knew that behind her back Marcie and Bob were still calling her "teacher's kiss-up pet." Mel's attention was focused almost completely on Livy and her project. The rumor Marcie and Bob had sparked was that there was more going on there than just "toy maker and his apprentice." The movie tie-in figures they had stressed over were getting totally lost in the Hannah hype and Farrell's success from last Christmas was practically forgotten.

Everyone knew that Bob Farrell had decided long ago that the VP job was his. He had been with the company longer, and he was older and more experienced. Joy was definitely in his pocket. But now, with Livy on the march, *his* promotion was very much in doubt. Things couldn't fall apart for Livy now. Or could they? She was becoming a bit of a celebrity herself, along with her doll, and she knew that one extra-nosy reporter could cause her a world of hurt. What if they discovered the real reason she came to JTC and everything else she had carefully tried to hide?

Having found the epitome of the "heartland of America" in Black Rock, Tennessee, JTC was ready for the big announcement extravaganza. The press, the cameras, the spectators on hand, and all of the country by TV, filled up and spilled from the giant tent they'd built around the Wendy's restaurant in the tiny Tennessee town. Wendy's, known for their child-friendly atmosphere and the good work of the Dave Thomas Foundation, was a natural fit.

Today, the winner would be chosen and Hannah's face would be revealed. Livy was not the only one with nerves on edge. The families of the finalists were undoubtedly glued to the proceedings with fingernails poised, ready to chew. The Hannah event staff was on pins and needles as they readied the voting machines, went over the latest rewrites of the script with the announcer, checked mikes and cameras, and tried to please the celebrity judges, some of whom demanded royal treatment at inopportune times. The company bigwigs, headquartered in another tent, farther out in the parking lot, seemed to be the most frantic of all. One would've thought that the future of JTC itself was on the line. Just possibly it was.

Livy was outside in the tent, nervously doing laps around the small enclosure.

"Calm down, Livy. You're pacing like a cat with one paw nailed to the floor. It's going well. Just relax," Mel advised. "This is just what you wanted. It's working according to plan."

If you only knew my plan, she thought. "Well, so far, so good. The response has been unbelievable, don't you think?" Livy asked.

Joy put in, "We should have taken more time. Everything's so rushed. Is it going to make it to market in time for the big push? What happens if the entire country is ordering dolls, and it turns out that they won't be ready by Christmas? That could ruin us."

"Oh, Joy! The engineers assure me that Hannah will be right on schedule. The prototypes are just about there. Why are you always looking for a reason to panic?" Mel asked.

"Because this is my company, and I have the most at stake. I think if it all went up in smoke tomorrow, you might not even care."

"Of course I care! I just don't stress out in front of everyone like you do. The captain of the ship has to keep his cool or everyone else will assume the worst and leap for the lifeboats. You should try being a little more upbeat if you want this company to succeed and, most important right now, this project to succeed."

Interrupting their conversation, Livy announced, "We're live in five so all eyes on the monitor."

An overhead helicopter camera circled around the Wendy's and the exuberant crowd that had gathered outside. As the video shot zoomed in on the excited multitude, they were given the cue to wave the hundreds of JTC-Loves-Kids signs they had been handed. The announcer stood at the door, poised and smiling, ready to lead the viewer inside to where an enthusiastic live audience waited for the fun to begin.

Mike in hand, the announcer began, "Good evening ladies and gentlemen and children across the U.S. and Canada! I'm your host, Randy Carlson, and we are gathered here at the Wendy's in Black Rock, Tennessee, to select the winner of the Joy's Toys Your Baby Is a Doll Contest! We have our distinguished panel of judges assembled here, and some of these people you'll recognize, I'm sure. You remember Joey from *Palmer Family Chronicles*, also known as Parker Hemingway."

Parker stood and waved enthusiastically to the crowd. Right on cue, a group of teen girls did as they'd been instructed and let out an appropriate swooning scream.

"Next, we have Jessica White, who is starring in the upcoming summer blockbuster *Peter Powerful and the Forces of Oberon*. And by the way, we at Joy's Toys have an action figure of Jessica that all of you will want to get 'hot' off the assembly line, if you know what I mean."

Randy took her hand, and she stood and waved to thunderous applause. He went on to announce the other celebrity judges: Jerry Stradling, a producer of many family friendly hits, and Dan and April Mendez, a chart-climbing brother and sister singing duo. "These judges," Randy went on, motioning to three more seated at the long, baby-bunting draped table, "are representing JTC and their affiliates. They are: Bob Farrell, Joyce Barker, and Joel Cartwright. They aren't famous, but give them a hand anyway, won't you? This is a tough job picking America's most appealing baby face.

"We have had these and a panel of one hundred expert judges, from photographers to modeling agents to stay-at-home moms, help us pick the adorable ten finalists you see before you. Thank you to all of the folks out there who sent us the pictures of your charming and endearing children.

The response was overwhelming, and we wish we could make a doll with the face of every one because they truly are beautiful. We have one more judge as well, and that is you, out there. You can vote online at JTCbaby-contest.com/winner or text message us at 800-555-5432. You can only vote for thirty minutes after the lines open up, so if you are unable to get through, please keep trying."

"Will our winner be baby A?"

And on down the line of finalists he went until the camera had focused on each one and the variation on the phone number or web address that would register a vote for that child.

"And there you have them, ten beautiful little girls, but only one can be our Hannah. We will be selecting our boy winner in a few months, so be sure to watch for that. All right, North America, the lines are open . . . *now*! Make your choice! We will be back here in sixty minutes to announce the winner. Don't miss it! Right now, let's take a sneak peak at just how wonderful Hannah will be and why we wanted to find just the right face for her . . . and soon, for him." Then a commercial for *Hold-Me-Hannah* using a computer-generated face was broadcast expounding on all her glories.

Somewhere back in New York, an expert hacker was insuring that the results came out exactly as planned. Just a few more keystrokes and the numbers would tabulate just perfectly. Baby F must win. Carlos must have his way.

Outside in the tent, Livy and the rest of the executives present exhaled . . . so far, so good. Still pacing, Livy asked Mel, "It's going well, don't you think? The celebrities worked out great, I believe. They probably brought us more viewers and more interest."

"It will be fascinating to see what our TV market share was for that five-minute slot," Mel wondered aloud. "Can you really believe that millions of people out there actually care what our doll looks like? It's amazing what a little hype can do."

"I just can't help thinking about all that you've risked with this undertaking. My father built this company starting with next to nothing and gave his whole life to it. I'd hate to see it all crash and burn if this doesn't work," Joy moaned.

Livy tried to assure her. "We're only going to add on to the foundation he built, Joy. This is going to be something he would be very proud of if he were here. Don't you think he would want to be the company out there, taking leaps like this and pushing the industry forward?"

"Maybe you're right. But he was always very careful, very sure that everything that went out there with *my* name on it was a good product."

"And this is good stuff, my dear." Mel put his arm around his wife. "It's true that he built this company as a monument to you, his only daughter, and he wanted it to be something that would last for generations. But I'm sure he wouldn't want us to just play it safe and stick with mediocrity."

"I know you wish we had a next generation to pass it onto. I failed you in that regard, didn't I? You always wanted children, and we couldn't have any. I'm sorry, Mel, that I couldn't give you someone to build your monument to."

This was getting much too personal for Livy's ears, and she suspected that Joy had had a couple of drinks to settle her nerves and that she would be sorry later for her candor.

Livy was about to exit the tent for some air when Joy called after her. "That's why I'm nervous, Olivia. That's why I give you such a hard time about this venture. This is my baby; it's all I have—the company, and this man that my father handpicked to run it and to take care of me. Only the best would do for Joy. Only the Harvard MBA with the proper pedigree would pass the test . . . and oh yes, his family's money to shore up the bottom line." She turned to Mel. "Tell me, was I a credit or debit on your balance sheet? Was I a liability or a company perk?"

She looked like at any moment she might erupt into tears. Livy had never seen this side of Joy before. This was a woman who never let down her guard. Mel looked embarrassed and confused.

Kyle, who was there watching the numbers roll in on the computer, sensed the tension. He put on his bunny ears, grabbed a festive Easter Basket, and began passing out goodies.

"I sort of went overboard with the kids' Easter candy this year so I'm thinking we could all do with a little chocolate overdose. What d'ya say? I have bunnies and chicks and these peanut egg things . . ."

Livy tried to lighten the mood as well. "It's almost May, and Easter was a couple of weeks ago, Kyle. You're slipping. But I am definitely due for some chocolate. It's been at least an hour." She caught Mel's eye and gave him a look that asked, "What's with her?"

He seemed bewildered too. They had enough to worry about without Joy having a meltdown, especially since, inside, Livy was having one of her own.

When an hour had nearly passed, Kyle totaled up the numbers, double checked with the others at their stations, and put the results in an envelope.

He was about to seal it when Joy asked, "Well, aren't you going to let us see the tabulations? We want to be the first to know who America's Sweetheart is, right, everyone?" Her words were appropriate but her tone was cheerless.

Livy couldn't help thinking that Joy didn't need chocolate; she needed some strong black coffee. Livy could use some herself.

When Kyle handed over the envelope, Joy peeked inside and said, "Fine, now I know." She closed the flap and gave it to the staffer to take into the restaurant for the announcement segment. She motioned for him to get going.

"Well?" Livy asked. "Who is it?" She had to know. Everything she'd worked for was riding on this little girl. Everything she'd pinned her hopes on was on the line.

"You'll find out with everyone else." Once again Joy had to be in charge. She had to prove she was one up on everybody.

The music cue brought up loud strains of "I Found a Million Dollar Baby (in a Five and Ten Cent Store)."

The camera once again zoomed into the restaurant and then to Randy Carlson who began in a singsong voice, "We're ba-ack. Hello again. I'm your host, Randy Carlson and we're here at Wendy's and just about to find out the results we've all been waiting for. Who is that lucky child whose face will become part of the fabric of American childhood? Who is that fortunate family who will enjoy the $50,000 prize and the cruise? They haven't given me the envelope yet, so let's do a little celebrity exit polling, shall we? April, how did you vote?"

April explained that she had voted for Baby F. "She makes me just want to pick her up and squeeze her!"

Dan, April's singing brother, went another way and voted for Baby A. After polling a couple more celebrities, Randy received the results packet from a young staff member and held it up triumphantly. The crowd roared.

The camera took one more sweeping pan of the giant photos hanging in front. "Which one is our winning girl? Don't forget, in a matter of a couple of months we will choose our boy as well! Drum roll, please." He opened the envelope and announced, "Well, April, a lot of people must have felt like you did, that she just needs to be picked up and loved. Our winner is . . . Baby F!" Thousands of balloons cascaded from the ceiling.

The audience clapped and cheered the winner but some few moans of disappointment were heard as well. Randy took the paper that had just been handed him and quickly announced the names of all the runners-up who would win cruises and dolls.

"And now . . . let's find out who this little winning stranger is and who her parents are." The staffer again appeared with another envelope and then whispered something in Randy's ear. He looked confused as he again lifted the mike to his lips. "Now this is a shocker. As for our little Hannah . . . we don't know who she is. I have just been informed that her entry blank specifically stated that she was to remain anonymous and that if she won, her prize money would go to charity. Now this is a surprise for everyone at JTC, I think. They seem to be at a loss as to what to say about this. Oh, maybe not. Here comes the CEO of Joy's Toys. I'll let him take it from here."

Melvin bounded onto the stage with an energy that seemed to belong to someone half his age.

"Hello, everyone. My name is Melvin Jameson and I am CEO of Joy's Toys. As you know, we kept the applications blind until this very moment and we are just as surprised as you are to learn of *Hannah's*, for lack of a real name, . . . to learn of her family's wishes to remain out of the spotlight. I think it's a fabulous opportunity for Joy's Toys to be able to give back something in return for all that we have been given. I'm announcing right now that we will double the prize money that would have gone to the winner and we will give that to worthy children's charities."

The press in the front row looked dubious.

One reporter shouted out, "Are we to believe that this was not planned all along? It so conveniently adds to the suspense and mystique of the product. How could you not know that this entry was anonymous?"

"We kept all the personal information in separate files from the pictures. Only a number identified them until the computer spit out the personal information just moments ago. We learned about it at the same time, almost, that you did. We had planned to go to the family home with Randy here, balloons, the giant check, and the whole nine yards. But I do think that it is a wonderful thing that Hannah can share her winnings with other children."

"What charities will you be donating to?" the reporter persisted.

"We just learned about this, so that decision has not been made at this time. We'll do a press release later and let you know. For now, I'd just like to give my congratulations to all the finalists! You are all winners and you are all beautiful. We will be contacting you, the families of the finalists, very soon so you can claim your prizes. Enjoy your cruises! And all of you out there will love little Hannah . . . whoever she is. Thanks again for being here. Good evening to you all."

Mel waved at the audience and to the camera. Then he turned and silently addressed the giant photo of the winner projected behind him. *Who are you, little one? You have just the expression we all wanted: the longing for love, the anticipation of receiving it. It's all there in that little face. Well, sweetheart, here we go on a wild adventure together. I hope you are ready for the ride!*

Livy was making her way over to the tent. *Are they going to buy this? Will they think we set this up as a stunt? I thought I'd feel better when we got this far but . . .*

Carlos pressed the speed dial button on his phone. "Can you talk? Then just listen. Great job! Now that wasn't so hard, was it? You just stay on course and we'll have no trouble. No . . . obviously nobody suspects anything . . . keep it that way! I'll be in touch."

Chapter Twelve

Linda's next placement was in the home of Bill and Arlene Harris. When Mrs. Clancy drove up to the house, Linda was somewhat encouraged. It was a nice-sized blue house with an attractive porch and it was clean and neat. Walking up the path to the front door, Linda was greeted by a yellow-striped cat staring at her from inside the living room window.

"Hello, kitty cat," she said aloud. *It might be fun to have a pet*, Linda thought.

Mrs. Clancy rang the doorbell and gave Linda some last-minute instructions. "Okay, sweetheart. Stand up straight and tall and shake hands with Mr. Harris. Show him what a bright and good girl you are." Linda was holding her breath.

Arlene Harris answered the door with an inviting smile. She bent down to Linda's eye level and in her charming Carolina drawl said, "Come in! This must be our little Linda. I'm Arlene."

She was a petite, attractive woman with friendly eyes, and Linda felt things might work out here after all.

Mr. Harris stayed on the couch as Mrs. Harris led Linda to him by guiding her gently from the shoulders. "Linda, this is Bill. We've been looking forward to having Linda come to stay with us, haven't we, Bill?"

Linda offered her hand to him as Mrs. Clancy had instructed.

He shook her hand while his eyes sized her up. He grunted a somewhat forced hello. Instinctively, Linda retreated toward Mrs. Clancy.

"Bill!" Arlene noticed his less than enthusiastic greeting as well. She let out a nervous laugh. "Don't mind him, Linda. He's just tired because

I made him clean out the garage before you came." She turned and called up the stairs, "Jody! Billy! Come and meet our guest. Linda's here."

As if on cue, Jody and Billy marched down the stairs and into the room, dressed in their Sunday best. Billy, fourteen, looked like he was uncomfortable with the show and just wanted to be out playing somewhere in his cutoff jeans. Jody, on the other hand, fairly pranced around showing off her fancy pink ruffled dress.

Linda looked down at her own simple plaid jumper and white blouse that had been her most recent school's uniform.

Jody looked down at it too and said, "I'm Jody and we're the same age. Will she be in my class, Mama? Oh, I forgot—I skipped a grade." She grinned wickedly at Linda.

"Let's ask if we can get you into Mrs. Bartlett's class. She was Jody's teacher last year and she's fabulous. We can register you tomorrow, all right, Linda? Mrs. Bartlett will be sure to give you any extra help you may need," Arlene assured Linda while taking her Minnie Mouse bag from her and the small plastic bag of belongings from Mrs. Clancy. She handed them to Jody. "Why don't you take Linda upstairs and show her where to put her things?"

Mrs. Clancy went over the paperwork with Mr. and Mrs. Harris and pleaded with them to give Linda a chance. "She's had some disappointments, so we hope that this will be a good long-term arrangement for her. That *is* what you have in mind?"

"Yes, of course. She seems like a very nice little girl," Arlene said.

"Give her and your children some time to adjust, and she'll be fine. I think she would really like to have a nice sibling relationship. It could mean so much to her." Stephanie Clancy studied their faces. She was getting very good at reading people.

Bill didn't have to be read. He made himself clear to her. "This is not leading to an adoption, you understand . . . just a temporary home, right?" He turned to his wife but continued to speak to the caseworker. "We are not interested in *that* kind of long term," Bill stated firmly, his eyes returning to Mrs. Clancy.

As Mrs. Clancy walked to her car, she felt that familiar ache in the pit of her stomach. So many children, so many cases, and yet so few happy endings. She could see it plainly: the mother was idealistic and looking to feel good about herself and all the father was looking for was a check. And for some reason, Jody was looking for trouble; Mrs. Clancy could feel it.

It was always easy for Linda to make friends at the St. Anthony's home. There were kids of every color and age, and each had a different story to tell as to how they came to be part of the St. Anthony family. Linda's story was that she didn't know her story. Sister Marian had said that Linda could make up her own. Maybe she was a princess or a magic fairy. Who knew? At the new school, when Jody announced that she had a foster sister, everyone had questions and Linda didn't think they would like her fairy-tale answers. They wanted to make up the story, and the ones they created weren't nice.

One third-grade boy, Joey, mocked, "I know where you're from— another planet."

Anika, a former friend and now enemy of Jody's, put her hands on her hips and said, "Maybe your daddy took one look at you and threw you in the garbage can. So then, they heard you crying and had to find you someone to live with. Too bad it had to be with Jody." Anika laughed and laughed, and others joined in.

Jody told them to be quiet and to leave Linda alone. Jody liked assuming the role of the older or at least wiser one. She was the "big cheese" for a change and not just the little sister who was picked on by the big brother. She was in charge.

Jody showed Linda "the ropes" at school and at home. She managed to help Linda "lose" her homework. She showed her how to do her chores, where things went, and, unfortunately, she also showed her things she should be sure to do that Jody knew would get her in trouble with Bill and Arlene. She showed her things to get into that were forbidden, such as how to eat the ice cream that Jody knew was specifically saved for the ladies' luncheon Arlene was in charge of or how to find where Bill kept his wallet and "borrow" a few dollars. He wouldn't miss one or two, Jody said, and according to her, Bill had told her it was all right to take a little allowance.

When a $20 bill was missing on one occasion, Jody assured her parents that it was Linda's doing. "That's what you get when you let someone in your house who hasn't been taught not to steal," she counseled them.

The worst thing Jody taught Linda was to regularly let the cat out to get "some exercise." This time, six weeks into the placement, when Linda let him out, disaster struck, just as Jody had hoped it eventually would. She had always been jealous of the attention her mother gave that pet. He was treated like the favored younger child.

When Linda came down the stairs that morning on her way to get her coat for school, she spied the cat waiting by the front door, and she assumed he wanted to go out. She obliged. When the girls returned that afternoon, the mangled cat lay dead on the porch.

"Oh no! What happened? The poor kitty!" Linda cried and turned her eyes away.

"I told you never to let the cat out! You did it, didn't you?" Jody pushed the door open. "Mom! Linda let the cat out again and now he's dead! Mom, come see."

Her voice was frantic, but her face suppressed a smirk.

The neighbor down the street had shot it, just as he had vowed to do if it ever trespassed on his property. Then he had deposited the remains as verification of making good on his promise. Jody had always hated the cat and the trashy, violent neighbor as well—this was her way of making trouble for both. It was big trouble for Linda as well.

Arlene came running and flew into a grief-stricken rage when she saw the cat.

"Tiger baby!" She lifted the lifeless head and let out a wail as she turned to Linda. "That Delbert McCoy's gone and killed my cat! What have you done? This was my baby!" She grabbed her by the arm and shoved her toward the stairs. "You go to your room! I can't even look at you right now!"

"But . . . Jody said . . ." Linda stammered, trying to hold her ground.

Jody jumped in. "I told her, Mama. *Never* let Tiger out. I told her lots of times."

"No, you said to let him out for exercise," Linda protested.

"Jody, is that true? I know you don't like . . ." Arlene began.

"See, I told you, Mama. She lies. She lied about the ice cream and the money and now this. I've tried to be nice to her, but she just keeps doing stuff . . . like this. It's 'cuz she never had a mama to teach her any better." Jody caressed her mother's arm and half whispered in her ear, "She even runs around naked in front of Billy after her shower!"

Linda heard and shouted back, "You did that, not me! And it's not my fault I never had a *mama*!" She glanced pointedly at Arlene for a moment and then turned back to Jody. "And if I did, *my* mama would never teach me to be a mean liar like you!"

Arlene raised her hand, preparing to slap Linda's face but stopped herself.

"Go ahead and hit me. Everyone else does!" In tears, Linda ran up the stairs and slammed the bedroom door.

Later, when Linda's sobs quieted, and she sat in silent, lonely tears, she overheard Arlene filling Bill in on the events of the afternoon.

"I tried to warn you, Arlene," Bill said with an I-told-you-so air. "You just never know what you're getting into when you take these kids in. I don't know why you wanted to mess with her in the first place. That measly check is not worth the tension she's brought into our family."

"I know, honey, but I was just trying to be kind to someone in need. This is the thanks I get. My poor Tiger, dead."

A moment later she heard Bill asking for Mrs. Clancy on the phone.

"Yes, Mrs. Clancy, I know I said we would try to give her a long-term place, but it's just not working out. She's disrespectful and she won't try to get along with my daughter; it's damaging our family. My wife has bent over backwards for that child, and she pays us back with lying and stealing. You must find another place for her, right away. I understand your concern for the kid, but just talk to my wife."

The conversation was muffled for a moment and then she heard Arlene tearfully say, "No, we *have* thought about it. We have been living with this chaos for weeks now. I've tried to be openhearted and treat her like one of the family, but it's just not going to work any longer. Do you know that today she was responsible for the death of my sweet cat?" She paused. "No. There's no trying again. When can you pick her up?"

Linda didn't know whether to be relieved or sad at this point. She definitely did not want to stay, but she felt so lost, so afraid of what might happen next. She began to pack her bag and with her tears spilling onto Minnie Mouse, she cried aloud, "Oh Sister M! I want Sister M!"

Outside the door, Jody mocked in a high-pitched, Wicked-Witch-of-the-West style. "Sister M! Aunty Em! Sister M!" She broke out in cackles.

Within the hour, Mrs. Clancy arrived to take Linda away. She tried to take Linda's hand as they walked to the car, but the child shook it away.

"I didn't *do* anything! I didn't do *anything!*" She turned and faced the house. "I HATE YOU! I HATE YOU ALL!"

"Do you want to talk about it?" the caseworker asked gently as she helped Linda into the backseat.

"No!"

The car door slammed.

While driving in the solemn silence, Mrs. Clancy was formulating plans to get another job. This one was just too painful. How she wanted to go home, hug her own children tightly, and block out all this misery. *I can't be part of this anymore.*

There were few homes available, and Linda's wait for another home turned into months and months in a group home that felt like children's prison. It was not at all like the home where Linda had been with Sister Marian. The hard-core girls organized teams, which were more like gangs, and preyed on the younger girls to serve them, do their assigned chores, and give them part of their food as protection payment. Most of them had learned to swear like longshoremen and could be very intimidating. If they caught a little one crying, they taught her how to be tough by unrelenting, brutal name-calling.

The older predators had learned to use the phrase "We'll give ya something to bawl about, you baby!" If the desired toughness wasn't achieved in one or two sessions of verbal whipping, then the abuse became physical. Linda only let herself cry when she was trying to go to sleep at night, when it was dark, and the scary girls were in another room. She held onto her little cross and to her mother's picture, but it was Sister Marian she cried for . . . and for Jesus. Sister Marian told her to call on Jesus to watch over her, and she knew she needed Him now. If only they could find her daddy. Somewhere she had to have a daddy.

By the time Linda was ten, she'd had four more family placements, five more schools and two long stints at group interim homes. Both of them had lasted over Christmas holidays. There she had experienced two incidents of sexual abuse and some physical abuse as well. She had stopped trying to make friends and didn't care about her school performance although her tests all showed her to have higher-than-average intelligence.

By age twelve, Linda no longer cried herself to sleep at night. Some girls had stolen her Minnie Mouse bag, written profanities all over it, and left it in a toilet. She was too old for that now anyway. She now moved her few personal belongings in a pillowcase. She still carried her photo and cross with her whenever she moved, but they'd lost some of their meaning. Instead of feeling good that there must have been someone out there who had at least loved her at one time, Linda was beginning to feel anger and resentment toward her mother for abandoning her. While it was true that she may very well be dead, even that made her furious. A baby loses her mother. So she just gets dumped? Who would do that?

Why did my mother have to die? Other kids have real moms who keep them and love them, no matter what they do. With these fake moms, the least little thing happens and they throw me back into the loser's den.

If the scenario was that her mother hadn't died, but had abandoned her, her feelings were even more intense.

Why couldn't you love me, Mother? I was only a baby, your baby. Everybody loves babies, don't they? Why can't anyone love me? White families don't want me, and brown and black families don't either because I'm somewhere in between.

When she held her cross with the daisy, she got angry with Jesus and Sister M. too. Sister M. had told her the daisy in the center seemed to represent how new life, fresh and beautiful, can spring forth miraculously out of suffering and pain and even death. Linda was ready for that new kind of life to begin. When would Jesus see that she was in pain and waiting for that new and better life?

Chapter Thirteen

The spring blossomed and the summer sweltered, but Livy barely noticed. She was always flying here and there around the country and the world at large signing contracts with manufacturers and distributors and was busy with her team, working on marketing campaigns.

Bryan was always there at the door to greet Livy and help her keep her head about her. After the Japanese Hannah deal was negotiated, she and Bryan finally went to Ruth's Chris Steak House for their celebration steak dinner.

"Wow!" Bryan said as he pulled Livy's chair out for her, glancing around the establishment. The atmosphere was elegant, and the smell was heavenly. "This has to be the nicest restaurant I've ever been to. That steak smells so good!"

Livy laughed as Bryan moved to the other side of the table. "It's no one you know, I'm sure . . ." She saw that Bryan looked around, baffled. "I mean the cow . . . the steak . . . it's no one you know."

"Oh, good!"

The waiter appeared and brought water. "I'm Travis, your server today, and could I bring you something to drink this evening? Would you like a moment to look at the wine list?"

"Give us a minute, okay?" Livy answered him. "Hey, Bryan, you're always trying to get me to be a kid again. How about I help you act like a grown-up?"

"What do you mean? Aren't I acting like a grown-up? Did I wear something stupid again? Am I undone?" Bryan asked, checking his fly.

"No, you look great, silly boy. We're celebrating, right? How about I get you some wine and for once in your life . . . get you nice and drunk?"

"You're kidding, right? You know I don't drink."

"I know, but it's time to be a man, Bryan."

"And to be a real man I have to get drunk? Is that what you look for in a guy?"

"Just try some. They have a good selection here. I'm not trying to corrupt you for life or anything. Let's just celebrate with a little champagne."

"You go ahead. I'll toast with my water glass."

"Well, I'm not spending big bucks on champagne just for me."

"I'm not all that smart, and I'm a total klutz without alcohol; with it, I'd be in real trouble!"

"Why do you always say things like that?" Livy asked.

"Like what?"

"Oh, I don't know. You always try to make it sound like you were the dumb kid, the poor kid who didn't catch on, the one who never got picked for the teams or anything. Just looking at you, I know that isn't true. Don't get all full of yourself when I say this, but you're very good looking, and you seem confident, and you're not a klutz, so why do you act like you were?"

"Some of us just take a little more time to 'come into our own,' so to speak. I *was* really like that. The kids made fun of me all the time. Once, after gym, the other boys pantsed me and ran my underwear up the flag pole while I stood naked, crying at the bottom, trying to pull it back down."

Livy could relate more than he knew. "That must have been awful. I just can't imagine it happening to *you*."

"Only because you get to see the real me. They only saw the slow, clumsy kid I always was. You see more, like the kids in our family somehow did. They always stuck up for me. They were my team and didn't let anyone mess with me . . . not if they could help it. Have I told you about my big brother David? He was my hero, just like David in the Bible. He'd stand up to any old giant for me."

"It must have been great to have that kind of support system," Livy said, sighing.

"The only exception was Becky, my foster sister."

"Why? What did Becky do?"

"She's the gorgeous one who got herself in some boy-trouble and got thrown out of her house. So I kind of took it upon myself to keep other boys away from her. She didn't like that too much. She called me every name in the book and loved to embarrass me in front of the other kids. It hurt a lot sometimes. I was just trying to help. She's mellowed over time, though. I guess she was hurting too."

"I thought all the Kimball kids were perfect like you."

Bryan rolled his eyes. "Not exactly. We have all kinds of kids with all kinds of things to work out, so we're about as human as you can get." A mischievous smile crossed Bryan's face. "Did I ever tell you about the doorbell?"

"What doorbell?"

"Clayt—he's the practical joker in the family—always in trouble before he came to us. Well, he and I were down in Grandpa's basement digging around and found the wires to the doorbell. Clayt discovered that if he stuck a pin in the wire, it would make the bell ring. He could hear Grandpa get up out of his chair and head for the door to find no one there.

"So Grandpa's yelling, 'Darn fool kids!' He was so mad to think someone had doorbell-ditched him.

"So Clayt kept it up. As soon as we heard the chair squeak and figured he was comfortable, we'd ring it again, and again, and again. Pretty soon he was out the front door and out on the front lawn, yelling and scream-ing and swearing. I never ever heard him swear before or since. I have to admit, it was hysterical. Then he'd come back and find some kid had taken over his recliner and he'd yell at 'em and chase 'em off. Just when we figured he was comfortable, we'd ring it again. He'd get up again and out the door he'd go, waving his cane into the bushes and screaming. The neighbors must'a thought he was having a stroke or something. Then he'd come back to find some other poor kid in his chair who didn't hear the first one get bawled out. Probably nearly did have a stroke!

"Then finally, Jackson told on us and we got in big trouble." Bryan was laughing at the memory, and Livy was too as she imagined the poor elderly gentleman out there shaking his cane and swearing into thin air.

"Yeah," Bryan concluded, "we're about as human as any other family, probably more so."

"Human, but fun. How does your mother keep her sanity with all of you?"

"She is amazing. She's gotten very good at keeping us all very busy. There's always work to do with a farm and with that many kids, folding laundry alone can keep you occupied for hours."

"I can imagine. Does she ever get some time to herself?"

"Now that the twins, the youngest, are in school, she has a little more time. But even her spare time she spends on us. She loves scrapbooking. Looking at those albums, you'd think every one of us kids was someone really special and important."

"So that's kind of what you're doing for those kids in the projects. You're keeping a record, a little story of each of their lives." Livy was sadly quiet for a moment. She remembered what Garrett had said about there being no one to witness how wonderful she was. She tried to imagine someone, anyone, having pictures of her in his or her scrapbook. She was sure no one would.

"Livy? Livy?" Bryan asked for the second or third time. She finally looked at him. "I'm sorry. Did I say something wrong?"

"No, it's just that . . . . never mind. It's okay." She played with the napkin in her lap.

"Are you thinking about your family? Are you ever going to open up and tell me what happened with them?" Bryan asked gently.

Livy swallowed and began, slowly, "I had a family . . . thought I did, anyway. But I screwed up. I screwed up so badly that they didn't ever want to hear from me again. I tried lots of times . . . but they made themselves pretty clear."

"Do you want to talk about it?" Bryan asked. Livy shook her head. "And here I am. I just keep going on and on about my family. I should just shut up. I'm sorry. Back in Idaho, they were my whole lifeline, my frame of reference. Do you want me to stop mentioning them?"

"No. Don't stop. I love hearing about them and even imagining that I'm one of you . . . that you're really my brother. I want to meet them someday, I really do."

"Someday you will. I'll make sure of it."

The server returned and Livy ordered huge porter house steaks for both of them but didn't order any wine or champagne.

It was a good thing too as she had to fly to Houston the next morning, and she got sick enough on flights without having a hangover. What would she do without Bryan? Probably have a good time. Sometimes he was more father than brother, watching over her like a mother hen, giving her advice and at times making her feel guilty about silly little things, like buying $400 shoes.

He was constantly bugging her, saying things like, "Do you actually have that promotion yet?" No, she didn't. "Did you get that bonus yet?" No she hadn't. "So stop spending money you don't have."

She didn't mind, actually. He kept her grounded in reality, and it was great to have someone outside the office to share this triumph with, even if she had to do it cautiously.

Early in July, on the way into the apartment building, she let it slip that she was finally done working such long hours, at least for a while. Bryan seized the opportunity. He sat her down on the apartment entrance stairs.

"Hey, you can come over to the neighborhood with me! Josie has been asking for you."

"It's not safe over there, Bryan . . . especially for you."

"That's why I need you, Wonder Woman."

"No, seriously, you've got enough to write about by now, and you should tell them it was great but now you gotta get out of there."

"I'm not worried. It's like they don't even see me. Nobody bothers me, and things have calmed way down. Just come and see Josie and Frankie. It would mean a lot to them. Come on, Livy."

"How's Jimmy doing after what happened?"

"He's okay, I think. He talks about Aaron but not really about what happened to him. He says things like, 'If I grow up, I'm gonna travel. Aaron wanted to travel.' or 'If I grow up, I'm gonna buy me and Mama a house and get outta this place. Aaron shoulda got outta here' . . . stuff like that, and it's pretty sad. He seems ready to accept the possibility that he might not get to grow up. But then, he never really got to be a kid, and neither did Aaron."

Livy didn't want to think about that fateful day. She hadn't been able to get Josie out of her mind, nor the rest of them either, for that matter. And that was the problem. She didn't want to care and worry. She didn't want to get in over her head.

"Look, I'm not a bleeding-heart do-gooder like you, Bryan. I'm a businesswoman who is very busy right now, in case you haven't noticed."

"Uh-huh, and guess what? Children *are* your business; have *you* noticed? And you need a life outside the office."

"And you're in charge of that? So who made you my fairy godmother and social chairman?"

"Speaking of which, have you called Garrett?"

"Not that it's any of your concern, but no, I haven't. Why do you keep bugging me about it?" Feeling a bit perturbed, she got up to go inside. "And, by the way, he hasn't called me either."

He grabbed her hand. "I'm sorry, but you were the one who felt terrible because you thought you offended him, and then you don't call to apologize or tell him you hope he and his kids are doing well. Nothing. You're the one that has to call and open the door. I know you care, so. . . ?"

When she wouldn't answer, he gave up and changed the subject. "Why don't we do something with the kids for the 4th of July?"

"Okay, I'll bite. What do you do in Blackfoot on the 4th of July?"

"We race snowmobiles into the lake at Jensen Grove."

She looked at him like he was crazy. "I'm not even going to ask. But hey, I know what we can do. Why don't I take you and the kids to that new movie, that *Peter Powerful* thing? We have lots of passes at work, and maybe then you'll stop badgering me. We could go pick up the kids and get them out of the neighborhood for a while. The flick is supposed to be pretty good for all ages. Happy now?"

"Ecstatic! I'll arrange it!"

The next afternoon, Josie was ecstatic too when she looked out the window to see Livy and Bryan crossing the courtyard between buildings. She had been anxiously watching for about half an hour.

"Livy! Livy!" She called and waved from the window and then scrambled down the stairs along with Frankie. She raced straight to Livy's legs and embraced them because Livy's arms were full. "I missed you so much," she squealed.

Livy put down her shopping bags and hugged her. "I missed you too, baby. Look what I brought for you!"

Frankie looked at her suspiciously.

"It's all right, Frankie," Bryan said as he set off to round up the other boys.

"Yeah," Livy said. "It's just some apples and oranges, some veggies and some books and things from the warehouse at my work. They're promo gifts. It's just free stuff. You don't *owe* me anything, okay? Let's go upstairs and put this food away in your fridge."

She gathered the bags again and started toward their building.

Frankie stopped her. "I got it. You can't come up—my mama's busy."

"I'd like to meet your mama," Livy suggested.

"I tol' y'all, she busy," he said, gathering up the bags from her and walking toward the building.

"Wait, Frankie."

Livy caught up with him, reached inside one of the large bags and pulled out a smaller one, and then let him take the rest. He gave her a wary look and then headed for the stairs. She turned to Josie and gave her the bag to open.

A beautiful grin lit up Josie's face as she peeked and then reached inside. She held the little pink-flowered top up against her body in obvious delight. Then her smile faded away, replaced by a furrowed brow.

"Let's go try it on you," Livy said. But Josie just clenched her jacket tighter. "Honey, it's too hot to wear that hoodie today. It's going to be ninety-five degrees out here."

"I can't take it off. Mommy said."

"Why, sweetheart?"

Her little face fell and she whispered, "She say if I take it off, she don' be my mama no more."

Just then, Bryan arrived with the boys and they set off for the theatre complex. Jimmy declined the invitation on the grounds that it was for little kids—he was beyond that now.

Josie spent a good portion of the movie nestled in Livy's lap, hiding her eyes when huge fantasy monsters appeared. Soon she found she liked the safe and comforting feeling of Livy's lap and Livy's arms, with or without monsters. Livy liked having her there too, just as she'd feared she would.

At last, the time for Hannah's debut had come. It was mid-August, a bit early to push the Holiday buying season, but Livy and her marketing team had decided that they couldn't leave Hannah off the public stage for too long or the momentum that they had built for her would evaporate.

They were using the Wall Drug technique. Somewhere in the Black

Hills of South Dakota there was an Old-West style drugstore that alerted travelers for miles ahead about the wonders, the glories, and the ever-increasing nearness of Wall Drug. "Only 55 miles to Wall Drug!" "Hang in there, only 27 miles to Wall Drug" and so on. Soon, the traveler absolutely had to see what all the fuss was about.

The Hannah commercials had started slowly after the winning face was announced, and built and built, counting down the days to her unveiling. And just like with Wall Drug, it worked. Hannah was a big splash indeed! The night of Hannah's debut, as it were, JTC was to host a huge banquet and bash for toy retailer executives from across the country. All the big-box bigwigs were to be there, and all of them would have the chance to meet the brain behind the baby doll sensation.

Bryan wouldn't let up on Livy. Every day he asked, "Have you called Garrett yet? This is the perfect excuse. You just need a date in a hurry for this gala and you thought of him. You wondered how he's doing, blah, blah, blah. It's a natural. Just do it!"

She resisted and made excuses why she couldn't or wouldn't call him. Finally, to get the big Idaho spud off her back, she picked up the phone.

She heard Garrett answer and that feeling was back—the rolling stomach and thick-tongued impairment she always felt around him.

"Hi, Garrett. Uh . . . I . . . Hi, how are you? It's Livy."

"Hi, Livy! How are you doing? That's a dumb question, isn't it? You must be in orbit."

"So you noticed, huh? You've seen our contest and everything?" He'd been paying attention.

"How could I miss it? It's everywhere I look. I knew you'd make a success of it!"

"You're nice to say that after I was such a creep the last time we met. I'm sorry."

"You weren't a creep. It was my fault. I should have explained my situation."

She fiddled with the phone cord for a moment and then said, "I'm sorry I didn't call."

"I can imagine you've been really busy." He stammered a little. "I guess that's why I haven't called you. You're probably never free."

And because I was a creep. She gathered her nerve. "I've thought about you a lot . . . about some things you said. Are you all right? How are the kids handling things?"

"We're going to be fine. We just take it one day at a time." He paused a moment as if choosing his words carefully. "Livy, I do have some news. My law firm has lined me up with some big New York clients and decided that I need to be working out of the New York office."

"So what does that mean?"

"It means I'm moving there, very soon. You know how moving can be. But it should be an exciting adventure."

"Wow. That's a promotion, I'm sure. That's great."

He paused an awkward second or two and said, "I've kind of come to a decision." He paused again. "I decided that it's time. For the kids' sake and mine, it's time to let someone into my life again."

"So you're moving on, starting over. I'm glad for you. Shelly would want you to be happy. You deserve some real happiness."

"Thank you, Livy."

This could be the best or the worst possible time to ask him out. But she forged on. "Well, I'll tell you why I called. This may not fit if you've already moved in that direction, but . . . um . . . I . . . we're having this sorta party to celebrate the doll's success. And I need someone to, uh . . ." *What am I? A fifteen-year-old with braces who's too scared to talk to boys? Spit it out.* "Well, would you like to come?"

"When is it?"

"It's really short notice. It's a week from tomorrow.

"The first Friday in August."

"I would like to come. I'd love to help you celebrate."

"Really? You would?" Her butterflies started a little dance.

"But . . ."

"But?" *He's letting someone else into his life, stupid.* She fashioned the long phone cord into a noose.

"It's just that we're moving that weekend. I have people coming over to help box up stuff and people dropping in to say good-bye. You know how it is."

"Sure. I understand."

"And I wanted to tell you . . . oh, hold on a second."

In the background Livy could hear a female voice asking, "Garrett, honey, Staci's fallen asleep in her clothes. Do you think I should put her pajamas on her?"

"Sure," he replied. "She'll be back to sleep in two minutes."

Livy felt a wave of disappointment sweep over her. Of course he would want to go on with his life. He obviously had. He found someone, and she was there with him now. Naturally, he wouldn't wait for Livy to learn how to love, to like kids, and to trust. But he didn't know how far she had come on all of that with Bryan's help. Now she was too late.

He was back on the phone. "I'm sorry, Livy. What were we saying?"

"Well, you're busy there. Maybe I'll run into you when you come to town. Or we could have lunch sometime. I hope you'll like it here."

"Thanks. I was wondering if you might want to . . ."

"Well, I've got to get my other phone. I have to take this, sorry. I'll talk to you later, okay? Bye."

"Livy wait . . . I wanted . . ." Click.

She glared at Bryan as she put down the phone. "Why did you make me do that? I feel like a fool—*again*! He's moved on. He's got some woman with him right now. You got me all worked up for nothing!"

For punishment she ordered Bryan to go with her to the gala event.

Chapter Fourteen

Livy rented a tux for Bryan to wear as her escort but at the last minute, he said he couldn't come. He told her he was sorry, but he had to rush to be with a grief-stricken child. She was crushed. Neither of the two men she cared about would be there in her moment of triumph.

When her big night arrived, Livy donned her new red-sequined designer gown. It couldn't have been more perfect if it had been designed especially for her. Long, fitted, with a slit up the side, it accentuated her long, shapely legs and model-like height. Her hair was piled high with jeweled accent pins and wisps of curls to frame her face. The success she had dreamed of was here in her grasp, and as she gazed at herself in the mirror, she marveled. Leaning forward, she pinched her cheeks, studied her face, peered into her eyes, as if to verify it was really she, herself, in the reflection. Gone was the lonely, frightened child who usually stared back from the glass. This lovely vision was almost beyond her ability to take in. She had made it. Hannah had made it. Despite the panic, the setbacks, and those who tried to tear her down, it was happening. It was real. The new life she had plotted up, planned for, and dreamed of was here.

Please let this be real! Please don't take it away!

She stepped out of the cab, took several deep breaths and made her entrance into the crowded hotel ballroom with outward confidence and flair, despite her very extensive collection of inner butterflies. She was thoroughly surrounded by as many rich, intelligent, and powerful people as one room could hold, and about as much palpable arrogance. Then, all at once, it felt as if a sea of stares tsunamied on her and time stood still.

"Fraud!" a sudden shout sounded in her mind. And a choir of distant

voices chimed in, *"You don't belong here. Who do you think you are?"*

A short, stern-faced, white-whiskered gentleman approached her and from his expression, she was sure he was going ask her to present an invitation or a driver's license to justify her presence here. Instinctively, she backed away from him and toward the nearest exit.

The man grabbed her elbow and barked, "You! You come with me!" He dragged her over to a table full of champagne-sipping hotshots and commanded, "Don't let her get away." Then his face burst into an enormous laughing, wicked grin. "Ladies and gentlemen, this is Olivia Thomas, and I'm claiming the first dance with her. I'm going to go jump-start that band leader. Be right back."

"Olivia Thomas!" A dozen enthusiastic hands thrust out for hers. "How wonderful to meet you!" "Congratulations!" "You've really turned the toy world upside down!" Their compliments came in gushes, rinsing her fears away. Names, company affiliations, and praises for her work swirled around her like a microburst of approbation.

She was already dizzy, and she and her partner hadn't even hit the dance floor yet. When he returned to escort her from the table, he could barely pry her away from the clutches of her admirers. The band was now playing "Lady in Red" which he had requested especially for her.

"I suppose I should introduce myself. I'm Richard Flemming," he said as he slid an arm around her waist.

"Of Townsend-Flemming?" she asked, noticing that his silver head came barely to her shoulder.

He seemed totally unfazed by their difference in height—he was probably 5'7" and she was 6'3" with her heels. Yet he was able to skillfully sashay her around the now-crowded dance floor. "So you've heard of us."

"Of course I've heard of you. Everyone has. You're the new force to be reckoned with in entertainment software."

"And . . . we're expanding into technology-based toys and educational lines."

"I didn't know that."

"I'm very impressed with what you've been able to do over at JTC. I was surprised to learn you're so young and . . . attractive."

After some small talk, he moved his lips as close to her ear as he could reach and asked, "So, what will it take to make you mine?"

"I beg your pardon?"

He raised an eyebrow, spoke louder over the band and repeated,

"What will it take to make you mine?"

A voice behind him said loudly, "All the tea in China, and you still can't have her." It was Mel, tapping him on the shoulder. "She's mine . . . and JTC's, of course."

"Oh, it's you," Flemming growled. "How did you find us so quickly? We were just getting acquainted, and I haven't even had a chance to explain what I can offer."

"It's always easy to find you, Flemming. I just follow your oil slick. Ms. Thomas has a very promising future with us, so I think I know where her loyalties lie. Am I right, Olivia?" He extended his arm to Livy, an invitation for her to change partners.

She shook Mr. Flemming's hand and said, "Mr. Flemming, it was wonderful to meet you." She quickly winked at Mel and continued, "One never can tell—it's nice to know that a girl has options. Thank you very much for the dance." Then she took Mel's offered arm.

Mel had been with Joy, seeing to the details of the gala, and schmoozing some very important guests. He hadn't had the chance to find Livy before this moment.

"So, did he stain your dress?" he asked.

"What are you talking about?"

"They don't call him the *Phlegm* for nothing. Richard Flemming is about the greasiest, slimiest con man in the New York metro area. You stay away from him. I don't think he was even invited. In his past ventures, he lured away some of my best people, and when he'd stolen as many of our ideas as possible from them, he exploited what was left of their genius and abandoned them in the dirt. Good old Richard. We go back a long way."

"Well, sir, I consider myself warned. But I do have to keep an eye on my best opportunities, don't I?" She changed the subject. "I'm really not much of a dancer. Now *you've* been warned."

"I'll be careful. I hope you don't mind when I tell you that you look beautiful tonight, Livy. Your success is very becoming, and in that gown, well, let's just say all eyes are on you for lots of reasons."

She was thinking, *You look mighty fine in your tuxedo too, Mel.* But she didn't dare say it. The look of pride and approval in his eyes was the most beautiful and satisfying thing of all. Dance? She felt she could fly.

"Where's your date?" he asked.

"At the last minute he couldn't make it. I'm really disappointed that he wasn't here to see this. He's some kind of social worker and was called away."

"So, is this something serious that I should be aware of?" Mel inquired, one eyebrow raised.

"We're just friends, I guess, but really good friends."

When the music stopped, Mel led her by the hand to the podium and turned on the mike.

"Ladies and gentlemen, could I have your attention please? For those of you who don't know me, I'm Melvin Jameson, President and CEO of JTC." He held his arm out to where Joy stood. "My lovely wife, Joy, is our chair and she makes me do all the dirty work . . . like speeches. First of all, I want to thank you for joining us on this wonderful occasion. We're celebrating the birth of a very remarkable little girl . . . our Hannah! We want to thank you all for your efforts in making this project such a fabulous success. We owe so much of that success to you and your partnerships with us. I can see that we will all be richly rewarded. In fact, as of five o'clock this afternoon, Hold-Me-Hannah broke the record for first-week in-store sales, a record that had held for about seventeen years. We knew she was something special!" He stared right at Richard Flemming in gloating satisfaction.

The audience clapped and cheered, and Mel held his arm up to quiet them. "Right now, I'd like to introduce you to someone very special—the creator and visionary behind this project. She and her team have worked tirelessly to pull off this major coup. I'd like you to meet Ms. Olivia Thomas! Please give her a great big, well-deserved round of applause." He held her hand up in a gesture of victory, and the crowd erupted in thunderous applause. "Olivia, would you like to say a few words?"

She hadn't prepared a speech, but took the mike confidently. "Thank you for your kind ovation. It feels really good to know that you like what we've done here." The crowd started to cheer. "It feels even better that the buying public likes what we've done here." They cheered louder. "I'd like to thank Barbara Donaldson, my assistant, and my whole team: Janey Gray, Sean Monson, and Jeff Howard. They're the ones struggling to hold themselves up over there at the open bar. We've been under a little pressure lately, as you can imagine." The audience applauded again. "And of course, I thank Mr. Jameson for all his wonderful support from the beginning. Hannah would not have been possible without his sustaining and guiding hand. Thank you all for being a part of this wonderful night, and I hope you're having a great time."

She waved at the crowd, and they clapped again. Joy stood with Bob Farrell in the back of the hall during the speeches. They had clapped absently, unenthusiastically. Livy had noticed but she didn't care. *They can't argue with millions of dollars, now can they?*

Finally, Mel led her to the side, away from the group. "What can I say, Livy? You've done it! You and your team have pulled this off, and I can't express how pleased I am with you. I want you to know that what I'm going to say has nothing to do with Richard. This is your night, and I was going to mention this anyway," he looked around to make sure that no one heard his next words, "I'm going to do everything in my power to make sure the VP job is yours. No one could be more deserving." He took her hand warmly and leaned in to give her a kiss on the cheek. "The board meets next week."

Do you know I love you, Melvin Jameson? And I just about have you right where I want you, she thought, as he dropped her hand and started to go.

He went in search of Joy, who had started dancing with the head of a new European toy distribution company. When he reached Joy, she glanced over and gave Livy a plastic, insincere smile. Livy returned one just as toxic, and then began to mingle smoothly and exultantly through the crowd, savoring every delicious minute.

Could it get any better? Who'd have ever thought that she, Livy, the lonely lanky loser would literally be Cinderella at the ball (complete with wicked-stepmother Joy)? She glanced up at the entrance, expecting to see a clock striking twelve, but instead saw Bryan across the hall, looking absolutely like the most beautiful man she had ever seen. He almost glowed. It *had* gotten better. Bryan was here to share in her glory, and by rights he should. He had given her the idea. It was all she could do to keep herself from running to him. With an expression like a lost lamb, he scanned the crowd trying to find her and appeared completely out of place. He was gorgeous in his tuxedo but still—and it might have been the white socks and bowling shoes—he had Idaho written all over him somehow. And that was just how she liked him.

She cut to the side of the room, sneaked up behind him, and covered his eyes. "Guess who?"

"Lucille? Is that you?"

She playfully slugged him, remembering their encounter with the homeless woman from Christmas day. "No, silly. It's me, Vice President,

Olivia Thomas," she whispered enthusiastically in his ear.

He pulled her aside, out of public view and enveloped her in his arms. Then he swung her up joyously into the air. "Wow! That's fantastic!" He took her hands and stepped back to admire the view. "Sheesh! You *do* clean up real good lookin'!"

She grabbed his hand. "Bryan, I want you to be the first one to see this display!" Livy guided him excitedly to a room where the newly unveiled and celebrated dolls were royally exhibited. The different variations of skin color, eye color, and other distinctions made each one unique, and yet they shared a common expression of hopeful anticipation that echoed back to the original winning Hannah face.

Indicating the one that was originally created, the one most similar to the photograph, now widely recognized as Hannah herself, Bryan said, "She's amazing, Liv . . . so remarkably like the picture. I'm amazed at how well they achieved the likeness."

"Of course. We do good work. She had to be perfect, and I think, if I do say so myself, she pretty much is. These are hooked up to the security system for this event, so I can't let you play with her, but she really is marvelous. Come and see this demo DVD." She loved watching Bryan's expression as he studied the video with fascination and delight. He was obviously impressed with his "sister."

"Mom and Dad will be so proud!"

"Oh, Bryan, stop. They don't even know that I exist."

"They *do* know and they love you already!"

They returned to the ballroom, and Livy realized that she had met everyone she had wanted and needed (for business purposes) to meet. She just wanted to spend the rest of the evening with Bryan. She wanted to fly, to laugh out loud, and to rejoice in her astonishing triumph. What a fabulous feeling to have someone so dear to her there to share the most marvelous night of her life!

Carlos was beside himself as he watched the news about the success of the doll. *They owe me, big time! Do I know how to pick a winner or what? Their big windfall is going to be my big windfall as well! A lousy $100,000 is not going to cut it.* He finished his tall beer and wiped his mouth with his forearm. Rubbing his hands together, he began excitedly formulating all new schemes. *It's playtime again.*

He couldn't wait to set up another appointment and watch her squirm when he laid his hands on her and demanded more . . . much more . . . or else! He relished the possibilities that the words "or else" opened up. He could ride this wave all the way to Christmas and beyond. Happy holidays indeed!

He vowed once again to find and silence Patti . . . if she wasn't already dead. She would be the only one who could poke her nose in and spoil the fun. Nothing and no one else could stand in his way.

After their phone conversation, Garrett lamented turning down her invitation for the party. But when he saw the write-up in the style section of the New York Times, he *really* regretted it. The article touted it as the most anticipated affair of the year. All the elite of retail would be there and representatives from children's agencies and on and on. It was all in honor of Livy's doll creation. It was a huge deal and would mean the world to her. When she'd invited him, he had thought it was a small get-together of friends from work. He hated those kinds of things where he felt like a stranger. But this? He had probably offended her, big time. No wonder she practically hung up on him.

He decided he would go and surprise her. Knowing her, if she asked him, after all this time, she mostly likely couldn't think of anyone else or whomever else she had asked had turned her down. Garret didn't want her to be alone. He'd rearrange his moving party and show up at the gala.

Hating tuxes, he wore his best suit and ducked into the ballroom through a side door. The big shots were making speeches. He made his way to a little corner where he could watch and listen unobserved. *She is really something. Could she ever come to care about me again? But whenever I take a move toward her, she runs away.*

He watched as Livy stepped to the mike and into the light. She was absolutely radiant, so charming and lovely. The feelings he had held at bay were renewed and amplified as he watched her confidently standing before them all in triumph. His heart was hers for the taking, like before. *But why is she so skittish around me? She acts like she owns the world up there.*

Could it be that she is afraid to show me that she still cares? He wanted to go to her, take her in his arms, and tell her how proud of her he was. How much he loved her and wanted her.

Now she was coming right toward him. She hadn't spotted him yet. Just as he was opening his arms to her, she crept up to a fellow in front of him and put her hands over his eyes. Next thing Garrett knew, the guy had her in *his* arms, swinging her up in the air. The way they giggled at each other, he knew they were very close. *Wait. It's that doorman guy. Little brother indeed.*

He escaped the ballroom, feeling the fool. He pushed through the outer doors and sat down on the stairs to sort it out. In a few moments Livy and her date came rushing past, holding hands.

"Hey! Let's blow this joint and go cow tipping. What do you say?" Livy said as they skipped down the stairs.

"I wish we could go to Rupe's Drive-In for super shakes and burgers," Bryan said. "That's what we always did when someone did something worth celebrating. It's right across the railroad tracks from the giant potato at the expo. But I guess New York will have to do."

They hit the street and immediately he squatted down like he had that day in the park; this time she knew just what to do. With Bryan, dapper in his tuxedo, and Livy fabulous in her designer gown, she got the piggyback ride of her life. Bryan kept shouting her success to everyone they passed. "This woman is a genius! This is the queen of Madison Avenue!" He'd stop people and ask, "You know that new Hold-Me-Hannah doll?" They all did. "Well, she created it. She's the mastermind. Isn't that great?"

Finally, she was sufficiently embarrassed and made him stop, but not for a good long time. This moment, with this guy on this magic night, was just too delicious to put an early end to.

He must be exhausted; he's carried me all over Manhattan. She climbed down from his back and pushed him down to rest on a bus stop bench. "You know, Bryan, I remember when I first came to this town. I'd never seen it—you know, actually been here—until the day of my interview with JTC. All that time at business school I never made the 'pilgrimage,' as Garrett called it. Everybody else came up lots of times, but I never did.

"So that day when I came in the taxi, I was blown away. We came in from the Lincoln Tunnel and right into the heart of the theatre district: Broadway. It was fitting. I felt like I was auditioning for the part of 'rising star.' It wouldn't really be me, but perhaps I could pull off the performance of the role. I was excited and confident and terrified all at the same time. Those giant buildings were intimidating and the monsters I imagined inside, even more so. But the confident part of me felt this sense of destiny. 'I can do this. I'm ready!' And I did it, Bryan! You know, veni, vidi, vici! I did it! I came, I saw, and I conquered! I created the marketing coup of the year!"

Bryan cleared his throat in mock insulted pout. "Hail, Caesar."

"Oh, of course! I'm sorry. WE came up with the must-have toy of the year! I'm sorry, Bryan. Am I a drag or what? It's all about me, me, me. Let's talk about you. What about your life? What do you want to conquer? What are you going to do when you've got all your case studies and you write up your thesis or whatever? Then what, Bryan? Are you going to go on playing basketball in the projects, counseling endless troubled kids, and never ever win? What can you conquer?"

"I'm not in it to conquer. Just the opposite."

"What? You want to be the loser?"

"Not at all. My mom always said it was like playing chess backwards. That's the game she and Dad live, and I'm living it too, I hope."

"Chess backwards? I'm confused," Livy said.

"Well, instead of knocking people down, the object is go out onto the battlefield and try to pick up as many as you can."

"There are so many little pawns out there suffering and barely holding on. They're the inconvenient and sometimes invisible victims caught in the middle of everyone else's wars. There they are, out on the battlefield, left to suffer and struggle on their own—neglected, abused, unwanted, and unloved. How could something so precious, so marvelous be left behind?"

"It's easy, I guess," Livy said softly.

"It all started when my Dad found my mom out there and brought her home. They've been out there working ever since. And now, I suppose I am too."

"But there are those who make it off the battlefield on their own, and they aren't going out there ever again. It's too painful."

"But that's how you win, Livy. The struggle is not in vain; the pain has purpose when you can turn it around and lift another. That's how I want to win."

Chapter Fifteen

Every Saturday, as the summer went by, Josie perched on her bench, anxiously waiting for Livy and Bryan to come. Her face would light up when she spotted them coming up the street. Out the gate she'd skip, singing, "Livy! Livy!"

Whenever Livy had to be out of town on business trips, Bryan was a poor substitute. Hard as he tried to cheer Josie, her affections were centered on Livy, and her disappointment was always clear. Livy arrived one afternoon, after having been gone two consecutive weekends, to find Josie in tears.

"Josie, my girl, why are you crying? I'm here and I brought you something. I've missed you."

Before Livy could present her with the box she had brought, Josie wrapped herself around Livy's long legs and sobbed.

"I thought you were never coming back and I think my mommy's gonna die. I'd be all alone, 'cep for Frankie."

She gathered her up in her arms. "Honey, why do you think your mommy's going to die?"

"Last night, I was in my bed, in the dark and I heard her crying out. That man was shouting and banging things, and I didn't dare move. When I got up this mornin', Mama be on the floor and I couldn' wake her up. Frankie said she was breathing, and she be okay, but I thought she was gonna die."

Livy could imagine a scenario where the mother had brought home some lover, had a rather indiscreet and rough romantic adventure, and ended up drunk on the floor. But how do you explain that to a terrified seven-year-old? Didn't the woman realize her kids were in the house? But this wasn't Livy's problem; she couldn't handle this kind of thing. Part of her just wanted to sit down with Josie and cry. What had Bryan gotten her into?

When she had let Josie cry enough to feel some relief, Livy gave her the box. Inside was a numbered, first edition, dark-skinned, dark-eyed Hold-Me-Hannah. It was beautiful, and so was Josie's face when she embraced it.

On one particularly warm September Saturday, Bryan and Livy noticed a change in the little gang.

"Hey, Jimmy! Where's Frankie?" Bryan asked.

Livy looked around to find Josie, but she wasn't there either.

"He's probably shoppin' around for my birthday present. I'm fourteen today, Bryan. Did ya'll know that? Fourteen! I be gettin' as tall as you, pretty soon," Jimmy replied.

"Happy Birthday, dude. A little older, bigger, and wiser, eh? I shoulda' brought a cake," Bryan moaned.

Jimmy looked disappointed. "Das okay. Nobody in my family said nothin' nietha."

Then Bryan pulled something from behind the back of his shirt, tossed it at Jimmy, and said, "Hope you like 'em."

Bryan had brought him some basketball shorts. Jimmy tried not to show that he liked them, but Livy could tell he did.

Livy asked Jimmy what she should give him for his birthday and he replied, "You can teach me all about . . . . you know what, pretty lady. My place or yours?" All the boys howled with laughter and were flabbergasted at his boldness.

"She was thinking more along the lines of a video game, I think. She works for a toy company, you know." Bryan tried to steer the conversation to something a little safer, but Livy took Jimmy's bait.

"I can teach you all you need to know right here and right now." Then the boys really howled and catcalled. They sat down on the pavement as if to watch a show.

She looked Jimmy right in the eye and said in a somewhat sultry sexy voice, "Sex is like nuclear power."

"Whoa! That's what I'm talkin' about. She's had some serious sugar!" Jimmy waited for the juicy part to follow.

"That's right. Sex is serious stuff. Used wisely, it can give life and light to the whole world. Or used unwisely, it can take down everything in its path. Jimmy, I suggest you stay away from it. You're only fourteen. Be a kid for a while, okay? Just be a kid."

The boys were surprised at Livy's intensity. There was a lot more to her story than she was telling.

"Somebody done somethin' to her, man," Ricardo said.

"Maybe somebody knocked her up and didn' leave no forwardin' address when he took off," Jamal suggested.

"Happens all the time, so what?" Jimmy said. "I was just askin'— havin' a little fun." With that, he took the ball from Ricardo and started dribbling toward the basket.

"When you want some fun, go shoot hoops or go bowling or hang with your friends. Don't mess around with something as powerful and dangerous as a little 'sugar,'" Livy said.

Just then Frankie raced into the playground screaming, "They're gone! My mom and my sister are gone!" He was panting and could barely get the words out.

"What?" Bryan asked. "Slow down and tell me what happened."

"The police came and took my mom away and some white car that said NYCDFS on it took Josette!" He was frantic. "I hid, and they didn't get me. They said my mama was workin' her street, and one of her johns was a narc and he found cocaine in her stuff. She goin' to jail! But where'd they take Josette? What do NYCDFS mean?"

"It means Division of Child and Family Services, and she's going into foster care. And as soon as they find you, you'll go there too," Livy said in matter-of-fact tone. A dull ache manifested itself in the pit of her stomach.

"Don't let 'em take me, Bryan. I don't wanna go to no foster care. I've heard about that from my friend. They beat ya' and starve ya' and stuff like that."

"No, cases like that are rare, Frankie. Most foster parents are very kind people who just want to help kids who need a place to stay. My family takes kids in. You'll see. She'll be okay, and so will you. We'll figure this out." Bryan put a comforting arm around his shoulder.

"Yeah, I'm a foster kid, and do I look starved to you?" Ricardo revealed. "I've been with these people for two years, and they're pretty good to me."

"You're a foster kid? Where's your mama?" Frankie looked shocked.

"With her boyfriend, I guess. He made it clear, he didn't want no kids around, so she dumped us and took off. I say I'm better off now than with her." His voice caught and betrayed the toughness in the words. "I do miss my lil' man Miguel. He's my little brother. He went to some other family."

Now Frankie really looked worried. "Some other family? I just want my mom and Josie back. I can take care of her. I always do."

"I know you do, buddy. You're the best big brother," Bryan agreed.

"Can I stay wid ya'll until she comes home? Bryan, please, I can't go with no stranger."

"Maybe. We'll work something out."

"What? What can you work out?" Livy asked. "If you just up and take him home, they'll get you for kidnapping. Not even a do-gooder like you can just pick up a stray kid off the street and just say 'Wow! Finders, keepers.' Even though it seems like that's exactly what *they* do—the agencies, I mean."

"I meant I'll have to talk to my superiors; maybe I've got some resources in this kind of thing. But what do we do in the meantime? That's the question. Frankie, do you have any other family members around here that you could stay with?"

"No, nobody. My mom might have people back in Haiti. I don't have a dad."

"We'll talk to them. We'll find out what's going on. There may not be anything else we can do right now, but we can at least find out what's happening and where Josie went. Maybe it would be better to try to work with the system," Bryan advised.

"No. I don't wanna to go to no home, and besides, who's gonna wanna take me home wid'em? They probably just throw me in juvie with the real criminals and gangsters."

"The system stinks. I'm sorry, Frankie. I wish I could say something or do something that would help," Livy said. She turned and walked toward the entrance of the playground.

"Jamal? Can I stay wid you for now? Just ask your mom if it's okay if you and me have a 'sleepover' for a day or two."

"I think dat'd be okay. My mom's pretty cool. I'll just tell her that your mom's sick or somethin'."

Frankie was just starting to calm down when the white Buick sedan pulled up to the playground court. Sure enough, it said NYCDFS on the doors. Two men in suits and a tall, heavy-set woman got out. Josie was not with them.

One of the men spoke to Livy at the gate. "We're looking for Francois Martine."

Before he could say another word, Frankie dashed out the gate and down the street. One of the men got in the car and gave chase, and the other took off after him on foot. Frankie was fast and able to get about three blocks away before they caught up with him. The woman and the group at the playground watched the chase unfold.

"I take it that was Francois?" the woman asked.

Livy nodded and added, "He likes to be called Frankie. And please don't treat him like a criminal; he's done nothing wrong. He's a good kid."

"It's our job to do what's best and to protect society, no more, no less." The woman was emotionless.

"Yes, ma'am. You be sure and protect society from kids, now," Livy said caustically. She turned and walked a few steps away, staring blankly into space.

The woman merely huffed.

Bryan approached. "Can he go home and get some things of his own and his sister's to take with him? And can we find out where the little sister went? They need to stay together. They need each other."

"Since he's obviously not coming willingly, I don't know if we can stop at the apartment at this point. We can't run the risk of his trying to get away again. And as for where they're going, it's confidential. You can talk to the family court judge if you want the okay to get information. That's about all I can tell you."

When the men had come back with Frankie, she told them to "secure him" in the back seat.

Did she mean they were going to cuff him? Livy wondered.

The warm wind kicked up and seemed to push the sedan away from the solemn crowd of friends. Bryan walked the boys back to their respective buildings in silent procession. Livy lagged several paces behind. She felt that sick ache she felt when someone had died or something terrible was going to happen. What could be more terrible?

She should have known. She did know. She had simply pushed the warning signs away—unwilling and unable to bear the obvious truth. She stopped in front of Josie and Frankie's building, debating whether to go inside. Unhesitatingly, Bryan took her hand and they climbed the crumbling cement stairs to the apartment. It was a landfill of pizza boxes and fast food sacks. It smelled of cheap wine and dirt. The refrigerator was empty with the exception of an unidentifiable leftover in aluminum foil, and a half-drunk can of Colt 45. Shreds of what had once been curtains fluttered at a broken window. Josie's bed was nothing more than a pile of dirty laundry on the living room floor covered pitifully with a ragged pink blanket and pillow. Frankie's rickety camp cot was neatly made.

Without a word, Livy marched across the hall to the opposite door, Bryan right behind her. In answer to a knock filled with all the anger and frustration Livy was struggling to control, a stringy black woman glared suspiciously at them through three thick security chains. Bryan's harmless manner and Livy's semi-celebrity status convinced her to finally open the door and talk with them.

Bad things had been happening for a long, long time, she said, and filled in some of the details. Many different men had been coming in and out of the apartment for years. Some seemed almost nice to the children. Some were dirty and violent.

"That boss-man," the woman said, "he think he own Madeleine, and Josie too. She tol' me he always leave his calling card in the way of beatin's and bruises and fifty bucks on the dresser.

"I'd go over there an' half the time fin' Madeleine and some man passed out on the floor from drugs, so I'd make them kids come have some food. That Frankie, he's a good boy. He'd always do me some chores, to pay me back, he says. He tried to protect his little sister, and he took care of his mother too. Though she usually high or on a passed-out-low. That little Josie be dead without him. I's the one who got 'em to school, if they went at all."

"So did you call family services?" Livy asked.

"No. Las' week I took her to school and the teacher stopped me in the schoolyard askin' about the bruises on Josie. Said she'd been to the nurse's 'bout seventeen times. They'd called services but nobody did nothin'. I tol' her what I tol' you and we called 'em together. Looks like they payin' attention, this time."

The subway ride home seemed to take forever. Livy and Bryan still hadn't said much to each other, and there were only two stops remaining until they reached her station.

Finally, Livy said, "Bryan, why did you take me there and get me in the middle of this?"

"You're not in the middle of anything. I wanted you to go with me and give me some credibility. And don't tell me you don't care. You really are good with them," Bryan told her.

"Did you know what was going on with that mother?"

"I had some idea. But Frankie's just such a good kid. He's tough and amazingly responsible."

"Why didn't I see this? Josie's so sweet. How could she be surrounded by so much ugliness?"

"Well, this could be a turning point for them both."

"Yes, but which way will they turn?" Livy asked rhetorically.

"Can they turn to you?" Bryan asked pointedly.

"Me? You think I should be their foster parent? Why not you? They all love you."

"Single guys my age, on temporary assignments, are not considered good candidates for this kind of thing."

"Single women who work until nine or ten at night aren't exactly ideal either, are they?"

"You don't *have* to always work late. You choose to. The office is your whole world. You could diversify your life portfolio a little."

"No. I can't do it. I care about those kids, but it would be temporary, and it would hurt too much when they took them away."

"It's all about you, is it? What about the hurt they feel?"

"That's the hurt I'm talking about, their hurt. The system will keep trying to give them back to their mother until she has either killed them, killed herself, or gets twenty-five years in jail, and then they'll finally think about terminating her parental rights. By then, the kids will have been yanked in and out of care situations eight or eighty times. I can't stand by and watch that—watch them get tossed around and have their lives ruined. I certainly don't want to be part of their pain."

"Then don't stand by. Do something. Fight for them. They need someone on their side."

"*You* do something. You're the one with the connections. You must know someone who could help. I can't do it, Bryan. I know I can't."

"Why not?"

"Because you can't give what you never had."

Bryan jumped in right on top of her words. "And you can't have what you won't receive."

After another long stretch of silence, Bryan asked, "Have you ever tried to call Garrett again?"

"No, and he hasn't called me either."

"Take a risk, Livy. Just show him that you care. He's alone in a new city."

"Alone? I don't think so. He has someone."

"You don't know that. There's love all over the place if you'll just grab some of it. Stop being afraid."

"I love you, don't I? Why *do* I love you, anyway?"

"Because I loved you first." He said it like a kid taunting, and then sang, "Nanner, nanner, nanner."

"I think it must be that you're low risk." She said it half teasingly.

"Yeah, I guess I'm not much to lose."

"You know that's not what I meant." She wanted to say that he was one person that she did trust to love her, no matter what. Her "brother" would never turn against her and never abandon her. He was her refuge, her sanctuary. She said she loved him and that realization itself was a little epiphany. Being able to say it right out loud was a major breakthrough. Garrett was right—Bryan was safe. She put her head on his shoulder for the rest of the subway ride.

Watching out the subway windows, she noticed the graffiti flying by. It reminded her of some "tenement art" she had studied near the playground that had struck some deeply buried chord within her. A young artist was screaming to the world, "I'm here. I'm not invisible. I want to be seen. Hear my voice." Suddenly Livy could hear, ever so clearly, Josie's frightened plea. "I'll be all alone . . ."

Chapter Sixteen

"I want my girls sold out by Thanksgiving!" she'd said at the first meeting. Olivia's prophecy was fulfilled more completely every day. It was only late October and dolls were getting as scarce as '65 Mustangs and were practically worth as much. The company hadn't over-produced the dolls, like they had with products past. Stores everywhere were running out and ordering more. They'd receive a few at a time; the plan was carefully devised to keep the scarcity mentality. Dolls were on back order everywhere. Sales on eBay were skyrocketing along with the highest bid.

The media picked up on the already well-known doll and her popularity. Local talk shows across the country gave Hannah sighting alerts for listeners still desperate to find a store that might have one left for a hopeful little girl to open on Christmas morning.

Livy was featured in an article entitled, *Olivia Thomas: The Woman Behind JTC's Baby Boom,* in one of the most prestigious business insider magazines. The inquisitive writer, Kent Duckworth, was frustrated to find Livy unwilling to expose any life details prior to her college days. He played up the sports angle. "Ms. Thomas credits her drive and will to succeed to her competitive days as a forward on the University of South Florida Women's Basketball Team. 'She had a passion about the game,' said one of her former teammates, Julie Keating. 'She had something to prove and wasn't going to let anyone or anything stand in her way.'"

Curious Kent just ached to know what it was she had to prove. He would start once again with Mrs. Keating, and dig a little deeper. The real story to be told had little to do with a doll. He'd bet the farm on it.

Carlos followed the story closely and counted his cash. A portion of every doll sold was given to his "charity."

The rich witch was getting tired of his demands, and he wondered how far was too far. He suspected he had a little more wiggle room, yet. This was just too much fun. Would she tell? Never.

He made his way to her office, this time disguised as a window washer and wearing a low bandana over his head. He ducked when he saw Mr. Jameson in the hall. The secretary failed to recognize him and let him into her office without question.

She was on the phone and motioned for him to go ahead and get started on the large glass panes. He nearly laughed out loud as he took the squeegee from his belt and got to work.

When she hung up, he turned around and said, "That's going to cost you extra."

She very nearly screamed. "You! You're never to come here!"

"I'll be quick. I need dolls. Lots of them. I been lookin' for a little somethin' to kick-start my black market activities. Each baby's going for around $1200 bucks out there. You know that? I was gonna sell your real one for less than that. My guy will set it up. There'll be invoices, and it'll all look legit. Don' worry."

"When does this end?"

She was at the very edge of losing it. He better not push it too far.

"Now don't cry. You've been such a good girl. I've been thinking maybe you and me could . . . you know. . . . Go off together when this dries up." He moved in close to her face. "Or should I just kill you?"

The woman at the child services agency was thrilled to meet the creator of the famous toy. "I saw you on *Good Morning, America* last week! I'm Sylvia Barrett, by the way." She reached out excitedly to shake Livy's hand. She was not as thrilled to share with Livy the current status and location of Francois and Josette Martine.

"We have to be very careful in these cases. Heaven knows what might happen if we tell just anyone where they are placed," Sylvia explained. "You have no idea of the kinds of things we've seen."

"I wouldn't be surprised. But I'm not just anyone. I have no ulterior motive. I don't really need the money, and I know these kids personally and want to help them out. Does that count for anything? Can I just fill out an application to be a foster parent? Then if you approve it, you can help me find Josie and Frankie and . . ."

Livy could not believe that she had just uttered those words. *Me? A foster parent? Not even in a parallel universe. What has Bryan done to me?*

"Oh, but there's a thirty-day training and a background check and by then," Sylvia leaned over the counter to speak more privately, "I'd be willing to bet the state will have sent them back to their mother. Happens every time. You just get someone picked out and ready to take some kids in, and the parent gets clearance to take them home."

"And everyone lives happily ever after, right?" Livy asked.

"Ha! I'd say eight out of ten times the kid is taken out of the home again and again and again. This place needs one of those revolving doors."

"Can you at least tell me if they're together? They really depend on each other. Don't take away the one family relationship they have that's working!"

"Unfortunately, I can tell you nothing. I'd lose my job. You're not related to them and have no guardianship paperwork. You have no standing. I'm sorry."

"I'll fill out the application and do the training and hope for the best. Is that all right? Is that a start?"

The woman merely shrugged.

Bryan had no standing either. He was doing case studies, period. He was not officially anybody. The kids he worked with were ones assigned from outside sources. The kids in the projects were just that, his private projects, fieldwork, support subjects for his findings.

It was a brisk fall morning, and Livy fought to stay awake in her third parenting class that week. She hadn't been sleeping well and these 8 AM classes were a challenge to get enthused about. Not because she didn't acknowledge she needed them, but because they were taught by staff psychologists who couldn't have been more boring. Elmer Fudd would be an improvement over this guy. She settled in for another session of note-taking. The rule was no cell phones in class, but Livy left hers on vibrate, just in case something came up. Fifteen minutes into the class, it buzzed.

"Hello?" Livy whispered as she leaned way over her knees to keep from disturbing the class.

"Ms. Thomas? This is Sylvia at the child welfare office, and we need you to come down here right now."

"Didn't I sign the roll or something? I'm at the child welfare office right now, in the parenting class."

"Could you step outside? They need to talk to you."

Livy excused herself and made her way out to the hallway. Two women and one gentleman were already waiting at the door. They had wasted no time.

"Ms. Thomas, we need to speak to you regarding Josie Martine," the older man stated. He extended his hand to shake hers. "By the way, I'm Dr. Langford, this is Mary Crawford, and this is Daria Nelson." They all shook hands and exchanged pleasantries.

"I've been hoping to see her, find out how she is, anything at all, and I haven't gotten anywhere."

"So I take it that you're still interested in her case," he said.

"I'm interested in *her*. Is there a possibility that she could be placed with me?"

"So you're taking the classes currently?" the middle-aged woman asked.

"Only a couple left. Has something happened?"

The group closed up their little circle to counsel with each other. At last, they turned to Livy. "Since the child has asked for you by name, we think we can expedite matters in this case. We need to act quickly because she will need a place to go in the next couple of weeks. Would that be something you could work out?" the woman asked.

"It's what I've been working toward. I can't believe it!"

"Would you like to see her?" Daria, the younger blonde, asked.

"Of course I would. You have no idea how much I've worried about her. Is she here? And what about her brother, Frankie?"

Dr. Langford led her over to a vacant room. "We have some upsetting news for you. You might want to sit down."

Of course, such a setup made Livy doubly anxious. "What's happened? Where are they?"

"Francois has run away from his placement, and we're fairly certain he's taken up with a neighborhood gang and has been a runner for some older youths dealing drugs. The last time the social worker spoke with him, he had a wad of cash two inches thick in his pocket that he couldn't explain. He disappeared a couple of days later," Daria told her.

"Tell me you didn't take the cash away from him and then send him on his way? You know someone's going to come looking for it. He'll be—"

"We're not stupid, Ms. Thomas. We were working with the police to devise a plan to get him out of the situation safely. But now he's taken off, and we're very concerned, naturally," Dr. Langford said. He drew a deep breath and loosened his tie. "But we really need to talk about Josie."

"Is she all right? Tell me she's all right."

"She's fine, Ms. Thomas. It's just that she isn't going to be able to stay with the family she's been with. They're taking in some severe abuse cases, and it's better for everyone if Josie can find another arrangement. We can let you have some trial visits, and if you still want to take her, we'll get the paperwork signed and make it happen. How does that sound?"

"It sounds great!"

"We thought we would start by letting you take her for Thanksgiving Day. We know that you're a very busy executive and in the limelight. It will probably take you a week or two to line up someone to help you care for Josie. But we assume you do have Thanksgiving Day free, am I right?"

"Yes, of course. Thank you so much! We'll give her the best Thanksgiving a kid ever had!"

The agency had a rule against cohabitation for foster parents, and Daria looked concerned. "Who's 'we', exactly? You're not living with someone, are you?"

"Oh no." She almost laughed at the suggestion. "It'll be just me and the doorman . . . for dinner, I mean. We're like . . . well, we're friends and he's the one who introduced me to Josie in the first place."

"Well, you can look forward to Thanksgiving then."

She stepped from the building and into the ominous growling wind that tugged angrily at her coat and hair. Overhead, pendulous black clouds obscured the daylight—a prelude to a menacing storm. Leaves and dust whipped through the air, and Livy shivered as her gloved fingers fumbled in her purse to retrieve her relentlessly ringing cell phone. It was Bryan.

"So . . . do you have something to tell me?" he asked excitedly.

"How did you find out?" she called out into the roar of the gale.

"I have my sources, you know."

"Oh, Bryan! I'm so happy, but I'm so scared. What if I do everything wrong?"

"Livy, just by asking that question you're showing that you have only her interests at heart. How far wrong can you go? You love that little child."

She thought about it for a moment. *I do love her. I really do.*

"So, are you free, Bryan? I need you to go with me over to the apartment to pick up a few things that she's asked for, like her doll. The apartment manager is expecting me."

He met her with a warm hug at the subway, and they soon found themselves at the housing complex. Livy hadn't been back since DFS had taken the kids. Seeing the place made her realize that she had missed the company of the boys as well. Bryan had continued his visits, while Livy had just maintained that she was too busy with everything going on at work.

They crossed the familiar playground and the sounds, sights, and smells brought back the real reasons why Livy had not returned. Hopelessness and despair seemed to hiss from the neighborhood like a snake lying in wait. They arrived at Building C and knocked on the manager's door.

A man with a mostly toothless smile answered. "Oh, it *is* you. I wondered when they tol' me Olivia Thomas be coming by if it was *you*. I seen you on TV the other day. What you doin' wid a kid from the South Bronx?"

When they declined to explain, he invited them in and gestured to a small pile of belongings he had gathered in front of his desk. "Not much left of the little girl's things. The place was ransacked pretty bad wid'in a day or two. I just found 'dese things here: a few shoes, some underwear, and a blanket. I didn't find one of 'dem dolls. Guess somebody stole dat firs' off."

"What about the boy's things?" Bryan asked.

"Even less of 'doze. What I got is still down in the storage closet. You wan' it too?"

"Maybe later," Bryan answered. "Do you ever see Frankie? That's the brother. Have you seen him hanging around?"

"Ever' now and again, I see him. Wid 'doze gang boys. I seen him."

"If you do get the chance, tell him we want to see him—Bryan and Olivia. We want to talk to him," Bryan said.

They gathered up Josie's belonging into a small trash bag and headed back to the subway station.

Chapter Seventeen

When Livy at last showed up for work, it was well after lunchtime. She was a big shot now and recently promoted to Vice President of New Products Marketing, so what was a few hours, especially when it was used for a good cause?

The intercom on her phone crackled and then buzzed. She picked it up. "Livy Thomas."

A cold and irritated voice: "Miss Thomas, would you come into my office, please?"

He didn't identify himself; and only by extension number Livy knew it was Mel. Maybe a few hours did matter.

Miss Thomas? He hasn't called me that since our first interview about working here. She racked her brain for every possible explanation as she made her way down the corridor to Mel's office. *What's gone wrong?*

When she arrived at Mel's plush corner kingdom, his assistant, Ron, greeted her coolly and with tangible discomfort. "Have a seat, Ms. Thomas. He'll let us know when they're ready for you."

Just then, Kyle exited the office and looked at Livy with the look she suspected he gave his children when they disappointed him: anger mixed with sorrow. Not Kyle too! He was one of a very few people at the office whom Livy counted as friends. Mel was another. What had happened?

"Livy, I tried to warn you." Kyle lowered his eyes to his shoes and slipped out of the office.

Tried to warn me about what?

Ron's phone buzzed, and he picked up. "Yes, sir. She's here. I'll send her right in."

Livy suddenly felt the familiar wave of grief and disappointment that she had so often experienced as a child. It always followed that "you screwed up again and I don't want to see your face anymore" scenario that dotted her growing up years. Her days as empress seemed to be over, big time.

She stood up, smoothed out her suit jacket, took a deep breath, and entered Mel's inner sanctum. She would not lose it. No matter what.

Mel and Joy Jameson were there along with two other members of the board. Bob Farrell was also present. *What is he doing here?* None of them looked friendly. They were seated in a semi-circle around Mel's side of his massive mahogany desk. One lone chair faced them on the other side.

"Have a seat Miss Thomas," Mel ordered.

I won't relinquish what little high ground I have. I will not be pinned or cornered. "I think I'd rather stand." Her defenses were definitely up.

"Suit yourself, *Livy.*" Joy sarcastically punched out the first use of her nickname. Joy never called her Livy. "This won't take long."

"We would like you to empty out your desk and be gone by 4 PM this afternoon. Otherwise, we will have the police escort you from the premises under arrest," said Hemmings. He was the silver-haired eighty-year-old crony of the founding father, who had tried to grab Livy's backside at every meeting. No one ever took him seriously except Joy, but he was most definitely serious now.

Livy did her best to stay composed, showing neither fear nor anger. "May I ask what this is about?"

"As if you don't know!" Joy blurted out.

"I'm sorry, but I *don't* know. What's happening?"

"I'm sure you noticed that Fitz was just here. He left this file with the computer entries (traced to your computer): dummy invoices to retailers that don't exist, padded expense sheets, and it seems that dolls have been disappearing, as it were, out the back door. Taking advantage of black market sales of your own project! Embezzlement of hundreds of thousands of dollars funneled through fake charities. That's what this is about!" Mel's voice had escalated several decibels in fury and now softened in disgust. "I saw such promise in you. I mentored you. I championed your ideas and believed in you, sometimes taking your side and your opinion over Joy's. How could you stab us in the back this way? Your seven-figure bonus on this wasn't going to be enough for you? Why Livy, why?"

Joy jumped in and answered for her. "Because people of her ilk are never satisfied. They'll take you for all they can get."

"There has to be a mistake. I wouldn't sabotage my own project. You know how hard I've worked, how committed to its success I've been. There's some other explanation. I wouldn't do this, Mel! You know me. I wouldn't do it!"

"I never would have thought so, Livy, until with a little digging by Farrell here, we found out that you have a criminal record—one that includes grand larceny and attempted murder. Funny how you neglected to mention that on your job application."

Livy swallowed hard. "I was a juvenile. That was supposed to be expunged!"

"As he said, it took some digging, but when you throw in the possibility of hundreds of thousands of dollars going missing, files start to open up, and all kinds of dirt surfaces," Farrell explained.

"See? She doesn't even deny that she has a record," Joy put in.

"No, but you don't know the circumstances. I was in the wrong place and I was—"

"Just like you are now. There's no place for you here." Joy triumphed in spitting out the words.

"You two," Livy hissed, referring to Bob and Joy. "You have always been against me. You made this up to get me out of here."

"It was your buddy Kyle who brought it to our attention. For such an odd duck, he really is an astute accountant. He said that he tried to go to you first, but you wouldn't reply to his emails or answer his voice messages, you've been out of the office most of the time for days—you were obviously avoiding him. He felt he had to come forward," Mel said.

"I never answered them because I never got them. I've spent the last few days on a personal problem and I have to admit I haven't spent much time in my office or looking at emails."

"He hoped you could explain yourself and these discrepancies. Fitz doesn't want to believe you're capable of this either."

"You said 'either.' See, Mel? You don't want to believe it. You know there's something else going on here."

Hemmings stood and took the floor. "This product is one of the most successful undertakings this company has ever produced and has given us the market share and public acclaim that we've waited for. Not since Joy's father's *rocko-repeater* in the 50's have we had the number-one seller for a Christmas season and—"

"I gave you that product," Livy protested.

"And your greed will not take it away. We will not press charges if you tender your resignation, effective immediately, and arrange to return the money . . . and the dolls. The company doesn't want to lose the respect that we've gained. We don't want some dirty scandal. I'm sure you can see this will be best for everyone," Hemmings said.

"So, I'm just supposed to admit guilt, print you up some phony funny money, and just go on my way? I don't have it. I didn't do it!" Livy turned to walk from the room.

"You should have seen this coming, Mel. I told you she was trash and that I didn't trust her," Joy said. "You can dress her up in a suit, stick some diplomas in her hand, give a chance, but she's still trash."

Livy faced her. "You've always hated me and never had the guts to say why."

"You hated me too—don't deny it."

"I didn't hate you; you're not worth the energy. But I do hold you in utter contempt, and I'll tell you exactly why. I think you have as much business sense as Homer Simpson and about as much class as Coney Island cuisine. I think you're a suspicious, conniving phony who's really afraid of her own shadow. Why? Because you know everything you ever got you was handed to you on Daddy's silver platter . . . even him!" Livy threw her gaze pointedly at Mel.

"I knew it was Mel you wanted all along! You've always tried to get your nasty little black claws into him!" Joy stood and leaned over the desk threateningly. Her poisoned words were almost whispered, "We're on to you, Livy. Give it up! I know this is all your doing."

"Ladies, please. Let's not cat fight!" Farrell was enjoying this.

Livy kept at Joy. "I'd like to see you try to make it in the real world. You'd be home eating bonbons and disorganizing the garden club in a week!"

She stopped to see what, if anything, Mel would say to all of this. He made no response, but Hemmings raised a hand to take control. "That's enough. We won't be giving you a reference, Ms. Thomas. So please enjoy the wonderful world of fast food or an exciting career in hotel maid service. We want you out by four o'clock. Mel, do you have anything else to say?"

Mel seemed momentarily lost in thought, but those words brought him back from wherever he had been. "Uh . . . no. You're excused, Ms.

Thomas. Just go. We'll be in touch."

She started for the door and then turned to face them. "I *do* hate you. I hate you *all*!" She walked out and slammed the door.

A half hour later, Mel sat uneasily at his desk. It just didn't feel right. He thought he knew Livy, and while she was ambitious and anxious to get ahead, he'd never have believed she could betray the company this way. It felt so personal. She had betrayed *him*.

Joy knocked at his door and at first just stuck her head in. When he didn't seem to object, she approached his desk. "I know how hard this is for you, Mel. But I really did try to warn you about her. I didn't want to bring this up in front of everyone, but you might find this interesting. Do you know why your 'wonderful Olivia' was willing to join in a crime spree?" Joy handed him a photo Farrell had found while gathering dirt. "She was young, desperate, and *pregnant*."

"What's this?" Mel asked. He took the photo and saw Livy hugging a little girl.

"She's her kid, Mel. It was in her desk. I'd bet money on who our little Hannah is. Seems she's dumped her on some relative or somebody in the projects. Can you believe it? That somebody was helping her clean us out. Get over it, Mel. She's just not as wonderful as you thought, is she?" Joy came up behind him and put her arms around his neck. She whispered seductively in his ear, "Let's go home, darling. Let me help you try to forget all of this."

Livy walked stoically past Ron's desk and managed to get all the way to her office on some borrowed power outside her own. She felt like a water hose with the water pressure suddenly turned off. When she got to her door, Barbara was already clearing out the secretarial area.

"They just sent me a memo telling me what was going on. They said that I was welcome to apply for some other in-house position, but I can't work for them now. You wouldn't do this, Olivia. I know you wouldn't. What are you going to do?"

Outwardly rock solid, Livy only shook her head. She opened her inner office door and collapsed into an avalanche of grief, anger, and despair.

She let it out in a mournful barking sound. Her breaths came shallow and quick, and she was hyperventilating. She didn't know what to do. She couldn't calm down.

Who would do this? Who *could* do this? Why didn't I check those emails? Maybe then I could have . . . what? I still couldn't explain it. But I might have been prepared for what was coming.

For the last several days she had been concentrating on Josie and Frankie, and not paying much attention to work or anything else. The child welfare representatives would never give her Josie now. Before, they might have said that she worked too much. Now they'd conclude she was unfit. Who'd take care of Josie now?

At last, she pushed herself to stand up and walk around the room. Using the boxes that someone had left for her, most likely Barbara, she began to gather her things. She picked up the photo of herself with Senator Harrington and let out a wry laugh. *Oh yes, Senator, I'd love to meet you for lunch. Say my place? Prison cafeteria at 1:00 sharp? The bigger your dreams, the more likely they are to turn to horrific nightmares.* She took the diplomas from the wall and laid the Senator's photo on top.

She lingered at the photo of herself receiving the award for "Rookie of the Year" from Mel. She remembered feeling so thrilled to have pleased him enough to make him beam at her like that. There was no spouse or family member there to share in her moment of triumph, and that look of total delight from Mel was precious to her. His obvious pleasure at her success on the night of the *Hannah Gala* was incredibly fulfilling and she'd surely never see that approval from him again. She gently added the award photo to her pile and laid all of it in the box. She just wished she could crawl inside of it as well and disappear altogether.

A knock at the door interrupted her reflections. Through the door, Barbara said, "Ms. . . . Thomas . . . Livy? Bryan, your friend, is here to see you. He called while you were in Jameson's office, and I told him to come right over. Is that okay?"

Another knock. "Livy, it's me. Can I come in?"

Livy dragged herself to the door and unlocked it. As soon as Bryan had crossed the threshold, he took her in his arms. For a moment she let him really hold her, afraid her knees might not. Then she pulled away, angry and frantic again.

"Oh, Bryan! Now I'm an embezzler, a liar, and a cheat! How could they think that? How can they do this to me?"

"You're none of those things. Barbara said they fired you, and they're threatening police action. What happened?"

"I honestly don't know. Kyle, our account . . . their accountant, found some discrepancies, money deficits, doctored invoices, missing shipments of dolls. It was all carefully hidden in some phony charity, but they traced it somehow back to me. They say I have to pay it back or go to jail. How can I do that? I don't have it. He said it's hundreds of thousands of dollars!" She dumped the file they'd given her into his hands. "Hundreds of thousands of dollars, Bryan! What am I going to do?"

"Someone obviously hacked into your computer and used you as a front in case they got found out. So the proof is circumstantial. They don't have a motive, right? Why would you do it? You have too much to lose to pull something like this. They'd never win in court."

"They don't want it to go that far. They want to duck the scandal. They just want me to pay up and go away."

"And if you don't just go away?"

"Of course I'm not just going to roll over and let them do this to me. Right now I feel like burning the place down! But I don't know if I even have the money for a lawyer. I've been spending like there's no tomorrow."

"What about Garrett? He's a lawyer," Bryan began.

"No! They dug up my past . . . the things I always tried to hide from Garrett. They're things that now even make Kyle and Mel believe that I'm capable of this. Garrett might too. I can't tell him."

"Can you tell me?" Bryan asked.

"No, Bryan. I don't want you to think—"

"Don't you know by now that there is nothing that will change how I think about you or how I feel? You can tell me anything, Livy."

"Can I really?" Livy sat down and remained silent for a few moments as she decided if and where to begin. "We'll see." She twisted her long black locks as she began her story.

"Remember I told you I thought I had a family? Well, it wasn't mine. It was a foster family." She looked to Bryan for a reaction but there was none. Just attentive listening. "Before Ann and Donald Lewis took me, the places I'd been in—they just hadn't worked out. We were almost there—almost a family. I was sixteen and just starting my junior year, and for the first time, I started to feel comfortable. I don't know that we loved each other exactly, but I figured I'd stay with them at least until I was released from the system. At last, I sort of belonged somewhere. I started to call them mom and dad and everything.

"And then Vic Archibald came along. He was so cool, so dangerous, the perfect irresistible bad boy. Predator that he was, he spotted me, the shy loner, desperate for love, and he used that as a tool to get anything he wanted. He threatened to leave me unless I gave it to him. He pushed and pushed until he took what little was left of my innocence. Most of it, along with my self-respect, had been stolen by others long before. He said he wouldn't love me anymore, and I gave in.

"Of course, after that, there wasn't anything I wouldn't do to keep him. Anything he wanted. And he knew that too. I got totally sucked into his world. My foster parents could see he was trouble. 'Slick white trash,' they called him. They saw what was happening, but they couldn't make me stop. They'd ground me, and I'd sneak out to see him.

"I'd catch him flirting with other girls—just letting me know he had others waiting in line. It made me want him even more. I was so jealous I couldn't see straight. I thought if I could get him away somewhere, have him all to myself, he would stop. I was telling him my foster parents were gonna kick me out and started talking about going somewhere . . . just us. Running away together sounded so romantic.

"What I didn't know is that he was in trouble and running away sounded pretty good to him to. So we made this plan. But we needed money.

"I actually got a job at a burger place and worked there for a little while, but I knew it wouldn't be enough. When I found out I wouldn't get my first check for nearly a month, I just walked out. I did some babysitting in the neighborhood and did extra chores—anything I could—but it still wasn't enough.

"The plan was that on Sunday night, while Mom and Dad Lewis attended Bible Study, he would come for me. I didn't know where we were going or what we'd do when we got there. I just trusted Vic.

"So Sunday came, and they were gone, and I had thirty dollars. I was so afraid that Vic wouldn't go if we didn't have enough money. I was desperate. So I started looking around the house for something to show him—anything. I found some cash in a dresser drawer and a heart-shaped diamond necklace and matching earrings Don had given Ann for their anniversary. I don't know what I was thinking. I took it all.

"So Vic finally shows up in a new Ford truck, and he's got nothing. He says he used his last dime to buy the truck. Of course, I wanted to believe him, but he was already near drunk, and there were beer cans all over the seat and floor. So I showed him the money and the jewelry, and he thought we might make it. So we took off, but first he wants to stop at the mini-mart where they always let him buy beer, even though he was underage. But this time, the guy says no.

"And so I'm waiting out in the truck, watching, when he starts pounding his fists on the counter and screaming. And when the guy still won't give it to him, he pulls out a gun. He didn't shoot him, but he goes totally berserk and pistol-whips the clerk unconscious . . . he's bleeding all over the place. Vic robs the register and then comes running out with the money and a case of beer, waving the gun and yelling, 'Scoot over and drive!' So I did."

"Oh no, Livy," Bryan said sorrowfully, "What then?"

"When I start thinking more clearly, I slam on the brakes. 'Vic! You stupid! You robbed a place that knows who you are!'

"He says, 'Shut up and drive. Anyway, the guy was new. He doesn't know me.'

" 'But the camera will,' I tell him. 'We have to go back. Turn yourself in. They'll just give you probation or something.'

" 'Turn myself in?' he says. 'Are you crazy? This was your idea.'

"I say, 'We're juveniles, and maybe they'll go easy on us. You didn't mean to hurt him.'

" 'What if the guy dies?' he screams.

"I scream back at him, 'I'm not going to have our baby in jail!' "

"Oh Livy," Bryan moaned. "A baby?"

"So then he tells me to get out of the truck. When I refuse, he picks up the gun and says it again.

"So I did. But I *still* wanted him. I said, 'Please, Vic. You said you loved me.'

"And he gets this really cold, hard look on his face and says, 'I never did. I don't want no baby. And I don't want you.' And then he slammed the door in my face.

"By the time I walked the five miles back home, the police were waiting for me. Don and Ann pressed charges for the things I stole from them, and I was also convicted as an accessory to grand theft auto, armed robbery, and attempted murder."

"He stole the truck?" Bryan asked.

"Of course he did, and he had the money and jewelry too, when they caught him—told 'em the whole thing was my plan. I got sentenced to a juvenile detention center until I was eighteen, or I could agree to go to a boarding school for problem kids and be handled there until I was of age. Then the case would be re-evaluated. Of course, I chose the school option.

"It was the weirdest thing; it should have been the worst time of my life, but it ended up being the best thing that ever happened to me. It wasn't just that they couldn't send me anywhere else. There was this teacher there, Mrs. Tolbert. She taught English and for some reason she liked me. She said I had imagination and was a good writer. A lot of the other teachers treated us like criminals, but she was always kind. She even loved me—in a teacher sort of way. She gave me something to hold onto all these years. While I was at school, I kept writing to the Don and Ann and begging for their forgiveness. I even called and asked if I could come home for the next Christmas."

"How did that work out?" Bryan asked.

"He said, 'Home? You can't come here for Christmas or ever again. You have no home here. Not anymore.' "

"That must have hurt."

"Sure, but I could understand how they felt. I really screwed up everything."

"But what happened with the baby?" Bryan asked

"There wasn't any baby." Livy paused and looked at Bryan for his reaction to all she had revealed. "I was mistaken, fortunately. I learned a big lesson about that. I kept wondering what would have happened if I did bring a child into that mess. No, there was no baby. I decided right then and there I would never bring a child into my mess of a life. I hadn't even been able to take care of myself, let alone anyone else. It's probably not even an issue, because since Vic, and after all that happened to me as a kid, I've never trusted a man to touch me . . . you know, that way. But I'm afraid I don't know how to love or be loved. I guess you noticed. I've never been part of a loving home, Bryan. I guess that's why I went off on Jimmy that day. Can you imagine Jimmy as a father?"

"Jimmy *is* a father," Bryan confided.

"Oh no. See? On it goes. People think that I don't like kids. That's not it. They make me uncomfortable. The ones in trouble break my heart and bring back so much pain. I know their suffering and I'm helpless to take it away. The spoiled rotten ones make me want to shake them and wake them up to all they have. And the happy ones, all snuggled in a loving father's arms, are the hardest of all. They have what I never could find: someone who wants them, someone who loves them."

"So who made you what you are today? Well, let's say what you were yesterday. I realize today is a little difficult."

"Mrs. Tolbert," Livy admitted. "I was at Odyssey Academy for two years. I guess it took that long for her to convince me I was worth believing in. She got the coach to let me play basketball. It turned out I was pretty good. She had me believing I was smart, too. If anyone else had told me that, I would have laughed in his face."

"So it was just that easy?" He was kidding.

She resumed packing the boxes while she talked. "No, not really." Olivia smiled, remembering her slow climb to self-confidence." She got me to stop feeling sorry for myself. I finally saw she was right. I could choose to be the victim and live in a world of excuses, or I could take charge and change my life."

"How did it happen?" He carried some file crates to the door.

"Well, first off, I changed my name. Linda became Olivia. Mrs. Tolbert suggested Olivia because I would 'live' my new life to the fullest. And then came a whole lot of hard work. She taught me that no matter what the rest of the world thought, there was one person who loved me enough to see me through, to die for me: Jesus. She sounded like you. She told me to imagine her or Jesus at my side all the time. I was supposed to feel their support and love in whatever I was trying to do. I felt like I had someone cheering me on, and to tell the truth, I didn't want to screw up with Jesus sitting beside me, you know? I haven't thought about that for a long time."

"So you were a believer then?"

"Well, sort of. It was kind of an on-and-off-again relationship. The more confident I became, the more I started to feel like I didn't need anyone, especially God. I got the basketball scholarship and thought, 'I can take it from here.' Then I blew out my knee and needed Him again—for a while. Then my grades earned me an academic scholarship, and I was pretty cocky. I could make it without Him again. See, I was always angry with God for my childhood and I started thinking my successes and achievements were in spite of Him, not because of Him. I was going to show Him and everyone else . . ."

"Show Him what?"

"That I deserved better . . . I was worthy of . . . I don't know, show Him what I was made of."

"He knows. He *made* you."

"Really?" Livy laughed sarcastically. "I always imagined that some poor unfortunate girl in the backseat of a Chevy made me. Everybody wishes I'd never come to this planet. Everyone except maybe you, I hope."

"You sure made this a better planet for me and Josie."

She reached for his hand. "Bryan, I'm so tired. I just want to go home."

"Let's get a cab. I'll take you home right now. Do you have your stuff?"

She went to a stack of books on the floor. "Not home to my apartment. I want to go somewhere where someone is glad to see me come home. Where someone holds me and says, 'They can't do this to you! Nobody messes with my little girl!' I want a daddy. I've always thought if he only knew that I existed or where I was, he would come for me and take me home. I still just want to go home." She was now sitting cross-legged on the floor, rocking.

"I'm always happy to see you come home. And they can't do this to you. We'll fight it." Bryan walked over behind her and sat down. He gingerly wrapped himself around her and joined in the motion.

She sank into him and soaked up all the comfort he could offer. "Oh Bryan, whenever I'm with you, my heart is home."

Barbara called for a taxi and helped Bryan and Livy carry her boxes down to the street. They naturally passed several staff members on the trip through the halls and down the elevator. No one knew what to say. Some were definitely aware of the situation, while others were shocked to see Olivia Thomas, the creator of the product of the year, obviously leaving in a hurry for good.

As she neared the door, Livy heard Marcie Jones's voice echoing across the reception lobby, "Hey! Here comes our new Vice President. Oops! There goes the new Vice President!" Bob and Marcie were posted by the door, happily ready to usher her out into oblivion. Bob had never forgiven Livy for her successes, her promotion, and more specifically for rebuffing his once-constant come-ons. She had even reported him for sexual harassment. Marcie *hadn't* reported him and had actually encouraged him. In her mind, they were a couple, a team. Surely she would get Bob's job, now that he would get Livy's promotion. But he had other plans.

Barbara held the door for Livy and Bryan as they carried their items outside to the waiting cab. Farrell sauntered up to Barbara and laid his hand on her lower back, a little too low, and whispered, "So . . . uh . . . Barbara, why don't you come work for me now? I'll be moving Matheson into that office when he moves up into my job. He's bringing his secretary up with him. So you could come on over to mine. I hear you're *very good*, and you're just what I need to spice up my new office."

It was the first time Marcie had heard that Farrell's actual plan didn't include her. "To hell with you! And this whole company too!" She took off in a huff. "How dare you do this to me?"

He didn't even acknowledge her outburst.

Barbara smiled sweetly as she removed Bob's roaming hand and replied, "I could never work for a snake like you."

"I guess even a snake would be too drastic a leap up from your last boss. I understand," Bob replied in mock sympathy.

Barbara picked up her heavy box lying next to the door, pretended to lose her grip, and dropped it right on his foot. "I'm so sorry! It slipped."

Marcie beelined back to her office, picked up the phone, and within minutes she had contacted *Inside Success* magazine. She was put through to Kent Duckworth.

Jones reached over, locked her door, and spoke softly, almost seductively, "Yes, Mr. Duckworth? I understand you did the article on Olivia Thomas of JTC?"

"Yes, I did. Who is this?"

"I'm not saying. You're looking to do a follow up article; that's the buzz I hear. I have some information that you might find interesting . . . for a price, of course."

"I'm listening and if I like what I hear, we can talk price. What ya got?"

"I'll tell you this much as an appetizer. The much heralded Ms.

Thomas just got herself fired." Jones's smirk could be heard on the phone. "Of course it's very hush-hush with Hannah being such a big splash."

"Fired? Wonder Woman? You're kidding. Why?" Duckworth asked in palpable shock.

"No more until I know you're paying enough to not make me hang up and call another rag."

"So why are you telling me? Aren't you afraid you'll get fired as well for letting this major cat out of the bag?"

"I don't need them. I already have another project of my own. But you're helping me with a little venture capital, right?" she said.

They haggled and came to an agreement on what this bombshell might be worth, and Jones continued. "This isn't going to be announced publicly so you already have a scoop, right there. But the really good stuff is the 'why.' I don't know all the details yet, but it seems that she has been dipping into the company coffers a bit more than was agreed to. Got greedy. Figured she deserved it."

"Well, I can see why they would want to keep this hushed. Their stock prices have gotten a bit inflated, and this'll definitely burst that bubble. How did it go down?"

"It seems that she's been funneling everything through those supposed charities. Remember, the winner was anonymous and the winnings were supposed to go to charity? A portion of each purchase goes to charity? Turns out they're bogus charities and received not only that money but a whole lot more and black market dolls to boot!"

"Oh my! This *is* good stuff."

"Now I don't know this for sure, but it seems to me that if the charities are bogus, then wouldn't it make sense that the contest was fixed? Anonymous entry? Ha!"

"It follows. And so . . . who is baby *Hannah?*"

"If I had to guess, I'd say she was Olivia's own kid that she keeps in a closet somewhere or she's dumped on a relative or something. Just came in real handy for this tidy scam."

"You know, I knew there was more to this woman than she was telling. I could feel she was hiding something when I interviewed her." Duckworth drum-rolled his hand excitedly on the desk. "You're sure about all this? She's fired in disgrace?"

"Positive. I just saw her crying and fuming as she left with all her files and junk from her office. Game over."

Chapter Eighteen

Bryan and Livy ducked in the rain as they ran up the apartment building stairs with all her boxes. She entered her key code in the door and wondered how much longer she'd be able to enjoy this place. The furniture was high end and chosen by a highly recommended designer. The art was impressive and tasteful. It was as tidy and clean as a hospital OR but it wasn't really a home. It was a portfolio, the evidence of her worth. One crayon drawing of Josie's, displayed on the fridge, gave it life and warmth.

Bryan put the boxes down by the closet and went to the kitchen. He shed his ugly plaid coat and laid it over the back of a chair. Then he filled the teapot and rummaged through the cupboard for the chamomile tea. He watched at the stove as Livy picked up the award photograph of her and Mel and carried it across the room to the huge window. She stood mesmerized, overlooking her million-dollar view, and breathing it in as if for the last time. When the kettle whistled, he poured her a cup and added honey, just how she liked it. Then he poured for himself and went to sit next to her on the floor. He patted the plush carpet as an invitation for her to sit down with him while they drank.

She sat down, took a sip, and smiled at him for getting it right. "Thank you. Bryan, I was just thinking about your mom and the battlefield. She was out there? And they ventured out again?"

"It's what they live for. Sometimes it goes well, sometimes not so well. Why do you ask?"

"Because I'm feeling like we're casualties in someone else's war right now—Josie and I, that's all." She was staring at the award photo, now lying at her feet.

"You really care what he thinks about you, don't you?"

"More than anything in the world." She was silent for a few moments and continued to gently brush dust off of the framed picture. Finally, she decided to go ahead and confide in Bryan once again. "You know, people kind of wonder what someone like me, someone not very comfortable with kids, is doing working at a toy company."

"It is kind of an interesting question."

"You know how you said that if this thing did go to court, there was no motive and none of it would hold up?" Bryan nodded and she continued, "Well, they might be able to find a motive if they do some more digging."

"What motive, Livy?"

"He's the reason I came here. Not just for a job; I came to find him." She was looking at the photo.

"Him? Mr. Jameson?"

She nodded and then said, "When I was dating Garrett and we were practically engaged, he took me home to meet his folks. His dad was a big-shot lawyer and his mother was a professor of something or other at Temple University. I felt so uncomfortable with them. I knew they thought I was not worthy of their son. They kept asking about my background. Where did I grow up? Who were my parents? What could I possibly tell them? They looked down their noses at me; I could feel it. Wouldn't they be thrilled to find out their son was marrying someone who had a criminal past?

"Garrett didn't know much either and asked me that night why I was being so evasive. He was angry when I wouldn't open up. If I did tell him, he wouldn't love me anymore, and if I didn't tell him, he'd feel I'd been dishonest and I was hiding things from him. I loved him so much and it about killed me when I told him that very night that it wouldn't work . . . we couldn't get married. He kept coming back and trying to get me to change my mind, but I sent him away. I pushed away the only man who ever loved me. He never understood why."

"And you came here to . . . ?" Bryan seemed confused.

"I'm getting there. So I had this overwhelming need to know who I was. I couldn't rest until I went back to the beginning, to the orphanage where I spent my early years, to discover anything I could about my identity. When I got there, I found out a woman had left a letter for me, just in case I did return. The woman who wrote the letter said that she had left me there when my mother died and that she prayed for me every day and hoped I had a wonderful life." Livy huffed in disgust. "Now isn't that sweet? Whoever it was just dumped me into this lonely existence, disappeared without looking back, and expected I'd have a wonderful, fabulous life. There was no signature on the letter. I don't have any idea who left it, and I don't care. But no question, the letter was for me, little Linda, who was left at the convent on Christmas Eve all those years ago."

"Livy, I'm sure she didn't just dump you. You can't possibly know the circumstances."

"Well, anyway, at least I know my own mother didn't abandon me. The letter told me my mother was dead. There was even a birth certificate that revealed my mother's name: Margarita Sotomayor of the Dominican Republic, and my father's name: Melvin Edward Jameson of New York. And the letter said my mother had wanted me to find him."

"Oh Livy! Melvin Jameson is your father?"

She nodded and stared out the window and spoke as if the memory were clearly painted there, "So when I was finishing Business School, I searched Mel out and applied for work with his company. I had to go through three meetings before I got to him. While I waited for the interview, I was paralyzed, so nervous! And then, there he was, this handsome, successful man, and everything I had searched for my whole life was hinging on that moment.

"But then as we talked and got going . . . it felt perfect, right from the beginning. I knew that he was impressed with me, and as he laid out his vision for my role in the company, I could just see it clearly, like it was my destiny, Bryan." The excitement of the memory still danced in her eyes. She stretched out her hands in the air. "I would come to work for him, make him proud and then I would tell him who I was. I would belong somewhere, to someone. I'd have a father at last. I could go back to Garrett and his parents with a family, all successful and worthy." Her hands dropped to her lap. "But of course Garrett had given up; he married Shelly after a year and a half."

She picked up the photo again and pointed to Joy seated at a table in the background. "And then there was Joy. See that pained expression on her face? She's always hated me. That's why I was so excited about the success of this doll. More than the money or the promotion, my excitement was that I knew he was happy with me, and she would even have to admit that I was worth something. Maybe she could accept me. But no, she only got worse. But I was going to tell him, anyway. With this mega achievement, it was now or never.

"The birth certificate and a letter are all framed and wrapped up as a Christmas present for him. And now? With this embezzlement and everything? I can never tell him. If I do, he'll think I planned all of this. They'll think I wanted to get revenge for his not keeping me when my mother died. I don't even know what happened. I don't even know if he knows a daughter exists. But I don't think now is the time to tell him, do you?"

"No wonder you're so devastated."

"You should have seen his eyes, Bryan. There was such disappointment and fury in them. He hates me now. He was practically shaking with rage as he handed me that file. How could he possibly believe that I would do this to him?"

"You didn't do it. We just have to prove to him that you're a victim of this crime, just like he is."

"How Bryan? Where do I start? He was my everything." She was now embracing the photograph like a teddy bear.

"Maybe your destiny is shifting a little."

"You might say that. I was flying so high. But what goes up—always falls flat."

"I just mean maybe God has other plans for you."

"Are you saying He wanted this to happen?"

"No, but you are here for a reason, Livy. You have some glorious purpose; I know it. With God's help, you made it through the darkness and came out into the light." He gave her a friendly smile and jab. "I know you have the strength to make it through this one too."

"But don't forget, with God's help, I'm right back in that darkness again."

"Come on. Don't blame God. Find who did it and blame him. This is only a temporary setback. Find the light again. God was that voice inside you that said, 'You can do it. You can make it.' He was the voice even when it came from Mrs. Tolbert or Julie or Garrett. They helped you work miracles in your life. God wasn't ignoring you. He didn't abandon you. He sent teachers who believed in you, a coach to push you, and I'm sure you can think of a lot of others."

She touched his hand. "Like you. I guess I should thank God for you. What would I do without you?"

Bryan deliberately dodged the compliment. "And like your boss, your father, despite what's going on right now, he has always seen your potential. Hasn't that been a blessing?"

"The hope of having my father is all that kept me going. Now I have nothing, nothing at all. Thank you, God," she said bitterly, snatching up the cups and saucers and heading for the kitchen.

"And so until everything's perfect in your life, you're going to be mad at Him?"

"I don't need 'perfect,' " she barked, nearly breaking the dishes as she carelessly slammed them into the sink. "But He could throw me a bone once in a while."

He stood up, still looking out at the city. "Do you want the Creator of the Universe to kneel before *you* and ask forgiveness? Are you saying everything must go according to *your* plan?"

"No," Livy protested. "But why can't his grand design include anything for me? Just once?"

He followed her and leaned against the counter to look her in the eye. "You remember what you told those kids? Being a victim doesn't get you anywhere. You were right. So don't be one now. I hate to break it to you, but the trials of life are a chronic disease. Jesus won't take them all away, but He'll get you through, if you trust Him."

"You can't possibly understand," she said, pushing him away. "So give it up, okay?"

"I do understand."

"How could you, Mr. Perfect-from-the-ideal-family, Mr. Always-been-loved? Mr. Always-been-needed-and-wanted, what do *you* know about the kind of rejection I feel?"

"More than you know."

"Yeah right. Because you got picked last for the baseball team? Wow. My heart bleeds for you. Do you know what it's like to feel like your whole existence is just one big mistake and the entire universe just wants you to go away? Do you know what that's like?"

"Yes," he answered softly, sitting down at the small kitchen table.

She followed and sat down across from him. "What it's like to feel like you've done everything you could possibly do and still, it will never be right—you'll never be good enough?" She realized she was yelling at him.

He yelled back, "Yes, I have. Are you finished? Do you feel better now?"

"No, I'm not finished. Do you know what it's like to have lost every-thing just when it was right in your hand? To want to pray for God to make it all better, but then you remember that you tried that, and life still sucks? It's never going to get any better, Bryan. Never. Exactly where do I go now? What do *you* think God wants me to do?"

"I don't know everything, Livy. All I can say is that I love you, and I *know* He loves you too."

"Well, just not enough, I guess."

"Only enough to send His son to die for you."

For a moment, she stared at him in silence.

He stood up, kissed her on the cheek, and for a moment his arms sur-rounded her in warmth and support. "Just try again, please. Say a prayer; let go and let Him take the lead." He looked at her for another minute and then sat back down. "So . . . about Josie and Thanksgiving," he said, abruptly changing the conversation.

"Can you believe it?" she asked, her tone going from angry to just sad. "I almost forgot about that in all that's happened. The family services people will never let me have her now."

"They don't know anything about all that. Let's at least have a kickin' Thanksgiving before it gets crazy. We can figure out how to cook a turkey."

"I thought turkeys were your friends, and you couldn't eat them," she answered. He wasn't having much success in brightening her mood.

"I've never actually been introduced to the ones at the grocery stores. I think I can deal with those."

"I'm no cook—you know that."

"Come on, Livy. We can look forward to that one day. We'll take Josie to the parade! Maybe we can find Frankie and make it a day to remember for the both of them. And . . . uh . . . we'll invite Garrett to come and bring his kids."

She gave him a dirty look. "Enough with the Garrett thing. He's got a girlfriend."

"You don't know that for sure."

"I do know it. I heard her in the background at his house."

"That could've been a cleaning lady for all you know."

"I just know."

"You could ask him, and if he's available, he'll come, and we'll all have a blast."

"I'm not calling him. I'd feel like a fool. As usual."

"Well, too bad, psycho—you're wrong."

"Thanks, but do you mean psychic by chance?"

"Oh, yeah. Anyway, there *was* a woman there, and she was his mother-in-law, by the way, not some new love. She's been helping him occasionally with the kids while he settles in."

"And how would you know?"

"Uh . . . because I called him and invited him for Thanksgiving. He's very excited about coming. I told him to act all surprised when you call and ask. He's expecting to hear from you."

"How dare you? You called him? When?"

"Right after we found out you could have Josie for the holiday. You weren't ever gonna do it."

"And he's coming? Really?"

"Yes."

She didn't know whether to throttle him or kiss him. She finally settled on throwing her arms around his neck.

"And his kids are coming, and Josie and I are coming. It's going to be fun, and we'll get you through this. Let's make turkey shaped cookies and pie and, of course, mashed potatoes."

She was warming up to the plan. She grabbed a pencil and paper and started making a list of ideas. "Oh! Bryan, I know it isn't Christmas yet, but can we do a widow run? Do you think that Martha and Lucille—are those their names? Do you think they're still there?"

"I'm sure they are. I visited them not too long ago. But I don't know about a widow run on Thanksgiving—that's not the accepted tradition." His words were teasing, but his tone sounded serious.

"Please? Only this year I play the mom and I don't have to wear pajamas and a robe! The kids can do that!"

"Lucille will be amazed at how well you're doing."

"Yeah, if she only knew. I'll be joining them in the park any day now."

Trotting and singing joyfully around the park on Christmas morning was one of her most treasured memories.

"No, wait. *Wait!*" she exclaimed. "I have a better idea. Let's invite Lucille and Martha over for Thanksgiving dinner too. That would be better than a meal at the shelter, wouldn't it? But then—I'm trying to show some faith here—I want the real thing, the *real* widow run. I have to have faith that all this mess will get cleaned up by then. So Bryan . . ." she mustered her courage, "Will you take me home for Christmas? I want a real Idaho Christmas with hash browns and hot chocolate, a widow run, and everything."

When she looked at Bryan's face, she felt like Oliver Twist holding his bowl and brazenly asking for more gruel—like a motherless child hoping against hope that someone would take her in and want her.

Bryan was quiet and looked to her as if he were struggling for the way to tell her what she feared most: that once again, she was not wanted at any family's Christmas table.

He looked up to the ceiling and mouthed, "Help me, Lord."

"You said I'm family, now, remember? I want an Idaho Christmas. We'll take the kids and make it special for them. Do you think Mom and Dad would let me do that?" Still Bryan didn't answer. "Fine then. Sorry I brought it up."

"Livy, I have something to tell you . . . um . . ." Bryan lowered his head to avoid Livy's gaze.

Livy lifted Bryan's face, searched his eyes, and read the story clearly. "Don't you say it, Bryan Kimball. Don't you dare say it!"

Livy's heart sank into a familiar abyss. She knew what was coming.

Bryan finally found his tongue. "Mom and Dad would love to have you, I'm sure, all of you, but—"

"Please don't say it. Not today of all days." But then she said it for him. "You're leaving. Am I right? You're leaving me."

He was slow to answer, but finally he pursed his lips, took a deep breath, and said, "I got the call this morning."

She shook her head. "You can't go."

"Well, you knew that I was temporary, that eventually I would get an assignment for projects somewhere else, and I would have to go. I've been here almost a year and that's the maximum."

"When? When do you have to go?" she demanded.

"Definitely before Christmas, maybe very soon. I'm not sure how it's all going to happen. Evidently, there's one more assignment, one last thing that I have to do. It's not settled yet, but it'll be soon, and then I have to go."

"No, Bryan. Not now, please. I need you."

"I'm still here for you for now. And you know that even if I go, you're still my sister and my love for you doesn't change. I can't always be right here with you, but I can always love you."

"Please, can't you wait until after the holidays? You missed Christmas with your family last year. Can't you stay until you take us home for Christmas?"

"I don't know. I'll make it if I can, but you, of all people, know how hard this time of year is for lonely, troubled kids. It's when I feel most needed, when I can make a difference."

"You can make a difference for me and two troubled kids right out there in Idaho! And Jimmy and Jamal and the rest? Who will write their stories? What about *my* story?"

"I have been writing your story. It's the most important one," Bryan confessed.

"That's what I am? That's all? I'm one of your projects? That's why you wanted me to open up and *share* with you because I'm part of some thesis project?"

"No. I really care about you, and you know it."

"Do I? Do you? All this has been research?"

"You're the whole reason I'm here this long. I had to beg to stay. Livy, I'm still around just to be with you."

"Oh really? If you love me, take me with you. I don't have anything holding me here now."

"Livy, I can't. It doesn't work that way."

She stamped her foot in exasperation. "And why not? Why doesn't it? Who gives you marching orders anyway? I'm not asking you to marry me or live in sin, for heaven's sake. You're my brother; I need you. I thought you were the one person in the world who would never abandon me."

"I'm not abandoning you. I would stay if there were any way. I hope when you pray, God helps you understand."

"Oh stop. Can't you see? He doesn't care what happens to me or you or anyone else."

"Oh Livy, if you only knew. It's going to be all right. Everything's going to be all right."

"What are you talking about?"

"You have to take it from here, but you'll be all right. You stay and fight this. No matter what happens now. You have to help Josie. You need to give things with Garrett one last chance. And I want you to go home to Blackfoot with or without me. That will always tie us together."

"Oh, right!" She went looking for her coat and purse.

"Livy! Where are you going?"

"I'm leaving *you!*" She charged for the door.

"Leaving me? This is your house. I know you're upset, but where are you going?"

"I'm not upset; I'm just determined. You can work it out. *We* are all going to Blackfoot for Christmas."

"But it's not up to me. Please, Livy, stop."

Livy was having none of it. She had lost enough for one day, and this was one battle she intended to win.

"I know you can work it out. Like I'm sure Josie and I are just going to show up in Idaho without you. 'Hey folks! We're here! Ho, Ho, Ho. You don't know us, but Bryan said we could come.' Nope. You are going to take us home and if you *really* care, you can figure out how." She abruptly walked away from him and grabbed her coat. "Right now, I'm going to get a bed for Josie to sleep on."

Bryan trailed right behind. "Livy, please. I know that you're hurt and upset but—"

"I'm so far beyond upset; you have no idea!" Slamming the door in his face, she ran for the elevator.

Downstairs, she stopped to button up her coat and was opening the outside doors when Bryan stepped out of the adjacent elevator.

"Livy, wait."

She darted out into the thunderstorm, down the stairs, and was about to head across the street where she would catch the bus. She turned back to Bryan who was standing on the stairs and yelled out, "No matter what, Bryan. We are having Christmas in Idaho!"

Quickly glancing across to check for the marker of the bus stop, she spotted Frankie standing in the rain. He was carrying Josie's doll covered by his jacket. His eyes met hers, and he held up the doll, communicating that he thought she could get it to Josie. Just then, someone in the periphery whistled for him, and he seemed to panic. He dropped the doll and ran.

"Frankie!" Livy, so frantic to catch him, to protect him, didn't notice the light had changed. She darted into the street after the boy—right into oncoming traffic.

Screeching brakes and blasting horns shattered the drone of the windy downpour. It was then that Bryan did that one last thing that he had to do. Livy caught a blurred, slow-motion glimpse of him running down the stairs toward her. He was shouting her name and then suddenly he was practically tackling her, heaving her out of the way of the speeding bus coming right at her. She heard a terrible thud just before she hit her head on the lamppost in the median. Then she was swallowed up in wet, cold darkness.

Later, when the police had compiled their report, the fire truck and the ambulance had come and gone, and after the crowd had dispersed, Bryan stood watching, hovering, wishing he could follow the ambulance, waiting for someone to come for him. No one noticed when he simply vanished into the frigid evening mist.

Kent Duckworth had worked at record speed. He had a preliminary article written up for the magazine but was not going to wait for publication. Under the company byline, he would go straight to CNN. By 6 PM much of the nation had heard of the scandal brewing at Joy's Toys and that America's little sweetheart and the charities were all a fraud. Olivia Thomas was a fraud—caught red-handed. From there, Duckworth received invitations to appear on FOX, MSNBC, and other networks. He included highlights from his inside source who had confirmed that the company now believed "Hannah" was Ms. Thomas' own child. In the middle of an interview on *Satellite Business News* with hostess Jessica Barnes, new information surfaced.

"And so the whole contest was a setup, Jessica," Duckworth was saying, "a scam for personal gain and—"

She interrupted Duckworth in mid-sentence. "I have just received information on a related story. I'd like your reaction, Kent. According to reports just coming out, Olivia Thomas has been taken to General Mercy Hospital in critical condition after an apparent suicide attempt. Witnesses say that she threw herself into oncoming traffic. Would you like to comment on this story? I assume that you were not aware of this situation until this very moment."

The news hit him like a slap. "Oh, dear Lord! I was absolutely unaware. I'm stunned. Naturally, if someone sees her whole world tumbling down around her, it's got to be devastating. But this is just tragic. When I met with Ms. Thomas months ago for interviews she seemed to be a strong and self-assured person. Even with all that's coming out, it's hard to believe this has happened."

He hoped she was not pushed into this desperate frame of mind because of his damaging story.

Perhaps Jessica read his mind. "I'm now hearing in my earpiece that this happened around 6:30 PM this evening, about the time this story was airing. Could the public humiliation of this scandal drive her to this?"

"I doubt she was sitting around watching news reports and then suddenly ran out into traffic. I'd bet she had no idea anyone even knew her secrets at that point." He was saying what he hoped was true. "She just knew that her high-flying success had come to a bitter crashing end."

Patti stroked her daughter's reddish hair as she watched the broadcast. Then, she suddenly and almost desperately held her close. They had it all wrong! From the beginning she knew full well who the contest baby was and exactly what was going on. This had to be Carlos's scam. And now that poor young woman was being blamed for everything.

"My sweet baby angel," she whispered. "He still found a way to exploit you." That beautiful little face had remained etched in her heart and haunted her through the years. But what could Patti do about Carlos now? She had changed her name and her life and hoped he would never be able to find her. If she came forward and blew his cover, he would find her—find a way to finish what he began years ago. And what about her family? He would come after them too. Was it worth the risk?

Chapter Nineteen

Three and a half weeks later, Garrett looked up as Mel exited ICU. He looked like he hadn't shaved or perhaps even slept for a day or two.

Garrett cleared his throat and approached. "Mr. Jameson, I'm Garrett Garner, and I'd like a moment of your time." When Mel gave him a scowl, he continued, "I assure you, I'm *not* a reporter. I'm a friend of Olivia's."

"You're sure I'm not going to find parts of our conversation showing up in a tabloid somewhere?"

"Very sure." Garrett motioned for Mel to follow him to a quiet corner. "Livy and I go back several years. I can't stand to see what they're saying about her. It's not true, Mr. Jameson. That's not the Olivia I know."

"I can give you five minutes." He sat down in a chair by a large potted plant. "So how do you know Olivia?"

Garrett sat beside him. "We met when she was in graduate school. We were romantically involved, almost got married."

"Oh, I see."

"Please tell me how she's doing. I've come here several times and sat and sat in this waiting room. They won't let anyone but you in there, and they won't give me any more info than the press got. Tell me the truth. Is she going to recover?"

"Frankly, Mr. Garner, it's not looking very good." Mel ran a hand across his face and through his hair. "I can tell you still have feelings for her, but prepare yourself for the worst. She had severe head injuries, and the doctors put her into a medically induced coma to protect her brain from swelling. But now they can't bring her out of it. She's not responding and by now she should show signs of—"

"Can I ask why *you* get to be the one they let in. Considering you put her there?" Garrett tried to keep the anger out of his voice.

Mel didn't react. "ICU rules. Her insurance papers showed no next of kin. And for some reason, she had me down as the one to contact in case of emergency. Unfortunately."

Garrett felt like punching him. "Unfortunately. Oh. You just want to totally wash your hands of her, is that right?" *This guy is a real piece of work,* Garrett thought.

"That's just it. I *don't* want to wash my hands of her. When they decide it's time to give up hope, and it may be any day now, they'll ask me to sign the papers and pull the feeding tube. That's the last thing I want."

"Oh, dear God," Garrett said. His stomach made a violent turn. "Any day now?" He'd sat in another hospital, day after day, the year before, watching his precious Shelly slip away. It felt all too horribly familiar.

Mel laid a hand on his arm. "They talked to me about the real possibility of it, just today. I'm sorry."

"Oh, great. You're sorry." He let go now. "I know she didn't do those things to your company. I know her!"

"For what it's worth, I'm beginning to agree with you. And I certainly never wanted anything like this to happen."

"Please. You can't just let her die."

Mel said gently, "Do you want to take responsibility? I could tell them that you're a better person to—"

"No, I can't. I've been there before, and I can't." His voice wavered, and he felt like a coward. He stood up and dug a business card from his jacket pocket. "Here is my contact information. Please call if there's any change. If she comes to, tell her I want to see her."

Mel grabbed him by the arm before he left. "I will. I'll give her this card. I'm sorry, Mr. Garner. Truly, I am sorry. I'm hoping for a miracle."

"Me too." He headed for the elevator.

By the time Mel arrived at the office, it was 2:30, and Ron knew where he'd been.

Ron looked at Mel. "Well? Any change?"

When the boss merely shook his head, Ron began leafing through the files and messages strewn across his desk. "Oh, that woman called again, the one who says she has some very important information for you. I told her to put it in an email and that I would make sure that you got it. She's very anxious to give you her take on the scandal, I think."

"Isn't everyone? Doesn't she leave a name or even a hint of what she wants to tell me? Something? Caller ID?"

"No, she's using a calling card and says what she has is for your eyes and ears only. She won't tell me anything. I get the sense that she feels like she's in danger or you are." His hands went to his face in mock terror. "Oooooh! Are you scared? She's probably just a nut case. And now, having said that, I should tell you that I did give her your personal email, not the public one. She won't sell it or give you a computer virus, I don't think."

"Thanks, Ron. When I find she's a cyber stalker, I'll know who to blame."

Livy opened her eyes. Wintry morning sun shone through window blinds and caused her to squint. Unable to focus, it took her several minutes to identify the black box hanging in the air as a television suspended above her bed—her hospital bed.

Even more blurry than her vision was her mental state. At first she couldn't remember who she even was. When her identity at last came into focus, she couldn't clear her mind and remember what had happened. Why she would be there in that hospital? She felt a heaviness in her body that gave her the terrifying impression she was paralyzed. She had to struggle with all her mental might to force her limbs to move. With some intense effort, she raised her right foot, just slightly, and then her left. She felt stabbing pain as she flexed her right hand and irritated the IV inserted there. Aware of some discomfort in her abdomen, she tried to raise her head slightly to find the source. She could barely lift her head from the pillow. She lowered her eyes and was able to see what she guessed was a feeding tube protruding from her belly.

Why am I here? How long . . . ? Her mind was an indistinct jumble of flashes. Thus she continued for hours, frightened she might remain imprisoned in this confused and disabled state forever. Hospital workers came in and out of the room, but she couldn't find her voice to speak to them. She could blink; move her toes and her hands, but only minimally.

Slowly, over time, the first vague memory began to trickle across her consciousness, and then another and another. Through a fog, she could see Mel, angry at his desk; she saw herself in shock and pain that she felt to the core. But what was it about? She could not cross that hurdle in her mind. There was something else, something terrible trying to break through. And at last it did.

Bryan! Where was Bryan? The last images before she blacked out flashed through her mind. She saw Bryan running down the stairs, heard him yelling her name, and then experienced again the terrible slow-motion horror of that bus slamming into one of the dearest creatures God ever put on this earth. He couldn't be gone! Yet she knew he was. He could not have survived that impact. The horrifying sound of the brakes screaming and the slamming thud that followed resounded again and again in stereo in her head.

No, no! Don't let it be true—God please! What was she saying? Bryan had just begun to re-open the possibility that there really was a God, and then He does this? God takes Bryan away—wonderful, good-to-the-bone Bryan? How ironic that his death would be just the thing to refute everything he'd been trying to teach her.

Poor, innocent, deluded Bryan! An endless string of empty tomorrows stretched out before her. How could she go home and never again be greeted by his cheerful, goofy smile? What kind of God would take away the very last thing, the last person that she had to hold onto?

She wanted to scream. She wanted to rip the tubes out of her arms, run down the hall, and yell, scream, and beat on something. The anger and grief was building inside like a volcano. Livy's scarred and battle-hardened heart burst, and her whole body shook with loud wrenching sobs. She had found her voice.

Just then, the door to her room opened and a nurse bustled in, rolling some kind of contraption on a cart. Startled by Livy's cries, she nearly up-ended the thing.

"You're awake! You've come back to us!" she exclaimed in surprise. "Don't cry, honey. You're back!" The chubby, older, African-American woman rushed to the door. "I'll get the doctors. You stay with us now. We'll be right back."

Horrified at being caught in such a state, Livy tried to put it all back inside. She could barely stop the sobs and shaking. Unable to move enough to even wipe her tear-stained cheeks, she managed to turn her face to the pillow just as an entourage of doctors and nurses streamed through the door. They immediately began poking, prodding, and asking her to perform basic tricks like reporting the number of fingers they were holding up, wiggling her toes, tapping her forefinger on the bed rail, and identifying the current president of the United States. After these and other more complicated tests and scans, they tentatively pronounced with amazement that she would be fine—in time. She'd need therapy and extensive rehab, but there appeared to be no long-term brain damage. Something of a miracle, they said.

Maybe not brain damage, but there was damage all right. She knew in some ways, she'd never be whole again.

The sweet, waddling nurse wore a name tag that read, "Betsy Granger" and she stood at Livy's shoulder stroking her hair as orderlies wheeled her back to her room. She spoke gently and said, "You've been sleeping about three and a half weeks now, dear. They've been trying to bring you around and, well, I'd about given up hope on your waking up. Somebody somewhere has been praying for you," she said, bending down to Livy's ear, "and I have too!" She spoke in a whisper not meant for the rest of the group to hear. As she got Livy's bed situated and the IV in place, she reached for a tissue and gently wiped her patient's face. "I thought for sure you'd miss Christmas, or that we'd lose you altogether."

Gradually, the other medical team members left, and Livy was alone with Betsy. "Is there anyone that you'd like me to call?" Betsy asked.

She had to work hard to make the words come out right. "Do you know if there was a young man brought in at the same time as I was? He was in the same accident." Holding onto the faint hope that perhaps Bryan had made it, Livy challenged silently, *Here's your last chance, God.*

"If he was, he wasn't assigned to this floor. Do you know his name? I could check and see if he was admitted."

It took Herculean effort for Livy to say his name aloud without again bursting into tears. She pursed her lips hard until she had control. "His name was Bryan, Bryan Kimball. He was twenty-two."

"Do you have any other information you could give me that might help?"

"Well, his parents are Jake and Marilee Kimball, and they live in Blackfoot, Idaho."

"I'll see what I can find out. In the meantime, do you want to see Mr. Jameson? He's been here almost every day and for hours at a time. This guy sure has been worried about you. Sometimes he just came in and held your hand, and sometimes he would talk to you. Talk and talk. I kept an eye on him, though. He's already been here today, and I'm sure he'll be back tomorrow, if not sooner."

"Anyone else come?" She was hoping to hear that Garrett had visited. "Tall, handsome black guy with some killer dimples, maybe?"

"Don' know 'bout that. Mos' regular folks don' come past the 'no unauthorized visitors in the ICU' sign, but those reporters and looky-lou's keep trying to find a way, and I scared 'em off pretty well. I may not look it, but I can be trouble."

Livy could believe it and almost found a smile when she imagined Nurse Betsy driving off the trespassers, maybe even Garrett, with anything handy, including bedpans. Betsy left the room to make the calls.

Did Livy want to see Mel? It was like trying to piece together a dream when she'd been awakened in the middle of it. If Mel was angry with her, why was he here all the time? What was it all about? Joy haunted the dream. She was there and Hemmings and Farrell. Suddenly the clouds parted and the whole scene replayed in colorful detail. She'd been fired, disgraced, and humiliated in front of everyone in the office. Reporters? Looky-lou's? The whole world had heard? She remembered enough to know that everything she had worked for was gone.

Chapter Twenty

Mel gathered his messages and the files from Ron and opened the door to his inner office. "Did Kyle call?"

"Yeah, there's something in the pile from him. You really ought to reconsider the voice mail idea. It's all the rage, you know," Ron chided him.

"And wade through sixty-eight unheard messages? No, I don't think so. That's what I pay my trusted assistant to do."

He entered his personal office and sat down at his computer. Holding his breath, he pulled up the latest sales figures and the picture was grimmer than he expected. The scandal couldn't have come at a worse time. JTC had just begun production on the next run of Hannah dolls, the boy version and the Hannah sequel, Playtime Polly, soon to be unveiled. Orders from retailers were drying up as the public showed its disgust over the bogus charities, the contest, and the rest of the fiasco. So far however, returns were minimal. There were just too many dolls already wrapped and ready for Christmas morning.

The intercom buzzed. "Kyle is here to see you. I told him that you were not in the mood for the reindeer antlers right now, was I right?" Ron asked.

Kyle stuck his head in the door and looked for approval to enter while still wearing the jingle-belled headband. Mel rolled his eyes and motioned to come in.

"Well, somebody around here has to try to revive the Christmas spirit," Kyle protested. "It feels more like Halloween or the *Nightmare before Christmas*."

"Well, this company just might be the ghost of Christmas past. Have you seen these figures?"

"I compiled those figures. It's what I do."

"So what's up? Did you follow up at the bank on that hunch you had?"

"I did and found some interesting things, just as I thought I would. There was activity on the charity accounts and more company money transfers attempted just after you fired Livy. That would be sort of gutsy, don't you think, to be found out and just keep stealing? Then, after a day or so, according to bank records, the money disappeared, transferred to offshore accounts or Swiss banks. By the time we told the authorities and they froze the accounts, they were empty."

"I can't take you seriously when you're wearing those things." Mel reached up and grabbed the antlers from off Kyle's head. "Okay, so she didn't act alone. We never said that she did. An accomplice was always a real possibility."

"But what does your gut tell you? Mine says hacker. These transfers were made through Thomas's computer but using back-door codes that I'm not even sure that she knew. She was great with business but she always had the IT guys helping her with some glitch or another. She was no computer whiz."

"So maybe one of those IT guys was in on it with her?" Mel was playing devil's advocate.

"Yeah, so they put their heads together and decided to leave a trail that leads back to her, a well-hidden trail, but a trail nonetheless. An IT guy, a talented one with access to a few master codes, could get into any computer in the company without a trace. Yours or mine, for example, have a lot more sensitive information and access to money than hers did. Why leave a calling card? And to put her name on the invoice approvals, how stupid could she be?"

Mel was hearing from Kyle what his own gut had been telling him as he sat at her bedside every day. "Well, Fitz, you're the one who brought this to me with all fingers pointing at Olivia Thomas," Mel said, shifting some of his own feelings of guilt onto Kyle.

"True. But I wanted you to confront her and get to the bottom of it, not fire her that very day. She might possibly be a fall-guy . . . girl, whatever." Kyle tossed the guilt right back into Mel's court.

"When Joy saw the files you brought us, she went ballistic, beyond postal! She wanted Livy out. She and Farrell had already dug up the dirt on her past to try to get me to change my mind about the promotion. And I did feel misled and really disappointed in her. They got old Hemmings on the inquisition bandwagon and then other board members, and then your file simply clinched it. But if she didn't do it, why would she try to kill herself?"

"Uh . . . maybe because everything she worked so hard for had just been vaporized in one fell swoop? Maybe because Jones and Farrell and that Duckworth guy made sure the whole world thought that she was a cheat and a fraud? Or here's a lovely thought. Maybe she was pushed."

"Oh, dear God!" Mel meant it as a prayer. "Kyle, get that reporter, Duckworth, on the phone and tell him to get digging for the real story. This time, tell him to make sure he's got all the facts."

Kyle nodded, grabbed his reindeer headgear, and charged out the door.

Mel logged into his private email account and found six unopened messages. One from Joy, marked urgent, implored him not to forget his tux for their annual Christmas dinner soiree for dozens of their most elite and most boring friends. This year they'd have something to talk about! They'd be consoling him and sympathizing, all the while relishing the dirt. "Not tonight," he sighed. "I'm really not in the mood."

Searching for the mystery email Ron mentioned, Mel found an obvious candidate. The subject line read, "Open immediately. Confidential information."

At first, he dismissed it as just another consumer stating her outrage at the turn of recent events. But when he got four or five lines into the email, the color drained from his face and his hands began to shake. Mel's entire world took on a new perspective. Everything had changed. And when he called the number she gave, it was clear what had happened at Joy's Toys and who baby Hannah really was.

Mel got out of the cab in front of his luxury brownstone and asked the driver to wait. He dodged caterers and a florist as he raced up the stairs to the front door. Joy was in the dining room, choosing between two centerpieces, and asked Mel's opinion. He didn't answer and set off straight up the stairs to the bedroom. With a grunt, he pulled a large suitcase from the closet and opened it across the bed. After some haphazard packing, he knelt at his dresser and from the very back of his bottom drawer he removed a locked leather-bound journal. He stood and felt underneath the upper right sock drawer to locate the key that was taped there, and then yanked it out. Opening the journal for the first time in more than five years, he felt his legs go weak when he saw her face. He sank to the floor and for a few moments, studied the photograph. One word, one name, escaped his lips: "Daisy."

When Mel Jameson and his roommates landed in the Dominican Republic to let off some steam between their first and second years at Harvard Business School, he'd had no intention of doing anything that could be remotely considered serious or life altering. The tropical beaches, soft breezes, the seemingly inexhaustible supply of alcohol and scantily clad, enticing women promised the kind of freedom and irresponsibility he'd been dreaming of since prep school. So for just this summer, Mel was anxious to drown out the past, postpone the future, and explore the here and now in an endless round of partying and sleep.

Not that his life had been that bad, nor did the future look bleak and forbidding. Raised in a privileged, old-money family, he had been given all the advantages, and to his credit, he hadn't wasted them. A hard-working, involved student, he had excelled in his studies, played the expected sports with enthusiasm and grace, and explored all options and opportunities that came his way. His parents were proud, if distant and old-fashionedly in their do-what-is-expected-of-you way. They approved when he began dating Joy Parker, the daughter of a manufacturing tycoon who had made his fortune in the toy market. During this last year of business school, Mel would do the expected thing and ask to spend the rest of his life with Joy. Joy would do the expected thing and ask her father to offer Mel a future with Joy's Toys. Mr. Parker would scrutinize Mel's impressive scholastic record, notable pedigree, and family fortune and do the expected thing by welcoming Mel as part of the literal and business family. That was the plan. But that was later. This was now.

This would be his summer of abandon. The grind of school was on hold, a predictable June wedding awaited. He had only this moment to do the unexpected—no plans, no responsibilities, only a determination to enjoy a perpetual bachelor party of booze, babes, and beaches before real life enveloped him. He counted on his buddies to keep the party going. What he hadn't counted on was Daisy Sotomayor.

Margarita Guadalupe Elena Sotomayor Reyes, like her name, was long and complicated. It was not only her height, a lanky 5'10", which distinguished Margarita from the other employees at *Susurro del Mar Resort*. Her drive and ambition distinguished her as well. Orphaned by Hurricane Carmen at twelve, Margarita vowed not only to raise her younger brother Carlos, but also to raise their station in life. At fourteen, determined to stay in school, Margarita had come to the resort looking for night work. The only opening was in the laundry where the supervisor was always seeking someone desperate enough to put up with the hot, tedious, and backbreaking work. Margarita stuck it out for two years. It was a definite step up when she graduated to cleaning toilets and making beds.

Observing the lavish and carefree lifestyle of the wealthy American guests, Margarita saw a future that she dared to want for herself and Carlos. She watched Ramon, the front desk manager, charm guests with articulate and effortless English and realized that a command of that language was the key to her quest for a better life.

In the break room one afternoon, she mustered the courage to approach Ramon for help. He generously provided the tapes and books that he used and often took time to practice with her. Margarita soon earned his praise, his respect, and the position of night clerk at the front desk. By the next May, she was night manager.

In her post at the front desk, she was a beautiful and logical target for bad pick-up lines and unwanted attention from vacationing frat boys. She got so deft at fending them off that they could feel flattered and put down all at the same time. Some, like Mel's buddies, Matt and Steve, took it as a challenge to try and try again. Rather than discouraged they were inspired to new heights of creative flirtation. They couldn't resist the temptation that her name presented. "Like the drink, you intoxicate me." "Are you a salty Margarita? I'd like just a little lick to find out . . ." Their puns got more suggestive every time and she was quickly tiring of them. She was about to have them thrown out of the hotel when Mel happened along and casually advised them to back off and stop acting like jerks.

Several days later, after a long day of bodysurfing and girl-chasing, Mel desperately wanted a drink. Seizing this golden opportunity, Matt suggested Mel call down and request the *front desk special Margarita*.

"Mel, say, 'You know what I mean, the long, salty, sexy Margarita that's served up right in your room.' "

Mel innocently fell right into their trap and in five minutes there was a knock at the door. Matt and Steve positioned themselves to watch. The door opened and there stood a gorgeous bikini clad maiden with a tall margarita on a tray. She also wore her name tag on the strap of her bikini top. In her most sultry voice she asked, "Is this what you had in mind?" Mel's jaw dropped and before he could say, "Oh! Yes!" she threw the drink in his face. "Towel?"

The next night he appeared at the desk with a bouquet of daisies. Having heard about the incident with the drink, Ramon had nonchalantly mentioned to him with a snicker that Margarita was also the Spanish word for daisy.

"I'm sorry for the behavior of my friends and myself last night. They set me up. Can we start over?" Extending his hand and a bouquet of daisies, he continued, "I'm Melvin Jameson and from now on I promise only to associate you and your name with these lovely delicate flowers. Please accept my apologies . . . ?"

She heaved an annoyed sigh and gave him a wary glance.

"Please?" One by one he began to pluck the petals. "She forgives me . . . she forgives me not. She forgives me . . . she forgives me not . . ."

"Stop. You will ruin my flowers." She finally smiled. "I forgive you, *Male Bean,*" which was how her pronunciation of his name came out. She accepted the daisies and an invitation for lunch the following day. From then on he was Bean and she was Daisy. And they were inseparable.

Would she mind showing him around Boca Chica? What were the restaurants she recommended? Could he take her and her brother out for seafood? Soon, no excuses were needed to get together. Mel was feeling and doing things he never had imagined before, totally unexpected things. He was definitely not a morning person, yet when she was off work at 4 AM, he would often find himself waiting for a pre-dawn walk in the moonlight or a sunrise swim.

When, after some weeks they found a secluded spot on the far side of the island and made love for the first time, Mel was surprised at his lack of "mission accomplished" feelings that had accompanied previous conquests. He felt he was the one surrendering . . . not to her seduction, but to feelings of true tenderness and a longing for closeness. Though he knew the affair was wrong, every moment without her seemed empty and long, only a bridge to their next meeting. When mid-August came, he had to stand back and remind himself that this was just a summer fling. Well, wasn't it? She was merely forbidden fruit and therefore had extra appeal. They were not falling in love; that was not part of the plan. He was unofficially engaged, after all. He was leaving this place and this girl forever.

He had to begin thinking about returning to Boston and to his future wife, Joy. To buck the plan now would throw both families into turmoil. He knew that as wonderful and beautiful as Daisy was, she would never be accepted by his family. She was a gorgeous blend of Hispanic and Black, like most Dominicans, and his parents would never hear of his marrying someone of another race.

But there was something about Daisy. She had spark and substance. She was not merely a silly island girl infatuated with the rich boy from the States in the way so many of the girls there had been. Sweet and spiritual, she believed that God had saved her from that hurricane to do something good with her life. She had a destiny. She was smart and self-educated and had ambitions that rivaled his own. Few of the girls at Harvard had shown such determination. She wanted to go to Florida, study business, and someday own a resort herself. And Mel believed she could do it, too.

He suddenly wondered if *he* could do anything on his own. Here he was living on his father's money, going to his mother's chosen college (generations of ancestors had all gone to Harvard), about to marry the boss's daughter, and set out on someone else's long appointed track to "success." Forever. What if he were to break those chains, leave the expected things behind, marry Daisy, and live on an island? What might they be able to create together? What did he want? Who was he really?

In the end, he was a creature of his upbringing and generations of expectations. He would take the road most traveled, the sure thing, and the conciliatory thing. He would return to Boston, finish his MBA, and marry Joy next June. He would break Daisy's heart and perhaps his own.

As the days went by, he knew he had to say something. It was like the continual splurge before beginning a diet. *Just one more day,* he'd rationalize. *I need a few more delicious moments with her, one more sunrise, one more time to be lost in her arms and in her eyes. After the weekend, then I'll do it. I'll break it off.*

They had talked about his schooling in Boston, and she was aware that he would be returning soon, but he had avoided the question as to whether he would be leaving with or without her. She had dropped some little hints that he had carefully ignored. Would he return? That question was always left unanswered by a sudden change of subject. An obvious tension was building between them.

One breezy morning while walking through the tourist market-place, he acknowledged that the dreaded time had come. As he wandered through the little shops, he found a silversmith making and selling silver jewelry. His cross pendants were especially lovely, and Mel asked if he ever made a custom piece for someone. Mel's gringo Spanish was terrible, and the craftsman understood little English, but somehow they were able to communicate about what Mel had in mind. He paid him to fashion a beautiful cross with a filigree daisy in the center. It could be ready the next day. This delicate tribute would be the perfect gift for her to remember him by.

He made a date for lunch and got a reservation at the nicest restaurant in the city. They shared a marvelous romantic lunch of coconut shrimp with rice and key lime pie. Mel was even allowed to have a margarita. Daisy was having bean dip after all. Margarita interpreted this wonderful lunch as possibly a set up for a proposal of marriage. She had even confided to Ramon that she thought today might be the day. Everything at the restaurant was perfect. Candles set the mood, the bouquet of daisies made a statement of love, and Mel was especially charming and attentive. Things suddenly got very quiet as he contemplated how to proceed with what he had to say.

Margarita thought she saw his hands shake just a little, and she smiled to herself about his shyness. *Doesn't he know I'll say 'Yes'?* She tenderly took his hand and asked, "Is there something that you want to say to me, Bean?"

He couldn't formulate the words. There is no easy, painless sentence to break someone's heart. After an uncomfortably long silence, Mel spoke. "Daisy, I have something for you. I had it made special. It's something that I hope you will wear, and that you will think of me when you do." He pulled a small box from his pocket. It was not a ring box. He opened it for her.

Her face showed that she was touched and delighted. "Put it on me, will you please?"

He stepped behind her and fastened the clasp. "I want this pendant to say that I know that you come straight from the heart of God; He loves you and made you so nearly perfect that you leave the rest of us . . . in the dust." He stepped to her side, turned her face to him, and kissed her lightly. "I'm so grateful that He allowed me to spend this time with you. I'll never ever forget this summer; you know that, don't you?"

These were not exactly the words that she hoped to hear. "I love the cross, thank you. But what are you trying to say, Male Bean?" She was trying to articulate his name the best she could.

He laughed and then said, "I will always smile when I think of how you say my name. I will remember all those little things that make me love you." He had moved back to his side of the table and mustered the nerve to go on. "You know that I have to be going home very soon."

"What will you take with you to help you remember?" She paused, waiting for him to seize the opportune moment. He let it pass, and she prompted, "Can you take me with you?"

He shook his head sadly.

"But then next year, you will come back, won't you? When you are finished with your school, you'll come back, right?" Daisy asked.

"No, I won't be back." He kept his eyes on a pea that he chased around his plate with a fork. "But this has been the most beautiful summer of my life because of you."

"Is that all that I am to you?" She took the fork from his hand and let it drop loudly onto the china. "Just someone you spent a summer with, and now you go back where you came from and pretend nothing happened here? Is that what you are telling me?"

"No. I never thought—"

"No, you never thought. I would expect this of those stupid friends of yours, but not from you. I am just a cheap souvenir. Not even that. Souvenirs you take home with you and then eventually you throw them away. But you are throwing me away now."

"No, no, Daisy, my sweet, wonderful Daisy. You know that you're much more than that to me. You know that I love you, but our lives, our destinies, are so far apart. You have such marvelous plans for your life—wonderful dreams—and I know you will make them come true!"

"When I fell in love with you, you became my destiny. You became part of my plans. Didn't I become part of yours?"

"Daisy, before I came here, before I ever knew that I could love someone like you, there were lots of plans . . . lots of expectations and responsibilities. I have commitments to my family and to . . . someone . . ."

"To a . . . girl? You're engaged?"

"It hasn't been made official, but we're planning to be married in

June, after I'm out of school. I didn't know something like this could happen. I love you, Daisy, but I can't marry you. I can't stay here. I belong to another life back home. Don't you understand that I didn't just flash into existence the day I landed here?"

"Do you think that I just flash *out* of existence when you leave here? I am real. What you had here was real. You can change the future; you can choose to change things."

"I can't. I've played it all out in my mind. I want to stay, but I have to go."

"You are a coward, Male Bean!" She spit the name out with a vengeance this time. "Is that the right word, coward? You are afraid to do what you wan' and you only care about what other people think. I thought that you were a man. You are less than a boy. You are more of a fool than your jerk amigos. I'm so sad that I was fooled into thinking that you were different. You looked like a man! You loved like a man! But you are someone's little child! I was just your silly toy!"

She threw the rest of his margarita in his face and stormed out of the dark restaurant and into the afternoon sun.

She ran all the way up the palm-lined hill to the resort. She fingered the cross pendant as she tried to contain the tears that would advertise to Ramon just how wrong she had been. She wanted to go back and throw the necklace at Mel but she couldn't. It would be all that she had from him, the only reminder of a wonderful summer, her first love. Maybe he would go home and see that he belonged with her after all. Maybe then he would find the courage to follow his heart.

Mel gently placed the photo back into the journal, locked it, and tucked it into the side pocket of his suitcase. He had enough clothes and toiletries to get him through the next few days until he could send for the rest of his things. He just needed to get out of there. He zipped up the bag and headed down the stairs through the crowd of decorators, food servers, cleaning crew, and of course, Joy.

"Did you get the tux? And I hope you picked the better one this year. Turn around and let me look at you. It was so . . ." She had finally caught a glimpse of his face. The cold expression there chilled her very soul. Then she saw the suitcase. "Mel . . . Mel? What's going on? Where are you going? Our guests will be here in less than an hour. Mel! Don't leave like this! What's happened? You can't do this to me!"

He continued out the door and down the stairs toward the waiting taxi with Joy trailing frantically behind. "Don't I at least deserve an explanation?"

He kept his eyes on the taxi and said coldly, "Like the one I got all those years ago? Like that?"

"Please, Mel. Our friends will be here soon; can't you stay and we'll talk about this later tonight? What am I supposed to say to them?"

He finally turned and looked at her. "Tell them whatever you like. The truth never mattered to you before, so why bother with it now?" He tossed the suitcase in the back, got in the cab, and said to the driver, "Hyatt Regency, please."

Shortly after checking in, Mel received a call on his cell. It was from Mercy General Hospital.

"Mr. Jameson? You asked us to notify you if there was any change in Ms. Thomas' condition . . ."

Chapter Twenty-one

Nurse Betsy ambled into the room, approached Livy's bedside, and began attaching another bag to the IV drip.

"What's that?" Livy inquired. "It's lethal, I hope."

"It's just a little something to help you handle the stress. But it's not supposed to make you too sleepy. We want you alert for a little while yet. Don't want you slipping away again." She put down the side rail and helped Livy to slide over on the mattress so that there was room to sit beside her on the edge of the bed. "Honey, I made some calls. It seems that your Bryan wasn't brought to this hospital or any other in the area. That could mean that he either didn't need to go to the hospital, or that he was pronounced . . . at the scene. I felt like you needed to know, so I called Idaho. I was able to get a number for his folks in Blackfoot. When they answered, I think it was his mother, I said that I was inquiring about Bryan Kimball and she said," Betsy paused, took Livy's hand and continued, "Ms. Kimball said, 'Are you a friend of his?' and I said that I was calling from New York on behalf of a friend and she said, 'We're so sorry to have to tell you, but Bryan has passed away.' She said to please thank you for your friendship with their son. They seemed surprised you hadn't heard, and I didn't explain. She was so caring. I apologized for troubling them at a difficult time and passed along your love and sympathy for their loss. I'm so sorry, darlin'. Did I do the right thing?"

With some effort, Livy turned her head and looked out the window into the overcast sky. "You did. I had to know. Did you give them my name?"

"No, I just felt kind of awkward and wanted to get off the phone as quickly as I could. You can call them again when you feel stronger if you like. But at least now you know and don't have to torture yourself wondering. Was he someone special to you? Were you close?"

"More than you can imagine. And to think at this time last year, when I first met him, I thought he was a little pest, a hick. Oh, I would do anything to see that pest coming through that door. And it's all my fault!" Livy fought to hold back the flood of tears but couldn't.

"If I tried to hug you right now, I'd smash you, but if I could, I'd rock you like a baby," Betsy said and gave a slight, sad laugh.

"I wish someone could. Oh, how I wish."

Betsy squeezed Livy's hand and then went to check on other patients in the ICU.

Despite what Betsy had said, something was making Livy drowsy. She kept slipping in and out of a dream. Bryan was there. He kept saying, "I'm sorry about our Thanksgiving. I didn't know, Livy. I wanted to give you that day." He told her it was all going to work out, and she'd be all right. She could almost feel it when he kissed her on the head like he had so many times before. "When you feel alone, just think of me," he said. "I'll always be there."

She kept mixing dream and her surroundings. The many flowers around the room were now part of a funeral setting for Bryan. They were all there: 'Mom and Dad', Carolyn, Jackson, Stew, Michael, Clayt, Leslie, Elizabeth, even Becky, and sweet little Sarah, whom Bryan had not even had the chance to meet in person, and the other siblings. And all the rest were there too, including grandparents, cousins, nieces, nephews, in-laws, clergy from church, and all the people who must have loved him so. She had missed it. They were sad, yet celebrating a life well-lived. She couldn't even say good-bye. Her subconscious couldn't help contrasting the picture with the scene of her own possible funeral. Now in the dream, she had died too, and she saw that no one was there to mourn her. Reporters told the tale in an unfeeling ten-second sound bite. "Olivia Thomas, much celebrated, then disgraced former executive at Joy's Toys, died this morning. Now on to other news . . . In Toledo today, a new sandwich was unveiled . . ."

She tossed back and forth despite her entanglements and cried, "No one is there. There aren't any flowers."

"No flowers? Honey, look at this place!" Betsy declared. "There are more flowers than I've ever seen. He brings some every time he comes.

You're dreamin' up a storm. Now wake up! You're not supposed to go to sleep for a while. Do you want to see him or don't you?"

"See him?"

"Mr. Jameson. He's right outside the door, and he's brought even more flowers. Shall I let him in or not?"

Did she want to see him? What did he want? Now that her memory of his betrayal was clearer, she wasn't at all sure that she ever wanted to see him. The thought of him made her want to retreat back into the darkness she just came from.

But her lips moved and she said instead, "Let him in, I guess. I'll see him." She kept her eyes closed, putting off seeing his face.

Betsy propped open the door, just in case Livy needed her, and then motioned to Mr. Jameson to come in.

"I'll be right outside, darlin'." She pushed the cart back into the hallway.

Mel walked in carrying daisies in a small vase. He had tucked Garrett's card in the flowers so he wouldn't forget to tell Livy about meeting him. He shuffled slowly to her bed and dragged a chair alongside to sit close to her. He whispered, "Olivia, it's me, Mel. You have no idea how relieved I was to hear that you're awake. They tell me that you're going to be fine. I'm so, so glad. I want to tell you—"

Livy spoke to the ceiling. "Tell me what? That you're so relieved that I get to go to jail after all? That you're glad that I didn't die so that I can enjoy the wonderful world of fast food? That even though I've cheated you and JTC, I have your permission to live?"

"No. I wanted to help you. Livy, I'm sorry. I can imagine how you must have felt but to throw yourself into traffic?"

"I didn't throw myself into traffic; you, and certainly Joy, aren't worth that. I don't know. I can hardly remember what happened. I woke up here and I guess, unfortunately for you, I'm not dead."

"I thank God that you're not—that by some miracle you lived though the impact and that you're awake again. I'm not a praying man, as a rule, but I've been by your bedside every day doing just that—praying. I didn't even know how to pray or if God would listen to me. But you're here and you're going to make it. That's all I know."

"Well, just so that you know, it was Bryan that saved me, not you or God!" Livy exclaimed. "If it hadn't been for him, I would have been crushed by that bus, and it would be all over, and no one would have cared. How ironic that the person who had so many loved ones, the one who meant so much to so many, is gone and I'm still here."

"What? Who's Bryan?"

"I can't talk about him right now. Let's talk about going to jail." She still stared at the ceiling.

"No, Olivia. I'm so sorry about all of that. I know you're innocent, and we jumped to a lot of hasty conclusions. I should have known better. I know you. Please . . . look at me and say that you forgive me."

"What changed your mind? Do you feel sorry for me?"

"Everything inside me told me that it was all wrong. The whole thing nagged at me, and I wanted to get the chance to tell you I believed you. Then, just today, actually, I found out the truth. I think I know pretty much what happened, and it had nothing to do with you."

She softened a little. "If you had just listened to me . . ." She stiffened again. "Let me guess. It had something to do with Joy."

She finally looked at his face, checking for his reaction.

"I couldn't believe that she would do something like that to her own company. And she wouldn't have, except that she was being blackmailed. She used her position to maneuver everything to point to you if someone found that the numbers didn't add up. That was unforgivable. Livy, I'm so sorry I took her word and blamed you."

"She was blackmailed? How? Why?"

"I'm sure the whole world will know soon enough, but I want you to get it from me." Placing the daisies on the floor, he stood up, wiped the sweat from his brow, and began his story. He awkwardly started with the summer in the Dominican Republic when he was in graduate school and explained that he'd had an affair even though he was, for all intents and purposes, engaged to Joy. He knew then that it was wrong. It wasn't fair to either of the women or even to him. But it happened.

"What I didn't know at the time was that Daisy had gotten pregnant. I married Joy, even though I was torn by my feelings for Daisy. Well, the child was born, somewhere in the U.S., I guess . . . a little girl. I didn't know anything about it. And then when her mother died, she was brought to me. Daisy's brother, Carlos, and his girlfriend brought her. Only I wasn't there at the time. I was away on business and they brought the baby to the house. It was not a pleasant surprise for Joy. You can understand; she was hurt and angry and . . . it was more than she could bear."

Mel awkwardly stammered through the next words. "Things were different then, attitudes were . . . well . . . she couldn't find it in her heart to raise my half-black child while she couldn't even have a baby of her own."

"What happened to the baby?"

"I don't know. Joy paid those people, handsomely I gather, to get rid of my little daughter and to never let me know she was born. She paid them to get rid of my child, my little girl. She's kept that secret from me for thirty years now. So when your contest came up, it was a perfect opportunity for Carlos to come out of the woodwork and blackmail Joy into fixing the contest. The winning picture is—"

"Joy had the contest fixed?" The realization had come slowly. "What? You mean that picture of *Hannah—the winner? She's . . . she's . . . your baby?*" Livy's confused mind was swimming.

He nodded and stared at the floor. "If she didn't win, Carlos would expose everything. If Joy didn't keep paying, he'd tell the world all about who our little doll baby really was. Joy didn't want me to know what she had done, let alone the whole world. And you know the rest."

A shrill, shaking voice rang out from the doorway. "No, she doesn't know the rest, Melvin. Why don't you tell her the rest? I'd like to hear how it sounds when you say it."

Joy had quietly come in, unnoticed, while Mel was speaking.

"Joy! How long have you been standing there?" Mel asked.

"Long enough to hear your version of the story, and it makes me ill. Tell her the best part, Mel. It's my favorite part! Tell her or I will."

She paused and waited for him to start talking. He looked utterly lost.

She began again. "Olivia, he left out just one tiny little detail. He *did* know that his precious little Daisy was pregnant. She came to the states looking for him to tell him the good news. She tried to get his parents to stand up for their future grandchild and to make Mel marry her. But they wouldn't hear of it. They were having no part of a black child and its island trash mother. What would their social circle say? What about his great job at JTC? And our engagement? To them, and probably to him, it wasn't a marriage; it was a merger. How could he throw that away for this . . . this . . . little mistake? They convinced Mel that there was an easy way out, and he agreed. They paid the girl big money to have an abortion and just disappear. How much was it, Mel? What was the disposal of your kid worth to you? How much was it worth to her?"

In anguish, Livy looked to Mel to deny it, but he didn't. He was pulling petals off the daisies.

"How much?" Joy was relishing his humiliation.

"I don't know."

"Oh, come on, Mel. You knew. Was it ten thousand? Twenty thousand? What was it worth to you and the folks to get rid of her? For a little island slut, ten bucks, a bus ticket, plus the cost of the abortion might do, huh?"

Mel stood, shouting with rage, "It was a hundred thousand dollars. My parents had more money than they knew what to do with. At least I knew she could make her dreams come true and then some in Boca Chica with that kind of money. She deserved something out of the mess I caused." He stopped short. "What about you? How much did you pay Carlos to get rid of the baby? You can't act so pure. You don't even know what became of her. They could have killed her for all you cared."

"Oh, yes, you cared so much that you never checked to see if your precious Daisy went through with it. She couldn't flush your kid down the toilet, but *you* could and you never looked back." She turned to Livy. "I didn't want the baby, but *he* wanted her dead! Wouldn't the world love to know all about 'Mr. Toy man'? About the 'JTC-loves-kids man'? They'd have had a field day."

Mel's face reddened. "You have no idea what you're talking about. A thousand times I literally cried over that horrible mistake. And when we tried to have a baby and couldn't, it stung even more. I've been haunted by that trip to the clinic more than anything in my life. I couldn't undo it. I thought it was all over that afternoon. After all these years, I find out that I could have had my child; I could have had peace, but you kept it from me."

"You wanted her dead?" Livy was visibly shaken. "So do you know anything about what happened to her? What those low-lifes did with her?"

"No, but I intend to find out. All Carlos's old girlfriend told me was that she left her at a convent. She doesn't want me to know where. The woman said if my daughter had *wanted* me in her life, she would have come to me by now. But I'll find her, somehow."

Livy couldn't help but give a bitter laugh. "This is all very enlightening, but why me, Joy? Why did you have to try to destroy me?"

"Because every time I see you, I think of that other woman. You're young, beautiful, and black, and Mel has always thought you were so wonderful. It was like a knife in my heart, seeing you together. I didn't know if there was anything going on or not, but you were a constant reminder that he had loved *her* and had a child with *her*. I thought if you were blamed, then Carlos would see the jig was up and maybe he'd leave us alone. You'd be gone and we could just go on with our lives."

Joy turned and faced Mel now. "I know what I did was wrong, but I did it to protect you and JTC. I did it for us! I was desperate. He was going to broadcast it to the whole world. And now he probably will."

Mel turned from her and looked at Livy. "I've left Joy, Olivia. Of course that means that I'll be leaving the company as well, or what's left of it after all this. But if you can forgive me for not believing you, Livy, maybe you and I can start something new. I've always wanted to be in on the ground floor of something. We'll build a new company from scratch. What do you say?"

Livy thought for a moment and whispered softly, shaking her head, "No, Mel. I think you should stay with Joy. You deserve each other. Both of you get out of my room. Get out of my life."

"I know all this comes as a shock, but I hope when you're feeling stronger and ready to face the world again, you'll change your mind. I'll make sure that you get your share of the doll revenues. You know how much I believe in you, Livy. Through it all, deep down, I believed in you."

"And I believed in you too. But everything I believed was a lie. Now get out! Both of you! And I think maybe there's a cell available for you, Joy, at Riker's, now that I won't be using it. Enjoy the wonderful world of orange jumpsuits, won't you?"

Betsy bustled into the room with a hypodermic needle in her hand and pointed it at Joy. "Now you scoot! She said get out—don't you under-stand English? And you too, Mr. High and Mighty. On your way!"

Mel tossed the mangled daisies in the trash, along with Garrett's card, and started for the door, but then he turned back. "I don't know what else to say, Olivia, I hope you'll reconsider."

When he saw Betsy moving ominously towards him, he stepped up his pace to the elevator, down to the lobby, and out of the building. Once outside, he drifted through the cars in the hospital entry circle and hailed a cab to the Hyatt.

Joy shuffled down the hallway in stunned confusion. At home, guests were likely eating her food and drinking her wine, oblivious to the drama. She had simply left them there. She couldn't go home and face them now. She wandered out into the frigid December air just as a light sleet began to fall. She had not even brought a coat. After several blocks, she slipped on the slick sidewalk and scraped her knee through her stockings. Her black dinner dress had ripped from the hem to her waist and she sat there in the slush, freezing, bleeding, and dejected on the path. A heavy-set homeless woman with red hair happened along with her shopping cart and advised, "You'd better get into a good shelter tonight, missy. You don't have enough meat on your bones to keep a cricket warm." Leaving Joy a ratty, filthy blanket, she continued on her way.

Back in the room, Betsy said, "Are you all right now? You didn't need those people here tonight of all nights, causing you so much pain. It's good I gave you that stress medication; you might have really gone after that woman. Heavens! *I* should have let her have it." She held up the needle. "Would'a made my day."

Betsy got up and fished in the nightstand, at last producing a little plastic bag that contained Livy's personal effects. There was a ring, a bracelet, and the beautiful little daisy-cross that Livy had worn out of sight, on an extra-long chain, most all her life. Betsy took the pendant out and lovingly put it around Livy's neck.

She held up the cross and said, "There is someone who can hug you. You just let *Him* hold you, baby." She got another tissue and wiped away Livy's remaining tears. "It's okay. You can go to sleep now. It'll help you heal."

She tiptoed to the door and quietly stepped out.

Livy struggled to open the clasp of the necklace to take it off, but could not move her hands well enough yet. Finally, in anger and frustration, she yanked it off and broke the link that held the clasp. It tumbled to the sheet beside her. And at last, Livy slipped into sleep.

Chapter Twenty-two

Daisy listened as Mel's parents discussed her and her unworthy off-spring as if she were not human and had no more feeling or value than a piece of unwanted furniture. Mel made a few weak attempts to stand up for her but got very little chance to say a word. So it was decided. It would be best for everyone concerned. Daisy would be paid off, the baby would be gone, and that would be the end of that. "Now, dear, would you like some tea?"

Mel and Daisy had agreed that he would go with her to the clinic and stay with her until he was assured that she was all right, and that the child was no more. The money would be deposited in an offshore account that she could access as soon as she was safely and permanently out of their lives.

The couple rode silently in the back of the Jameson limousine, and it seemed to take forever to get to the clinic. Mel tenderly helped her to register and paid in cash for the abortion. She couldn't look at him. How could he ask her to do this? Did their baby and their time together mean nothing to him? How could she ask it of herself? He stayed and held her. He brushed her hair from her tear-stained face.

"It's better this way. You'll have a wonderful life." He was trying to convince himself as well. "You and I . . . it would never work. We're from two totally different worlds. But I do love you, Daisy."

"Then why . . . ?" She broke down in sobs.

"Please don't cry. Daisy, I can't stand to see you cry. Some things are just not meant to be."

"But some things just *are*."

A nurse approached and politely broke the tension. She guided them to an exam room where she explained that Daisy would be examined and then taken by gurney to her "procedure." Such an innocuous word for so devastating an event. Daisy wondered how the nurses and other staff members could be so casual and pleasant. For them, it was just another day at work while it was the end of everything for Daisy's baby. As they helped her onto the gurney, Mel kissed her cheek. He accompanied her down the long pink hallway to the surgical center. It was hung with black and white photographs of peaceful landscapes—scenes from a lifeless world.

"Please just go, Mel. I can't bear to see your face when this is all over."

"Daisy, I want to know that you're all right. I'm so, so sorry."

"Please do this for me. I don't want you to be here when I come out. I don't want to say good-bye again. Please, just go."

He squeezed her hand and watched them wheel her down the long hall and out of his life. He walked out into the cold fall morning and tried to console himself. She would be fine. He would have other children. Joy would never know, and they would have a good life together. This horrible feeling inside would pass, and life would go on. His would.

Daisy was all prepped for the abortion. She lay on her back, staring at the ceiling, feet in stirrups. Alone, she waited for the nurse to bring the doctor and for them to begin their work.

How will I feel when it's done? Will I feel better? she wondered. *Will I feel free to go on and begin an exciting new future? I'll be rich. I'll make the dream of owning my own resort come true. Carlos will be well provided for . . . but will this hurting in my empty heart and the void in my empty arms haunt me for the rest of my life?*

She touched the cross necklace that Mel had given her. She had lost him. His parents had taken him away from her; but she didn't need to let them take the baby too. Part of Mel was growing inside her, and she had come to love that little someone as she had loved him.

A quiet, tender voice from her very core spoke to her. "This baby comes straight from the heart of God too. She is my gift and my beautiful child. Mi hija linda."

No puedo. No lo puedo hacer. I can't! I can't do this! She pulled the IV from her arm, pulled the hospital gown closed, and ran down the hall to the changing room. It was only when she emerged, dressed and ready for escape, that a nurse confronted her and assured her "everyone goes through this," that "things will work out for the best," that "she would feel better when it was over," and of course, that "it wouldn't hurt a bit."

It wouldn't hurt a bit? Who was she kidding? My baby will be dead, and how could that not hurt?

She gathered up Carlos, and all she had brought with her to America and headed for Miami. Her grandmother's two sisters, Balbina and Eugenia, lived there and were happy to take her in and help with her pregnancy.

She passed the next seven months preparing for her baby and trying to keep her brother out of trouble. The latter was not an easy task. She suspected that he was becoming involved in drugs and violent activities. Miami was full of such opportunities for a boy of seventeen. Daisy never told him about the Jameson money, which now waited in an account in the Cayman Islands. He'd surely find a way to get at that cash and use it to buy drugs or for some other malevolent purpose. Daisy would not touch it either; it was cursed—blood money that only represented death and the disgust she felt for Mel's parents. Someday she would give it to her baby, the very one once marked for death. It would be washed clean.

Daisy—Margarita to everyone except Mel—was thrilled to deliver a beautiful 7 pound 8 oz. baby girl on March 24. She called her Linda. She had huge black eyes and curly black lashes. She had milk-chocolate skin and an adorable little nose and full pink lips. She was born with lots of wavy dark brown-red hair and was 22 inches long, very long indeed for a girl. Mel was 6 ft. 4 inches tall, and she would be tall like him, like both of them. When she'd grown a bit, and when her first teeth came in, she learned to use an adorable smile to get most anything she wanted, especially from her two doting elderly aunts. She had total command of Margarita's heart and was the happiest and most beloved of children.

In the months that followed, Daisy worked hard to provide for Carlos and for her little Linda. Leaving her baby in the care of her aunts, she went to work in one of the high-end Miami Beach resorts. She won recognition for her hard work and abilities. As promotions and raises came, she held to her vision of one day being in charge.

She had befriended a young girl by the name of Marielena Patino, "Patti" to her friends, who was employed in resort housekeeping. They had become very close, and Margarita openly confided in her new friend. Patti knew all about Linda, who and where the father was, and how he never knew that his child was born. Margarita used to share her dream that Mel would soon tire of his loveless marriage and realize he still longed for his island sweetheart. He would come looking for her, and he would be so thrilled to find her. He'd sweep her up in his arms, beg her forgiveness, and weep with joy when he saw that his little daughter was alive and so beautiful.

Early on, Patti confessed to Margarita that she was attracted to Carlos, and Margarita was torn as to whether to warn Patti or to encourage her interest. She knew many a floundering man had been saved by the love of a good woman. But the ruin of many a good woman had come from loving an evil man. Had Carlos crossed that line? Was he floundering or was he truly lost? Soon, they were spending a lot of time together, and Patti was sadly already under his spell and dependent on him for a fix.

Margarita prayed that somehow she and Patti could save him. Patti was strong enough to have survived living with her father, a talented photographer and an abuser when drunk. Her mother had left them for another man when Patti was only six. When she was fifteen, her father moved in with a new girlfriend, and left his daughter pretty much on her own in their trailer home. She had taken care of herself for three years now. Eventually, she all but moved in with Carlos and the family.

Carlos was in increasing danger. That meant all of them, including the elderly aunts and the baby, were in danger too. The gangsters he had become involved with were violent drug dealers who used this young inexperienced boy to run their errands and collect money. He found an opportunity to play both sides of the fence. He was Black *and* Hispanic, and he could work the middle ground between the rival gangs, skimming a share of the product for himself off the top. The danger was exhilarating, like another drug. Never on the street without a gun and other weapons, he thought himself invincible.

Margarita knew it was only a matter of time before he brought his violent world home. She and Patti planned to move to Orlando. Just this once, they would use some of the "blood money" to save their lives. She found the account number that had been given to her and withdrew just enough to leave some with her aunts, along with a letter of explanation, and a sufficient amount to begin a new life in a new place. They packed only the belongings they needed for the trip, and Margarita hid $15,000 in the bottom of Linda's diaper bag. They waited for a night when Carlos would come home doped or drunk. He'd simply wake up in a new life and realize it really meant the safety and freedom that was best for all of them. They could all begin again, again.

They didn't have to wait long. On December 21, Carlos did his part and came home high on something. He was not ready for sleep, however. He was wild and ranting about "something going down" and how "those guys are gonna pay."

They tried to calm him down and get him to go to bed, but he would have none of it. Regardless of Carlos's condition, the time had come to make their move. The Oldsmobile was packed and ready for their journey. Patti carried Linda out to the car and strapped her into her car seat. She backed it out to the edge of the street and left it running while she came back to assist Margarita in getting Carlos outside.

He raged and resisted and threatened to go for his gun because "he was going to get those guys." The two women managed to force him into the back seat. Patti climbed into the driver's side, and Margarita ran toward the passenger door. They were almost on their way.

It was then that the previously hidden black sedan sped up the street toward them. The blinding headlights suddenly flashed and two rifles bolted out of the open windows. Shots exploded into the night. One bullet pierced the windshield, missing Patti by inches and lodging in the upholstery of the back seat next to Carlos. Another sailed right over little Linda's head and through the back window. Several pelted the front windows of the house. Two more found a human mark. And now, Margarita lay bleeding in the street under the open passenger door.

By this point, Carlos had lunged from the car and was struggling to get a shot off. He was too wasted to handle the weapon. By the time he had it out and pointed in the right direction, the sedan was long gone. He screamed obscenities into the night, as if words alone could bring the perpetrators down. He turned to see Patti cradling his sister in her arms, praying, "Hail, Mary, full of grace. The Lord is with thee. Blessed is the fruit of thy womb, Jesus. Be with us now and at the hour of our death. Our Father, who art in heaven . . ." She held Margarita's daisy-cross pendant almost as if it were a rosary. Blood seemed to gush from wounds in her chest and groin.

"No! Not Margarita, no!" Carlos shouted incredulously and then he began to cry, loud and hard.

Alone in the car, the baby trembled. She could see Mommy was hurt, Mommy was going away. "Ma ma ma," she sobbed.

Margarita knew there was nothing to be done. Her life was slipping away into a red puddle in the street. She called out in a weak voice, "Patti, how can I leave my little Linda motherless as well as fatherless? How can this be? How can life be so unfair?"

"You'll be all right, Margarita. Carlos! Call an ambulance!"

He stood motionless, unhearing, unbelieving. Finally, he ran into the house.

"Take her from here Patti, please, promise me. Take her to her father. He can't turn her away now. Even *she* can't turn her away now," Margarita whispered.

"But he didn't want her, Margarita."

"Please Patti! He must see her. She needs her father. Please do this for me."

"Hold on, Margarita! She needs you. She loves you."

But Patti could see Margarita was dying. She knew it was true that Linda belonged with her father and if he only saw her, held her in his arms, he couldn't help but love her. Even the baby's grandparents would come to love her.

"Everything you need is in my purse and in her bag. I have his address and a birth certificate and money. Take it for you and Carlos. But there's more, an account number is there, but promise me it will go to Linda. Please Patti—don't tell Carlos. Promise me, Patti!"

Carlos came running out of the house with Aunt Balbina who immediately took Margarita from Patti's arms. She covered her in a blanket and gently rocked her.

Patti held onto Margarita's hand and whispered, "I promise. I'll take her. I'll make sure she's okay."

Carlos dragged her away. "Get in the car. The ambulance is coming and that means the police are too. We gotta go. Those guys may be stupid enough to come back. Get in and drive!"

"But Margarita!"

Aunt Balbina whispered, "You can't help her now. Go! *Que se vayan!* Get out of here!"

And they drove off.

Balbina held Margarita close until the ambulance arrived. The EMT pronounced Margarita Guadalupe Sotomayor Reyes dead at the scene. Balbina couldn't explain to the police why her grand-niece was outside in the street after midnight and no; she did not know the whereabouts of her grand-nephew. She hoped she never would again.

Patti drove for the first half hour in silent anger and grief. Neither of them knew what to say. She wanted to scream at Carlos for bringing home the violent garbage he had filled his life with. Margarita was dead because of him. He was sweating, rocking back and forth, and breathing heavily. He reminded Patti of her father when he was trying to come to grips with what he had done to her or her mother in one of his drunken rages. Carlos's remorse was real, but she wondered if, also like her father, Carlos would fail to learn anything from it. If this didn't wake him up, nothing would.

The prospect of change didn't look too likely when Carlos rifled through his jacket pockets and pulled out joints and cocaine paraphernalia. "What are you doing? Carlito! Haven't you had enough of that? Don't you see what it's done?"

"I know, baby, I know. But I just gotta calm down; then I can get myself together, I promise. I'll leave it forever. I promise. I will."

"Look at me!"

He kept his eyes on the joint he was fumbling to light.

"Carlos, I want you to look at me before you get high again. Do you see that I am covered in your own sister's blood because of what you've done? Now look!"

He gave her a quick glance and went back to his rocking as he took his first long inhale. Then another.

She grabbed the reefer from his shaking fingers, took a drag of her own, and then threw it out the window. "Now look behind you. Do it and keep looking this time!" He turned around and she said, "That is your niece, your own flesh and blood; she now has no mother—because of you. She is traumatized and scared out of her mind."

He started to blubber in stoned slurs. "I know it's my fault. I feel terrible. I loved Margarita; she took care of me. She was the only person who ever loved me since Mami and Papi died. But what do I do? What can I say? I can't bring her back. I can't. What do you wan' from me, baby?" He broke down into sobs. "What do you wan' from me?"

"For one thing, I want you to live, Carlos. You know if you ever go back there, they will kill you."

"No, I'll kill them first. If it's the last thing I do."

"No, Carlos. You've made too many dangerous enemies. They tried tonight, and they'll try again. I hope your aunts keep the place crawling with cops for a good long time."

"So where are we going? There are suitcases and food and everything in here. What were you plannin'?"

"We were going to take you away and start over. She knew something like this would happen, but she thought you'd be the one who ended up dead. She made a deposit on a place in Orlando, and we were going to have a new life there."

"So you two just decided to what? Kidnap me? I don' get no say in nothin'?"

"Obviously we had to get out of there. Why couldn't we have gotten away before this happened?"

Eventually, Carlos noticed they were on I-95 instead of on I-75. "Hey! I thought we were goin'—"

"We have a little errand to run first." Patti looked over her shoulder at Linda who had cried herself to sleep.

"She's not coming?" Carlos asked. Patti shook her head. "Good! I don't know what to do with a kid. So where ya takin' her?"

"Margarita wants her to go to her father. He deserves to know that he has a child, and she deserves a father."

"That dirt bag? I should have killed him two years ago, for my sister's honor. We're driving to New York? Tonight?"

"That's what she wanted and that's where we're going. It's almost Christmas, and who can turn away a motherless child at Christmas? This is the perfect time."

They took their time driving north up the East Coast freeway. They spent a night in an expensive hotel in South Carolina. Carlos slept like the dead that night and nearly half the next day as well. Patti dug some of the baby's toys from the trunk of the car and plopped down on the floor to play with her for a couple of hours. Linda gleefully soaked up the attention.

Soon, Patti and the baby were frolicking in the hotel pool, exchanging splashes. While feeding, changing, bathing, and dressing this little girl, Patti got just a taste of motherhood and found herself enjoying the flavor. It wouldn't be hard for someone to bond with this little one, Patti was sure. The father would instantly fall in love with her as Patti was falling even now. Did the wife have any idea at all? What kind of person was she? Could she find room in her heart for this little surprise?

Late in the evening of the 23, they arrived at their destination—a dignified ivy-covered mansion that seemed to take up a full block. More fortress than house, it was surrounded by a stone wall, and the driveway was guarded by huge iron gates. Curiously, they were open.

Carlos took one more drag on a joint, seemingly to get up his nerve. "What if he don' want her? What then?"

"How could he not?"

It was nearly eleven when they knocked on the massive door. They were surprised when a frail young woman in a bathrobe answered the door instead of a butler. Not one to wait for an invitation, Carlos barged right in, pulling Patti in right behind him. She was carrying the sleeping child in her infant seat.

"Excuse me!" the young woman began. She seemed angry and wary, but not frightened. "Who are you? I don't remember asking you in. For your information, I have servants, dogs, and a silent alarm. Now, what do you want?"

Patti put the seat down and stepped forward. She began, "We are sorry to arrive so late. We have important business with your husband. If you could ask him to come down please, we need to speak with him." Patti knew this woman was the person who would require the winning over. "We're so sorry to disturb you. We've come a long way, and our business is very important."

"My husband is asleep."

"Well, get him up. This is important, like she said," Carlos barked.

"You still haven't told me who you are."

"I am Carlos, and this is my girlfriend, Patti. Now, where is Melvin?"

"What is the nature of your business with my husband?" She gave him a look of utter contempt and sniffed at him, probably detecting the marijuana. "He doesn't do *business* with the likes of you!"

"Oh, he doesn't? Do you see this little darling over here?" He gestured to the child asleep in the car seat. "She is a Christmas present for you and the mister. She's his child."

"She is not!" she hissed.

"I assure you, Mrs. Jameson, she is. If you'll just wake your husband, he'll be able to explain it all to you."

"He's not here. He won't be back until tomorrow."

"Then you'll have a nice surprise waiting for him when he comes home. You can say, 'Oh Sweetie, it's Christmas Eve and look what Santa brought!' "

She eyed the child reluctantly and recoiled as if looking at a dead body. "I don't believe you. Is this some kind of prank? Where is the mother? What proof do you have?"

"Why don't you ask your in-laws about their grandchild, the one they paid good money to get rid of."

"He wouldn't do this to me. It can't be his." She peered at the child a little more closely, suspiciously. "How old is she?"

"She was conceived in Boca Chica, if that's what you're askin'. Didn't he send you postcards while he was having his way with my sister?"

Joy Jameson then turned away, pale and shaking, and crossed the room to a white satin sofa. She collapsed, too shaken to stand. "That son of a . . . ." She dropped her head into her hands and let out a stream of angry curses.

Patti followed and sat down next to her. "I'm so sorry. I know this is coming as a shock to you—one you weren't ready for. But she really is the sweetest thing. Her mother was Carlos's sister and my best friend. And when Margarita died, she made me promise to bring Linda to her father. Those were practically her last words."

"Oh really? You expect me to care? What a cruel joke! I risk my life to give him a child, lose it anyway, and you have the unmitigated gall to come here and wave his 'love child' in my face? Well, too bad, but we can't take this, this . . . kid. Look at her! I can't pass her off as mine . . . she's not even white."

"Oh yeah? Well, she's half-white," Carlos interrupted.

"Shut up, Carlos," Patti said.

"I'm not raising some Black child as my own."

"People adopt mixed-race children all the time. No one needs to know . . . the rest," Patti said.

"Not people in my world."

"Don't you think that Mel should have something to say about this?" Patti asked.

"Does he even know?" Joy asked.

"No, I told you," Carlos said as if speaking to an idiot. "He paid Margarita to get rid of it. He thinks of it as a problem that just went away. But as you can see, she couldn't go through with the abortion."

"If anyone is going to give my husband children it will be me and not some Black Hispanic slut!"

Patti got up, walked over to the infant seat, and knelt beside Linda.

"Just look at her. Her name is Linda. It means beautiful and that's what she is—and innocent in all of this. How it all happened is not her fault." She stroked the baby's cheek. "Please just look at what a little angel she is. I know that you could love her . . . if you gave her a chance."

Joy twisted her face away. "No. I can't do it. I know I can't. She'll never be mine. I'll always think of my husband with her mother and I'll resent her. I will never love her. I will *hate* her. Is that what you want?"

Carlos stood, coldly brushed his hands off on his pants, and said, "Well, I guess that's his problem now." He turned and motioned to Patti to leave. "Let's go."

Joy turned to Carlos, frantic now. "No. You can't leave her, and you can't come back. Listen, our family owns a toy company. We have money. I can pay you to bring her up in your family where she belongs. You're her flesh and blood, why can't you take her?"

"How much money we talkin' here?" Carlos asked.

"Carlos, don't you think that he . . . Melvin, should have some say in the matter?" Patti asked.

"Oh, yes, definitely. He needs to know and we can stay right here until he comes home, or should we come back tomorrow? What do you say, Mrs. Jameson?"

"No! As Mel already showed by paying for an abortion, he doesn't want this baby. I don't want it. Take the money, keep her, put her up for adoption, leave her on the side of the road. I don't care. Just take her away."

Carlos raised an eyebrow. "I don' know. It costs a lot to bring up a kid these days. A lot."

"I told you, I'll give you money. I can get $50,000 right now from the safe."

"Tell you what. You have a lot of nice things here and you know if $50,000 just suddenly turns up missing, someone's going to ask a lot of questions—ones that you will not want to answer. So if I take, say, a little jewelry you never wear, and this little statue over here . . ." He picked it up and handed it to Patti.

"What are you talking about? I'm not going to give—"

". . . and the money. See, that way you can say it was a burglar. You have insurance, and no one will think too much about it."

"And when the police ask and I describe you?"

"Remember, if you sick any police on me, Mel and I are going to have a nice chat. And you'll have your little Christmas present after all. We have met, you know."

"Just take it all and go. Don't try to contact us again, or I *will* have you charged with extortion." She turned and left the room to go to the safe.

Carlos turned to Patti with a triumphant smirk. "What do you thin' about that, Patti?"

Chapter Twenty-three

The doctors in charge of Livy's case decided she could return home for Christmas. She would, however, need in-home care on a three-times-per-day schedule to make sure she did not relapse or miss any necessary therapy or medication.

When Livy came home, Rachel, her aide, a sweet young woman of 20, got her situated in her bedroom with everything she needed: the TV, lots of DVDs, books, snacks, and anything else she could think of to keep her occupied.

"You know, Ms. Thomas, I think the wheelchair will be a good idea to get around the apartment when I can't be here. I know you've been up and walking around the hospital, but not by yourself. I'm sure it's a pain, but for my sake, if not yours, please use the chair," she said as she readied the blood pressure cuff. "You're still as unsteady as a baby taking her first steps, and I don't want you to take a bad fall when you're alone."

After checking Livy's vital signs and giving her a shower and several medications, Rachel was about to depart for the evening.

"Now, Ms. Thomas," she began.

"Call me Livy, please."

"Livy, if you insist, but the agency suggests we keep it more professional. Please let me know if you need anything or if you experience any of those symptoms on the sheet: numbness, dizziness, severe headache, or anything more pronounced than you're experiencing now. Just call anytime, okay Ms. Thomas? Sorry, I mean Livy."

Déjà vu—echoes from a year ago. It seemed like mere weeks since she and Bryan had had that same call-me-Livy exchange.

Rachel, in an almost mother-for-hire manner, tucked Livy nicely in bed with a good book, gathered her purse and keys, and took her leave.

Livy didn't last five minutes in bed. She'd been lying down for almost a month and felt as restless as a caged animal. She flung the blanket off, stepped into her slippers, and got herself into the wheelchair at the end of the bed. A long hallway led from her bedroom all the way to the front-door foyer. She could easily maneuver anywhere in the house.

She wheeled down the corridor, into the living room, and over to the huge window overlooking her New York world. She'd spent hours and hours at this 54th floor vantage point, vowing to experience, and to conquer everything, every challenge this city offered. Somewhere out there was Garrett. Why hadn't he called or visited? Didn't he care? He must have heard about the accident, but he obviously didn't care. Now even the cars in the traffic jam below seemed to mock her, as if they too were personally leaving her behind. The shadow of night crept across the skyline.

Rolling into the kitchen, she discovered more remnants of her former life. There on the counter was the picture of her and Mel at the awards dinner, right where she had left it. In the sink were the teacups she and Bryan had used on that fateful day.

Bryan. Where was he tonight? She reached for everything he had touched that evening—the teapot, the cups, the picture, trying to capture just a trace of him. Then she noticed it. There, draped over the back of a kitchen chair, was his ugly, horse-blanket plaid coat. He hadn't even grabbed his jacket when he'd run out the door after her. She wheeled herself over, gently lifted it to her face, and found a rush of memories of him in the scent. She awkwardly slipped it on and almost felt his arms surround her.

She glanced around the stark apartment. He had provided the warmth. Here on December 21, there was neither sign nor smell of yuletide. Not a touch of Christmas cheer. Bryan would be ashamed of her. She rolled to the hall closet and stood up to search inside. Behind the boxes from her office, she found the tiny festive tree and the precious Nativity scene that Bryan had brought her last year. She lovingly displayed them in front of the picture window. As she plugged in the lights, bittersweet memories of an Idaho-style family Christmas flooded her heart.

She studied each piece of the crèche and smiled when she picked up and caressed a little lamb. She could vividly recall one Christmas when she was about six, and she savored just a taste of Christmas spirit when she thought of it. At six, she was still at the Catholic group home and was excited to be in the pageant. She remembered being dressed as a little lamb with a big cowbell around her neck. The collar was a bit too loose, and when it was her turn, she ding-donged irreverently up the aisle and the audience laughed. She scampered to the front, crying and clanking, and hid behind a shepherd. When they laughed again, she ran offstage to find her nun. Of course she thought they were laughing at her because she was silly and because of that dumb bell. But it was only because she was so cute.

Sniffling, she asked Sister M why she had to wear it, and the nun hugged her and answered, "You wear that bell so Jesus will always know where you are. That way, little lamb, you will never be lost."

After that, she wouldn't take it off and she let the bell ring loudly and proudly all evening long. (She held onto it for two years after that, until someone at a shelter finally stole it from her belongings.) After the pageant, a sweet, funny-smelling old Santa gave her the doll she would cling to for the next seven years and through several different homes. She called her doll Hannah. But this "Hannah" had never felt so lost.

She returned to the closet and took out the *Tiffany's* gift box she had intended to give to Mel for Christmas. It was to reveal her secret to him. Thousands of times she'd imagined the reaction on his face when he opened it. That long-anticipated moment was lost forever. Now the lovely package would only serve as decoration under the tree.

More than four weeks had gone by since she had heard anything about Josie and Frankie. She longed know where Frankie had gone that night. Had they found him? Was Josie safe? Would they have any kind of Christmas? Maybe she could see the kids. She forced her feeble legs back to the kitchen and found the last crayon drawing Josie had made for her still displayed on the fridge. There she found the number she had scribbled for child welfare services. She picked up the phone and dialed. Sylvia connected her to Daria, the caseworker, who broke the news.

"It's good to hear that you're going to be all right, Ms. Thomas. You must realize, however, that when we heard, well, when everyone thought that you . . . had serious criminal and legal problems, and then you had that terrible . . . accident, we naturally took you off the parenting candidate list. You understand; I'm sure. Besides, it doesn't matter now," Daria stammered.

"What do you mean it doesn't matter?" Livy asked.

"As you already know, Francois ran away from his placement. And now Josette is back with her—"

"You sent her back to her mother? How could you do that? Do you know what kind of danger she was in? Do you know what abuse and neglect was going on?"

"Madeleine did everything we asked. We had no choice."

"Everything . . . like what?" Livy demanded.

"She went through her sixty-day rehab for the cocaine, and she has been in job training. She has vowed to stay off the street. She wanted her daughter back. What else could we do? She kept her end of the bargain; we had to keep ours."

"What about Josie and your responsibility to her?"

"She was happy to be with her mom again. She loves her, Ms. Thomas."

"Of course she does. But whatever happened to laws and punishment? Prostitution is illegal. Drugs are illegal. Neglect and child endangerment are illegal. The woman gets a pass and the reward of getting Josie back? Are you people insane?"

Daria sounded angry now. "She spent some time in jail, and she went to lock-down rehab. And as I just told you, Ms. Thomas, you are not a candidate for fostering or anything else right now, so none of this is any of your business. We are closely monitoring the situation. That's all you need to know."

"Let me tell you something *you* need to know. The only reason Josie is alive is because she had Frankie. He protected her. Now he's gone. What is she going to do when things get bad again? Who's going to feed her when her mother leaves again for days at a time? Who will hide her from that goon who repeatedly beat her and her mother?"

"She can call on us. She knows that. She'll be fine. I'll make sure she is."

"Oh, I feel so much better now. A seven-year-old will call and update you," Livy said bitterly. "Can I at least see her during the holidays?"

"It sounds to me like you would try to do more than just see her. Don't make us seek an injunction or a restraining order against you. You are not approved to be meddling in this case. You're obviously unstable. I'm warning you; just back off. You have enough problems of your own to deal with. You're not needed here. Good afternoon. Merry Christmas!" Daria said curtly and hung up.

Livy shouted at the dial tone, "This is not over yet!" She stood, trembling, supporting herself at the kitchen counter, and pondering Daria's statement. "You're not needed here." Because Olivia had always heard that, she had always felt it. She had said as much herself. That Christmas morning, a year ago, she had told Bryan, "A kid is too much trouble. They poop, they cry, they smell, they get into everything and poke their little noses into places where they don't belong, they're inconvenient and expensive . . . who wants to mess with all that?" The phrases joined a cacophony of others she had heard throughout her life. "You aren't wanted here." "There's no room for you." "I'm sorry; this family will not work out for you." "I don't know why we bother with you! Go back to wherever it was you came from." "Your Daddy took one look at you and threw you in the trash can." "No, you can't come *home* for Christmas. You have no home here." Obviously Garrett had no room for her in his life. Again, she heard Joy's voice, shrill and adamant, "I didn't want the baby, but *he* wanted her dead!"

I am not needed or wanted anywhere. Why didn't Mel just get his wish that I would never be born? Bryan said I was here for a reason. He saved me for a reason. "Bryan!" she cried out. "Why did you do that? You stupid, crazy boy!"

She could almost hear his words again. "I want you to go home to Blackfoot for Christmas, with or without me."

She knew he would be missed this Christmas and every Christmas from now on. A family in Idaho was aching for Bryan terribly, like she was. While it was true that his work had kept him from making the trek last Christmas, she knew he would have been with them this year, if it had been at all possible. The kind of love he described would be calling to him like a beacon, especially at Christmas, his favorite holiday. He would have found a way.

She could picture Marilee Kimball, knee-deep in some yuletide project or another, wiping off her hands on an apron and opening the door to see Bryan standing there. It would be just like him to surprise them. She would hug the daylights out of him, and when he was about to faint from lack of oxygen, she would let loose of him and yell, "Hey Jake! Hey kids! It's Bryan! He's home for Christmas!" Livy was designing in her mind an image of what she, herself, would like to experience—just once.

Go home. She felt it more than heard it.

Home? Livy knew them all and really did feel like she was a part of them somehow. They shared the pain and loss she now felt in a way that no one else could comprehend. Had he told them of the sister that he had so boldly claimed as part of the family? Maybe they already knew about her and would love to embrace her as one of their own. But when she confessed to them that it was her fault, that he had given his life for her carelessness, what would they say? What would they think of her then?

They love you already. A reassurance, a prodding. And then clearly and audibly, he said her name. *Livy, go home to Blackfoot.*

Startled, her eyes searched the room for him. He was here. She could feel it as distinctly as the weight of his coat on her shoulders. It was his voice or she was losing her mind. He *was* here telling her, urging her, to go.

"But Bryan, can they forgive me?"

It will be all right. They need to hear what you have to tell. And then her sense of his presence was gone.

She knew she had to go. She must tell them how sorry she was and how much she had come to care about them through him. But how could she face them? Maybe they could comfort each other.

But she couldn't make herself call. She might say all that needed to be said on the phone and that would be that. They might say they didn't *need* her to come; it wasn't *necessary*. Wanting desperately not to hear those words, she made up her mind to just show up at their door. She would actually be with them, be a part of them. She had to go and hope that they would let her stay to share her memories of Bryan and his "Kimball Christmas" with them.

She pulled out her day planner and turned to the listing for her travel agent. He had gotten her to Paris, Tokyo, and London. Certainly, he could get her to Blackfoot, Idaho. She picked up her cell phone and dialed.

There was no flight available, so close to the holidays, to the nearest airport in Idaho Falls, so she made a reservation for Salt Lake City on December 23 and a hotel reservation for that night. She booked a rental car for the three-hour drive to Blackfoot. She couldn't tell her aide. Rachel would tell the doctor, and Betsy would probably show up and chain Livy to the bed. No, she would be the perfect patient for the next two days, and then that morning, when Rachel had gone, she would leave a vague note and make her escape.

The press had lost interest in Livy's story now that they had learned she was going to live. Mel hadn't publicly cleared her name. Garrett finally called the hospital and learned that Livy had regained consciousness and had been released. If Jameson had told her about his concern, she hadn't welcomed it, or just as likely, Jameson hadn't said a word. Garrett called her home and cell numbers.

Her cell phone lay forgotten on the counter where she'd left it in her haste to escape. It received message after message from a frantic Garrett.

Chapter Twenty-four

All went according to plan, and she was able to endure the flight better than she expected. She landed at Salt Lake International, picked up her rental car, and drove to the beautiful Grand America Hotel. The luxurious lodgings were her Christmas present to herself. She awoke to the light of a beautiful winter morning streaming through the break in the curtains. She drew them back and gasped in awe at the view. The sky was crystal clear and the majestic mountains surrounding the Salt Lake Valley were beautiful—brilliantly white with new snow. She lingered for several moments, procrastinating the start of the next leg of her journey.

She gathered her courage, dressed in jeans and a heavy sweater, and then applied some casual make-up. Without it, she looked gray and sick. After bundling herself up in her powder blue parka, she dramatically flung the ends of the scarf Bryan had given her around her neck and over her shoulders in an act of resolve.

It will be fine. I'll like them, and they'll like me, and we'll all talk about Bryan. Maybe they'll invite me to stay for Christmas and then . . . then life will go on. But what if they hate me? That's very possible when they learn it's my fault that he is . . . gone. I must be nuts! The brain damage must be worse than the doctors thought.

The courteous young parking attendant at Grand America placed her large suitcase into the trunk, and she kept her purse with her up front. The hotel valet instructed her on navigating the complicated on-ramps, off-ramps, exits, and overpasses the locals had affectionately nicknamed "the spaghetti bowl" that would take her to I-15 north. Map in hand, she was on her way.

She was surprised at how pretty it was, especially after she had passed through the major cities and was out in the country among the small towns and farms. There weren't the thousands of trees she would have seen in the East, but the snow-covered countryside and the rugged mountains had a rural simplicity that was both charming and inviting. After two hours, she crossed the Idaho border and uttered a cheerful "Thank you," as she read the *Welcome to Idaho* billboard signed by the governor. *I will enjoy my stay, sir.*

Pocatello was the first city of any size that she came upon after crossing the state line. She had been on the road for nearly three hours and thought she should probably stop for gas and a snack. It had been hours since she'd eaten, and she didn't feel like she could crash a grieving family's Christmas (and a family of strangers, at that) on an empty stomach. She needed some intestinal fortitude. The doctor had warned her that while she may not have much appetite, it was important to remember to eat.

At the junction of interstates, she turned into the Gem State Truck Stop and parked her rental near the gift shop entrance.

She found The Trucker's Mama's Kitchen café and waited for the hostess to seat her. A cute, perky blonde of about eighteen finally approached and escorted her to a table near the window. She gave Livy a menu. As she looked it over, Livy wondered how many truckers had just up and had coronaries after eating at such places. The glossy photos displayed stacks of pancakes, six or seven high with loads of butter, accompanied by ham, bacon, and sausage *and*, of course, deep-fried hash browns. The lunch page advertised triple cheeseburgers with a full pound of beef smothered with the restaurant's proprietary secret sauce, all guaranteed to clog an artery in five minutes or less or your meal was free. Well, something like that. Livy ordered a fruit plate and a cup of coffee. When it came, she slurped up the coffee and mostly played with the fruit.

As Livy was forcing herself to eat a chunk of banana, a towheaded little girl of four or five at the booth in front of her kept peeking around her daddy to steal a look at Livy. Livy played along and pretended not to notice and then slyly made a silly face at her. The little girl giggled and whispered something in her daddy's ear. Not so discreetly, he turned around and glanced at Livy for himself. After he whispered something back, she replied loudly, "It is *too* the dolly-lady!"

"No, honey," the big man said. He wore a plaid flannel shirt and a baseball cap with a large "I" on it, and with his sun-weathered, freckled face, he looked just like what Livy thought an Idaho potato farmer should look like. "Leave her alone. It's not nice to stare. I think that lady you're talking about is in a coma or brain-dead or something." He tried to hush his deep voice, but Livy heard every word.

Livy piped up. "You're both right. I am the dolly-lady, and I must be brain-dead to be doing what I'm doing. I'm Olivia Thomas, and you are—?" She extended her hand across the booth without getting up.

"I'm Ray Proctor," he returned as he tried and failed to extend his hand over the booth-back and across the table. He made a little waving gesture instead, obviously embarrassed.

"Daddy, see? It is her." The child fished in the corner of her seat and produced a *Hold-Me-Hannah* whom she informed Livy, was really named Suzy. "She's sleeping now so I haf' ta talk softly. I really love her. Thank you for making her. She's my best birthday ever!" She held up five chubby little fingers. "I turned five, and my name is Wendy."

"I'm sorry about the brain-dead remark." Ray fingered the brim of his baseball cap. "The last we heard, it was looking pretty bad for you. We followed the story for a while after Wendy picked up on it. They showed you and the whole doll connection, and since she's enthralled with her Suzy, Wendy was very interested. It's amazing how that doll captivates her—that face—and how it keeps her busy and all. By the way, we entered Wendy's picture in your contest, you know."

"Really? She should have won. She's a beautiful child, Ray."

"So . . . uh . . . how did all that play out, anyway?" Ray asked.

"I didn't do what they said, if that's what you mean. Don't hold your breath for JTC to come out and make a big explanation and an apology, though."

"So you are all right now then?"

"Some might say yes, and then again . . ."

"What in the world brings you out to little old Pocatello, Idaho, for Pete's sake?"

"It's a long sad story that I just can't go into. I'm actually on my way to Blackfoot. Is it far from here?" Livy asked, trying to change the subject.

"Heck, no. It's just up the road apiece—half hour or so. I'm from Blackfoot myself. What ya gonna do there?"

"Well," Livy hesitated and then decided to go on. "Do you know the Kimballs?"

"Jake and Marilee Kimball?"

Livy nodded.

"My heck, yeah! Their farm is just up the road; they're my neighbors. Everybody knows the Kimball family. They make up a quarter of the town . . . well, pert' near. That's where you're going?"

"What do you think of them?"

"They are somethin' else." Ray laughed and shook his head.

Livy's heart sank just a little. "Do you mean they're weird?"

"Not weird, they're amazing! Marilee's just a regular woman, I guess, but she seems to handle more than any of us can even imagine. Like this one time? I was at the next check stand at the grocery store and she's got like six kids with her. You know, some are in the cart and some running around and stuff. Well, this woman come up behind her and says, 'You know, there is such a thing as birth control. How can you possibly take good care of that many kids?' As if she could have actually borne all those different kinds'a kids! She didn't even know that there was a bunch more at home and at school. And Marilee answers back without missin' a beat, 'Thank you! You're absolutely right. Which one would you like to take care of? Go ahead and pick one. I sure could use the help.' That shut her up fast. And yet Marilee, she's just . . . she's still . . ." Ray took off the cap and pushed back his thick brown hair as if it would help him find the right word.

"She's just, still what?" Livy really wanted to know what to expect. Bryan, of course, hadn't been objective; to him his family was perfect.

"Well, I guess she's so good with kids 'cause she still is one. Jake's even more that way. He's hardly ever serious," Ray said, laughing. "How do you know the Kimballs?"

"I don't really. I knew their son, Bryan . . . in New York."

"You did? They was real broke up when they lost him. I wasn't sure Jake was gonna find the strength to go on, and I never saw Marilee like that. He was a real sweet kid. Everybody loved him. It was so sad."

Livy didn't know why she felt so struck. Of course they would be devastated. "They took it really hard then?"

"Oh, they're doin' better, little by little."

Wendy had been staring at Livy with a puzzled face. "Will Suzy grow up to look like you 'cause you made her?" Wendy asked Livy as she placed Suzy back in her little seat.

"Suzy will always be your baby, won't she? And if she did grow up, I bet she would look like you. See? She has pretty blonde hair like yours," Livy said, pointing at her flaxen curls.

"Mommy says she made me out of Maalox. Is that good?"

"Must be, because look how beautiful you turned out!"

Wendy leaned close, staring at Livy for a moment, and then pronounced, "You are pretty. Are you Black?"

"Umm, that's a good question. I'm part Black."

"Part Black? Which part?" A light bulb seemed to turn on in her little head and her face lit up. "Do you have black feet? Is that why you came to our town?"

Livy tried not to laugh but couldn't help it. "Maybe that *is* why I came to Blackfoot. Actually, my feet are black, but they're part white too, is that okay?"

"Oh sure, it's okay. I just wondered."

Ray, a bit chagrined, chuckled a little too. "I guess we don't have enough diversity around here."

Just then, the waitress approached Livy's table with her check and exclaimed as she looked out the window, "Oh my goodness! Look at it comin' down out there!"

"What? Snowing?" Livy looked out into the black sky and frenzied air. "It was sunny when I came in!" Livy cried in panic.

"Yes, ma'am. It's December in Idaho and does tend to do that from time to time. Snows back East, don't it?"

Up and out of her booth almost faster than the waitress could finish her bill, Livy dashed to the cashier to pay and then out to the white blob her rental car was quickly becoming. Ray called after her and offered assistance but she was halfway into the car already and didn't hear. Perhaps she could get to Blackfoot before the snow began to accumulate on the road. While it certainly snowed in New York, she never needed a vehicle. Most of her driving experience had been in Florida, and conditions there never resembled anything like this. She started the engine and began the frightful last leg of her journey.

At first, harmless flurries of snow danced in the air and melted on the car-warmed asphalt. But with every passing moment, the darkness pressed in heavier around her and the winds raged more threateningly. Soon, those harmless flurries turned to a frenzy of giant flakes of blinding white that buried the road in wet, slick snow. The storm had come up behind her like a giant stalking animal and had overtaken her. There was nothing much between here and Blackfoot, and there was no turning back. And after festering over her conversation with Ray, she wanted to turn back. She couldn't decide what frightened her more: never arriving safely at the Kimball home, or what might happen when she did.

She knew her exit number, but most of the signs were now unreadable. According to her map, it was 19.7 miles from the last Pocatello exit to her destination ranch exit. Might as well be a hundred. She was creeping along at about five miles per hour now, her white-knuckled hands strangling the wheel in a death grip. More experienced snow-drivers and those Livy assumed to be less encumbered by common sense, raced by, swerving, on all sides. She'd have to speed up some or this twenty-minute drive would become a two-hour nightmare or worse. She gave the gas a little push and immediately began to fishtail. *Turn into the skid and avoid sudden braking,* the Internet snow-driving tips had said. She corrected slightly, resisted the urge to brake, and continued, terrified.

When the odometer clicked off the appropriate number of miles, and fifty minutes that seemed like hours had passed, Livy spotted the remote exit. From here, it would only be another 4.2 miles to the Kimball farm. She carefully moved to the right and followed the exit, which immediately became a downhill slope. At the bottom of the hill she could make out a partially hidden stop sign at the cross street. As instructed by the tips, she tried to gently pump the brake but a patch of ice and the force of gravity launched her into a quick skid. Instinct took over and she was braking for all she was worth. The car spun around and then, at great speed, sailed trunk first into a deep ditch across the intersecting road. A violent jolt marked the car's abrupt stop with the rear end at the bottom of the ditch and the front end sticking straight up, the front wheels not touching the ground. Livy was lying back against the seat, staring straight out the windshield into the blizzard. Thankfully, because the impact was in the rear, the airbag did not deploy.

Mentally, she did an inventory of her body. She concluded that she was okay—she had no broken bones and she had blessedly not hit her head. She may have sustained just a little whiplash from the rough impact but nothing more. Now, however, she was shaking violently, trembling not from the cold, but from the panic and the ordeal she had just experienced. Suddenly she had a disturbing thought. With the winds and the blizzard raging on, it was probably colder than twenty degrees outside the car, and the temperature was dropping rapidly inside. The car had stopped running and when Livy's quaking hand turned the key, the engine did manage to start. She tried to feel whether the heater still worked.

It wouldn't matter anyway. The interior of the car was quickly filling with gas fumes. The blow to the back end must have damaged the exhaust system.

She immediately stopped the engine. Opening the door to breathe some cleaner air, Livy's face was stung by little ice-blades and the freezing cold. She leaned out and looked down to see several jagged rocks jutting up through the snow below. There was no way to jump without further injury. A growl of metal against rock sounded as the car began to lean precariously toward the driver's side. Livy didn't have time to completely close the door. The rocks did it for her in rough and ruthless fashion as the car slammed down on its side upon them, catching a good portion of her hair in the jammed door and giving her what felt like a good swift kick in the face and shoulder. The seat back suddenly jerked forward and locked; her right arm was pinned between her chest and the wheel. She could barely breathe. The point of a sharp rock protruded through the shattered window just an inch or two from her face and it was edging its way further in as the side of the car settled down upon it.

Her quivering was now uncontrollable as the very real possibilities of more injury or freezing to death loomed before her. She was quite sure the car was not visible from the interstate above. Probably half an hour had gone by, and no other vehicles had passed in sight. This remote exit most likely didn't get much traffic at any time, let alone in a blizzard.

Nurse Betsy had said what a great thing it was that she had awakened and wouldn't miss Christmas. Now she would miss it, but no one would miss her. No one knew where she was or what her destination had been.

With half a hopeless smile, she remembered Fitz talking about nearly missing Christmas last year.

Kyle had accidentally locked himself in his private office restroom on Christmas Eve. His phone lay ringing on the desk as he settled in to spend Christmas on the floor. Debbie, his wife, along with the church congregation, and his older kids, called his cell, the office, the hospitals, his friends, and the highway patrol, trying to find him. For lack of any other place to try, they finally came into Manhattan for a rescue.

If Livy had been stuck in a bathroom on any one of twenty Christmases, no one would have missed her, she was sure. And now, this Christmas, once again, no one was looking for Olivia Thomas. No one would call the highway patrol or the hospitals.

Wouldn't it be strange, if after all the trials she had overcome and her miraculous recovery, she ended up frozen and forgotten in a snow-inundated ditch in the middle of nowhere in Idaho and only 4.2 miles from her destination? She was utterly helpless and dependent on a miracle. Again! For years and years, she had been out to prove that she didn't need anything or anyone. But now, there was nothing she could do to save herself. She pounded her left fist on the door in anger. The jagged rock inched closer to scraping her immobilized face.

The brooding winter day crowded in upon her, and she felt the temperature dropping fast when the sun abandoned her. Did she, or anyone else at this point, care whether she lived or died? All she would have to do would be to free her hand, start up the car, breathe deeply, and go to sleep. There were worse ways to go. *Let it go. I'll close my eyes and let it all go. What's the point? I can't face the Kimballs. What am I doing here anyway? I'll just free my hand, turn on the car and . . .*

"Ask God how he wants to use you," Bryan had said.

Ask God? Why bother? I don't even care anymore. I just want to die. She struggled to free her hand.

Then it was almost as if she could hear God asking, *Livy, what does it take to get your attention? When will you admit that you need me?*

She answered back aloud, "When will you admit that you've forsaken me? My whole life you've left me to struggle and suffer alone. Where were you then? Where are you now?"

It wasn't much of a prayer. She really didn't know how to pray, but that if she was going to have this conversation, she had better learn. She began again, a little more humbly and shaking in complete panic. She did want to live!

Please God, I have no one left to turn to, no way to help myself. You win. You win! So I hope that if you are there, you will hear me and if you care, you'll save me. I know that I've been rebellious and almost hated you at times because of my childhood. I've been so angry at you for taking away everyone I ever loved until I felt I could never risk caring again. Then Bryan helped me to love, and now he too is gone. The kids are out of reach. Garrett's moved on. Mel and all he meant to me . . . gone. She softened somewhat. *Bryan said to acknowledge your hand in everything in my life, but that's not quite the same thing as blaming you, is it? Please God, forgive me; don't hate me. If you save me now, I'll have to acknowledge your hand in it. Is there a reason to stay? If you show me the way, I will try to follow. Can you forgive my sins and my anger and ease my pain? Jesus saves. Can He save me now? Please, dear God, one way or the other, save me, rescue me, please. Whether in heaven or on this earth, save me, please God. I want to live, and I want my life to mean something to someone.*

Bryan had said that she had to have the faith to say what she said next. And at last, she surrendered with these words . . . Jesus' words: *"Not mine, but Thy will be done. Thy will be done. In Jesus' name I pray, amen."*

Still, no cars appeared on the road. But she was beginning to calm down and was almost resigned to her possible fate. As two hours passed, the temperature continued to fall. Her hands and feet were numb, and yet she was not afraid; she was somehow at peace. Her weak body's response to the cold was a desire for sleep. When she could fight it no longer, she surrendered to its call. After a time, she was aware of being warm and free and felt herself being drawn up and away from the frigid car and toward a wonderful world of light and love.

Chapter Twenty-five

Suddenly, the screeching of a saw cutting away at the metal of the passenger door above her shattered the peaceful silence. She was freezing again.

"Hang on," the big man called out. "We're almost there." Grating and growling sounds of the metal door being wrenched from its hinges followed. The stranger reached down to her but couldn't pull her out because her hair held her fastened to the door. He pulled himself up and out, and called to his son, "Clayton, get that rope from the back of the truck and start on the winch, and Jackson, you get Josh out here with the pocket knife from the glove box."

In a few moments, a little boy of about six or seven descended toward her, face first, while his dad held him by the feet. He held the open knife in his hand.

"Hi, I'm Josh," he said as casually as if they had met in the park in spring.

With that, he began hacking away at her hair with the same stylistic finesse he used on the sheep he regularly sheared. When she was freed from the door, he reached down and found the seat belt release and the seat back recline lever. The chair bolted violently backwards and so did Livy. Smiling, Josh ascended back up and out of the door hole as quickly as he'd come. Clayton was busily tying the rope around the frame of the car door while Jackson hooked up the winch. Soon the car was abruptly hauled up from the ditch. The father reached in and pulled Livy from the ravaged vehicle and carried her toward the truck. In route, she felt a sudden wave of nausea overtake her, and she quickly turned to her right and vomited on the uncut side of her hair and all over the stranger's boot.

"Thank you," she murmured, barely conscious. "I mean, I'm sorry."

"That's all right. I'm just glad we found you before you froze to death. I'm Jake Kimball, by the way."

"I knew you were; you had to be." Livy smiled weakly. He was just as Bryan had described—a large man with large hands, a weather-worn face, and a deep friendly voice. Under his stocking cap, she could see wisps of graying blonde hair. She said, "I'm Olivia."

"I knew you were; you had to be," Jake repeated. Livy dared to hope that Bryan had told them something about her but couldn't imagine how they knew she was here. She was too weak to ask.

Jackson bundled up the rope and put away the saw, attached a bandana to the mangled car, and climbed into the cab. Jake got Livy into the backseat, laying her across the bench with her head on little Josh's lap and covering her with a blanket. Clayton reached into the backseat of the car, got her purse, and brought it to her.

"She stinks like barf, Dad," Josh said and wrinkled up his slightly reddened little nose.

"You've stunk like that a few times yourself, Bucko," Jake said with a laugh as he took some snow and cleaned off his boots. He started for the driver's side. Then he turned his head to Livy and asked, "Do you think you need to go to the hospital?"

"No hospital, please. I've been there, done that. Please, could you just take me to your house?"

"Sure thing, but my son David, who's just graduated from med school, is home for the holidays, and we'll have him check you out. If he says hospital, you'll go, okay?"

Livy nodded, and they began the drive to the Kimball farm.

Proceeding carefully, the truck labored up the snow-bound country road and finally reached the long driveway leading to the charming old farmhouse. "We're home now, Olivia. Don't try to walk. We'll get ya inside."

With considerable effort she sat up and marveled at the little winter wonderland before her. She must be dreaming of heaven again. Icicles hung like stalactites from the gingerbread trim around the veranda of the stately old house. The icicles encased the Christmas lights and provided a misty prism for Christmas colors to shine through. The magical aura reflected onto the frosted trees and the bushes in holiday splendor.

Marilee Kimball held the door open while Jackson carried Livy into the house.

"So you found her, then?" Marilee commented on the obvious. She was wiping her hands on her apron.

She was just as Livy had pictured her in some ways: she was dusted with flour from Christmas baking, she exuded mothering and caring, but she bore no physical resemblance to Bryan at all. She had dark hair with a few strands of white in it, dark eyes, and a light brown complexion. Bryan must have taken after his blonde, blue-eyed father.

Jake answered, "Yeah, we found her in that ditch by the freeway exit—and not a moment too soon. She's dipping into hypothermia. We'd better—"

"Let's get her into a tub of warm water," Marilee suggested.

"First, let's let David look her over."

David, the eldest son, who was married, a father of one, and about to start his internship in Seattle, stepped up and examined Livy. After checking her vital signs and examining her as best he could, he explained that she mostly needed warming, food, and rest. From what he could tell, going back outside onto questionable roads in freezing weather in search of an emergency room was definitely not what the doctor would order.

Livy was vaguely aware of Jackson carrying her into the bathroom off the main hallway. Marilee was already filling the tub.

"Sweetheart, come and give me a hand with her, would you please?" Marilee called to the beautiful dark-eyed teen watching from the hall. She must be the "gorgeous one" with the cruel tongue that Bryan had talked about. She'd been with them since deciding to give up her baby for adoption. Her parents had thrown her out, and the Kimballs had taken her in.

With very little of Livy's own power, mother and daughter managed to get her out of the blanket and her wet cold clothes down to her underwear. They helped her to step into the warm water that felt scalding hot to her frozen flesh. She gasped at its sting. Gradually they helped her sit and lie back while they gently massaged her limbs. After a few moments, the burning subsided, and she was able to relax.

All the while, Marilee cooed a soothing banter of comforting phrases as if bathing a baby. "This should help you feel better. There now, let's give those pretty little toes a rub and get them nice and warm. Now, how's that feel? Are you doing all right?" She filled in the gaps with soft humming.

Livy's proud, independent nature resisted the helplessness and humiliation of being treated like a baby. But the humble, wounded inner child drank it in. Marilee then, careful not to get shampoo in her eyes, gently washed and conditioned Livy's ravaged hair.

"Honey, stay with her a moment. I'm going to find her some pajamas," Marilee said to her daughter.

She helped Livy to stand up and dry off, and Livy ventured, "You're Becky, right?" The girl nodded in bewilderment and Livy explained, "I knew your brother, Bryan, in New York. He called you the gorgeous one."

"You knew Bryan? That's what he said? After all the awful things I called him—he called me the gorgeous one? What else did he tell you?"

"Well, just that you were hurting pretty badly at the time."

"I was hurting but that was no excuse for how I treated him. When you hurt someone like that, over and over and then they die . . . it feels just awful. Especially someone like Bryan," Becky said.

"He'd forgiven you, long ago. I could tell. Imagine how *I* feel—"

Just then, Marilee returned with green flannels in hand. "Here you go, Olivia. You can put these on."

Soon, Livy was warmed, bathed, clothed, and coiffed. (Becky had helped her even out Josh's sheep-shearing job on her hair.) She was seated in a large easy chair facing the fire. The room, the whole house she supposed, was like the headquarters of Christmas Inc. The old parlor had very high ceilings, allowing for a tall, full, ponderosa pine, which smelled divine. On it was every kind of ornament imaginable, from the very classy to the child's handmade masterpiece. Loads of presents, many obviously wrapped by child hands, surrounded it. The other smells of the season wafted through the air: fresh baked gingerbread, the smell of the fire and something else . . . soup!

Marilee pushed through the swinging dining room door with a tray of soup, crackers, orange slices, and chamomile tea. "There's nothing better when you've come in from the cold. Don't you think so?"

She laid the tray over Livy's lap.

"This is wonderful, just perfect. Thank you," she replied lifting her cup to take a sip of tea. "I'm sorry to be a bother."

Jake and three very tall older boys came barreling into the room in full wrestling mode. One of the guys, probably Clayton, if she guessed right, was up on the back of the biggest one, Jackson, not jousting, but trying to take him down. Without warning, Clayton went flying up and over Jackson and above the couch and landed on his back on the bean-bag chair right next to Livy's feet. The thud rattled the entire room and shook the Christmas tree. Livy steadied her soup and her tea but was not surprised by what she saw. She had been warned. She could imagine a bouncing Bryan right in the thick of the roughhousing.

"Boys! This is neither professional wrestling nor the NFL. You could have spilled that hot liquid all over her. Save your tackling for the football field. Now stand up and introduce yourselves to Olivia," Marilee lovingly scolded.

Jackson was suddenly all chivalry and honor. With a hand on his heart he said, "Jackson Kimball, m'lady, at your service." He came around and knelt at her feet. He gestured to his brothers. "And these are my knaves, Clayton the bold and Stewart the dweeb."

"Sit down, boys. I'm sorry," Jake said, "I should have calmed them down before I brought them in. They really are good guys, though, trust me." He sat down in a big recliner to the left of the couch.

"Oh, I know they are." She finally asked, "How did you know who I was and how to find me?"

"Our neighbor, Ray Proctor, called and said that he had met you in Pocatello and you were on your way here. He said you seemed terrified of the storm, and he was concerned about you. He and Wendy didn't even try to make it home and so he called from a motel and asked if you got here all right," Marilee explained. "When you still hadn't arrived after a couple of hours, we were very worried."

Livy was incredulous. "He was *concerned* about me? You were *worried?* And you came out in that blizzard mess after me like the Red Cross! Is everyone in Idaho this nice? I'm just a stranger."

Jake smiled and shook his head. "Not anymore. After all, you upchucked on my boots, so you're practically family. And you can't get much stranger than this crowd, right, guys?"

Livy looked around the room, which had gradually filled with Kimballs of varying ages, sizes, and races, already dressed for the family Christmas pageant. Becky shepherded Sarah and Leslie, dressed as angels, and Elizabeth in her biblical garb, into the room. Little Sarah went over to sit on the floor beside Livy and laid a friendly hand on her arm.

David and his wife, Pam, proudly held up their six-month-old, William, wrapped in "swaddling clothes."

"We've got the Baby Jesus. Doesn't he look great?" Pam bragged.

He was an adorable little boy with fat pink cheeks, curly chestnut hair, and twinkling brown eyes. They'd bundled him up in a snowsuit and then wrapped him in ace bandages. The fat little mummy wiggled and wrangled 'til he managed to get his little arms free.

Livy knew all their names and their stories. The curiosity in the sea of eyes made it clear that they wanted to know her story and how the infamous doll-lady had ended up in their living room.

Elizabeth, a ten-year-old already dressed as Mary for the family Nativity, and according to Bryan, suspicious of everyone until trust was built, voiced the thoughts of all when she faced Livy and asked pointedly, "Well?"

"You're Elizabeth, aren't you? I can tell."

"I know who I am, but I'm asking about you."

That was Elizabeth all right. Strawberry blonde and one tough cookie. Bryan thought that she would grow up to be either a lawyer or an interrogator for the FBI. She was a no-nonsense kind of kid, and Livy knew she'd better answer, or else.

She felt too weak and tired to go into it all at this moment, but there they were, waiting for an explanation. She took a deep breath and asked, "Didn't *he* tell you about me?" They gave her confused stares.

She sighed with tired trepidation and searched for the right way to begin. Why had Bryan told her, "They love you already" when he hadn't said a word?

Marilee intervened. "We don't have to give her the third degree. She's been through a lot. Maybe she just needs to get some rest. We can talk in the morning." She stood up to help Livy upstairs. "Boys, go get the barn ready for the Nativity." And gesturing to the little twins, she asked, "How about my wise men? Have you got your props?"

The boys reluctantly started for the door.

Elizabeth pressed on. "She can tell us why she's here, and then she can rest."

Marilee looked at her with embarrassment and scolded, "Leave her alone. You're being rude."

"It's okay," Livy said. "Elizabeth is right. I probably won't be able to rest until I explain myself."

Now the little detective *was* suspicious. "Explain what? And how do you know my name?"

"I know all your names. I know all about you."

"What's her name?" Elizabeth gestured to Sarah.

"That's your newest sister, Sarah, from Ethiopia. And that's Michael and Leslie . . ."

Elizabeth gasped, "Mom, she's a spy. Why does she know all about us?"

"She's not a spy and . . ." Marilee began but seemed a little nervous, herself.

"Well?" Elizabeth tapped her foot.

"It's because of Bryan . . . I met him in New York. He never mentioned me in a phone call or anything?"

"Bryan? No, don't think so. We heard from him quite often when he was in New York, but he didn't tell us much about what he was doing. He mostly was homesick and wanted us to tell him what was going on at home," Jake said.

"I know I must have offended him all those times I tried to brush him off. I've shut most people out for years, but Bryan would not give up."

"Maybe he just forgot to tell us. He could practically forget his name sometimes," said Marilee.

Livy glanced at Becky who looked away.

"Anyway, I never met anyone like him. I resisted being friends with him at first, like I always do, but he was persistent and he made me love him. I felt like he was my little brother."

Jake interjected, "You know, a lot of people told us they felt that way. So you knew our Bryan?" He shook his head and smiled. "I'm sorry, you two just seem like an unlikely pair."

"I know this may sound strange, but he sort of *adopted me* as part of the family."

"Now *that* sounds just like Bryan."

"I never had much of a family, and Bryan convinced me I could be part of his. He told me all about you—how you open up your hearts and your home. He made you all so real. But now he's gone, and after all I've been through lately, I don't know, I just *had* to come. I didn't have anywhere else to go."

She looked to their faces. Jake was still smiling, so she continued. "I thought maybe I could belong here. I know this sounds so stupid and that I should have called first. But I just needed to be here for Christmas. I'm sorry . . . I couldn't bear it if you told me not to come . . ." She broke down. "I'm so sorry!"

Sarah was all angel now and flew to Livy's arms. "Sure you can come!" She hugged the daylights out of the newcomer. "You can come for Christmas or anytime you want!"

"If Bryan said you're family, you're family!" Jake said reassuring her. "Of course you can stay with us."

Livy looked to Marilee for confirmation.

"Really," she said, "our home is your home, okay?"

Olivia absorbed the hug and their loving words with a giant sigh of relief, as if all her life she had been holding her breath in anticipation of this moment.

Little Sarah put her hand on her head to offer Livy her halo. "You can be an angel, too! You can wear my costume."

Livy's tears turned to laughter. "I don't think it would fit, but I can't wait to see you little cherubs do your part." She replaced Sarah's halo. The hug had left it hanging over one ear.

"Well, okay then," Elizabeth pronounced as she joined in the hugging.

They were letting it all sink in when some sudden crashing and banging upstairs broke the spell.

"Mom!" yelled Josh and Jesse from the upstairs hall. "We can't find the Frankenstein and Fur!"

Marilee got up from the couch, laughing. She called back, "That's Frankincense and Myrrh. I think it's in the costume closet in the basement. Jake, could you go help them get ready?"

Jake escorted the bigger boys out the door. After listening to them tromping down the back stairs, Marilee turned to look thoughtfully at Livy. "So . . . *he* didn't send you?" she asked quietly.

"What?" Livy asked absently, as she tried to wipe up the soup that Sarah's excited hug had spilled in her lap.

"Nothing," Marilee said unconvincingly. "Never mind."

Just then, from the porch, there arose the clatter of eight heavy winter boots prancing across the wooden planks. As they trooped in, Jackson announced in a voice big enough to be heard by all the ears in the sizeable family and probably those in the neighboring farms as well, "The barn's ready. Let's get this show on the road!"

Elizabeth, sure that now Livy was one of them and could be trusted, jumped to her feet and pulled up her blue robe to reveal her little red legs. "See?" she confided. "I have to wear my long underwear and my snow boots underneath. Can you be my lantern partner?"

Livy looked puzzled and Marilee explained. "We make our procession to the stable in Bethlehem, otherwise known as the barn, and the little ones pair off with an older child to help them carry their lanterns." She turned back to the girls. "Sorry, my little darlings, but I don't think it's a very good idea for Olivia to go back out in the cold just yet. We'll leave her right here snuggled up by the fire until we get back."

"Oh no, you won't!" Livy said. "I didn't come all this way to miss the most important part of Christmas. I'm going out there even if it means coming down with pneumonia in the morning! I'm really feeling stronger and more alive than I have for a very long time."

Marilee snagged Leslie by the sleeve. "Run and get those rice bags you made me last year and put them in the microwave. Becky, get the comforter off your bed and Bethie, get the knitted hat Grandma made you." Off they all went to do as they were told, and Marilee shrugged her shoulders and turned to Livy. "All right. I guess you're coming by popular demand. Boys, go set up that old barn heater. We'll be ready in a little bit."

She got up and walked Livy into the adjoining den. Then she went to the other door and called, "Jake, could you put Jackson in charge of the pageant and then come in here? We need to talk with Olivia for a moment." Now that Marilee had Livy alone, she said, without turning to look at her, "Please, Olivia, tell me the truth." She sighed. "Was it really because of Bryan that you came?"

Livy was completely confused. No one even knew she was here. "Why else would I be here?"

Marilee turned and studied Livy for a few moments. She tried again, shaking her head. "It's just so strange . . . that someone like you and someone like my sweet Bryan . . . please . . . You're sure *he* didn't send you here?"

"He? Who? Why is it strange?"

Satisfied that Olivia was not holding anything back, Marilee led her to the couch. Then she reached for one of many scrapbooks on a bookshelf. She sat down, inhaled deeply, and opened an album of Kimball baby pictures on Livy's lap. The very first page took Livy's breath away. It was the contest-winning photo—it was Hannah.

Chapter Twenty-six

"*You* sent in the winning picture? *You* rigged the contest? I can't believe for one second that *you* were involved in blackmailing Joy."

"I took that picture, but I didn't send it in. However, I know who did. The only other person that had a copy was Carlos Sotomayor. Does that name mean anything to you?"

"Mr. Jameson mentioned that name," she answered cautiously.

"As soon as the scandal broke, I knew Carlos was behind the thefts and the phony charities and everything else. I knew exactly what had happened and how he had blackmailed that woman. The contest was the perfect opportunity, a scam made in heaven—or hell, more likely—just for him. I also knew Joy Jameson was behind the rumor that it was your child, and she blamed you to cover her tracks."

Marilee's anger and frustration were almost palpable. "I *wanted* to come forward right away, but I was afraid. Carlos once promised me he'd kill me if I got in his way. Believe me, he tried. I was afraid for my family—and for her," she said, nodding at the picture on the page. "Afraid he'd find her and ruin her life too. But I couldn't stand it anymore. All those terrible lies about you, maybe dying in the hospital—another life destroyed by Carlos—I had to tell Mr. Jameson. That much I *could* do."

Livy traced the tiny face with her finger. "It was you? *You* left her at the convent? All of these other children you've taken in; but you left *her* there," she said it so quietly that Marilee almost didn't hear. *Even this "perfect mother" couldn't love me.*

"Everything was so different then. *I* was so different. I don't like to even think about it. I don't want the kids to know the story, at least not until they're older. I only told Bryan a little about it because he asked and asked and—really—it had everything to do with him."

"With Bryan? Please tell me." She tried to keep the resentment she still felt out of her voice.

"I don't really even know you—"

"Please. I have to know." Livy looked up from the photograph and gazed intently into Marilee's troubled eyes. Something about Livy's expression convinced her to go on.

"Back then my name was Marielena Patino—'Patti' to my friends. My best friend was Margarita. She was the baby's mother. But *he* called her Daisy."

The floodgates opened, and Marilee told Livy the whole story. When Marilee shared the part about Carlos's gangs and the story of Margarita's tragic death, she still had to fight back tears.

"Margarita made me promise that Carlos and I would take Linda to her father. I know she believed that if Mel held her, he couldn't help but love her. But he never got the chance. Jameson's wife . . ." She choked on the words as she related the encounter at the mansion.

"Didn't *you* want her?"

Jake, who had come in quietly during the conversation, joined his wife on the couch and put a comforting arm around her shoulders.

She continued. "I loved that little girl so much. Driving back home after that horrid woman—well, I made such lovely plans. I wanted to keep her and be a family. But Carlos had plans too. And his were so awful, so ugly—so horrible—I saw exactly what Carlos had become. The trouble was she was *his* niece, his blood, not mine. I was just his strung-out girlfriend, an addict with a ninth-grade education. What did I have to offer her? Who would listen to me? I knew if I got in his way, he'd kill us both."

"How did you manage to leave her with Carlos in the car?"

"I prayed—harder than I've ever prayed in my life. So it seemed like kind of a miracle when I came upon that lovely little convent and orphanage, and Carlos was sound asleep. I had to leave her in God's hands, not in mine and definitely not in the personal hell Carlos would have given her. Leaving her there was the hardest thing I ever did in my whole life, but it was the only thing I could have done. I took that picture there at the door of the church. When she reached for me like that, I longed to pick her up and give her the world. But I had nothing."

"So you loved her? And her mother loved her?"

"Oh, yes. And her image has stayed with me all these years. That baby, that moment, her cries as I left her, changed my life, saved my soul."

"I promised Linda and myself, that from that day on, I would get ready. I would change, so if ever another child needed me, I would be there for her or him as I couldn't be there for Linda."

Livy felt like she was awakening from a lifelong, confusing nightmare. "But what happened when Carlos woke up?" Livy asked.

"It was hours later, and we were far from the convent. He was furious when I wouldn't tell him where I left her, no matter how much he yelled. He threatened to kill me, but still I wouldn't tell him. He dragged me out of the car and beat me until I was pretty near dead. At first, I think he was going to leave me there to die, but he decided to try again to get the information when I regained consciousness. Carlos carried me to the car and pressed on to hide out in my father's old trailer in Miami. I guess with a windfall of cash and stolen jewelry, he wasted no time in going out to fence the goods and cash in. When he came back, I was afraid he'd finish what he began. But he was too drunk and stumbled into bed. The next few days were horrible. I was too injured to leave and too scared to stay. I think he was waiting for me to be well enough to guide him back to her. Next time he left, I used my dad's dark room there and developed the photos I'd taken at the church. I loved this one. It was so like her." Marilee wiped her eyes.

"So I tucked one of the pictures into Carlos's wallet that he had left on the nightstand. I wanted him to feel something—some shame, I guess. Then I limped a few blocks to the freeway entrance and hitched a ride west. The only thing I could think of was that I'd always assumed my mother had gone to Seattle and maybe I could find her there.

"I got as far as a rest stop in Idaho Falls before I was too sick with drug withdrawals, and too bruised and broken to go any further. Out of money and all out of hope—that's how Jake found me. He took me home to his family. Those kind folks took me in and re-introduced me to God and how the world could be. With His help, they put me back together. It took a couple of years and a whole lot of love and prayer." She laid her head on Jake's shoulder. "Jake took a big chance on me," she said.

Jake kissed her cheek. "It paid off, sweetheart."

Now Marilee was touching the photograph as she continued, "So you see, in a way, she was our first child, and she is definitely the reason we're the family that we are. The reason I am where I am; who I am." Her hand quickly flipped through pages and pages of other little faces. "And these are the fulfillment of my promise to her."

"Bryan told me that Jake had picked you up off the battlefield, but I had no idea," Livy said. Decisively, she got up and locked the door to the room. "I just want to make sure that we get to be alone for just a few more moments."

Livy's face was glowing when she sat back down. "Now it all makes sense. I know why Bryan led me here," she said breathlessly. "I don't know how he knew, but he did!"

Puzzled, Marilee and Jake waited for Livy to go on.

"You left Linda at St. Thomas of Assisi Convent on Christmas Eve all those years ago. You were the one who left a letter and a birth certificate at the convent in case she ever came looking for clues to her past. It was you . . . wasn't it?"

Marilee nodded in astonishment. "How could you possibly know this? Not from Mr. Jameson. When we spoke, he said she never contacted him."

Livy came back around the couch, knelt in front of Marilee, and took both of her hands. "That's because I never told him who I was."

As realization dawned on her, joy flooded across Marilee's face. "You are my Linda?"

"I was Linda *Thomas*—for the saint of the convent. I changed Linda to Olivia after I was in trouble with the law. I wanted a new life and to start fresh."

"My sweet, beautiful little Linda? Let me look at you." With tears streaming down her cheeks, she cupped Livy's chin and studied her face. "I've always dreamed that someday I'd find you again, that I would know you're all right. It's like an answer to a million prayers."

"Mine too. You said you were a totally different person then. But I'm still the same; I'm still reaching," Livy said. And with just a little hesitation, she lovingly reached out for Marilee's embrace. "I'm home. I'm here where I belong."

Marilee pulled her to her feet, and they held each other, weeping.

Livy reached her hand out to Jake. "You know, I've been calling you Mom and Dad for quite a while now."

"It *is* a wonder that somehow Bryan found you and that he brought you to us," Jake said, joining their arms.

"Tell me about your family. What happened to you?" Marilee finally asked.

"Well, I was never adopted. Just lots of foster homes. Some nice. Some not so nice at all. I couldn't seem to fit anywhere. After I found your letter, I went searching for my father. And you know how that turned out."

"Why didn't you tell your father who you were?" Jake asked.

"The timing was never right. I had to prove myself first. And Joy hated me. I was going to tell him anyway but then when he fired me and believed all those lies, it broke my heart."

"Forgive him, Olivia. Tell him. He feels terrible about everything."

"When he told me himself that he'd paid to have me aborted and all, I was glad he didn't know."

Marilee sat back down, overcome with wonder and happiness, and with regret as well. "I'm so sorry, Olivia, my little Linda. I'm so sorry for everything."

Livy sat down beside her. "Sorry? You did the only thing you could do. And you risked your very life to protect me. Now you've taken a big risk for me again." She rested her head on Marilee's lap. "Now I know that I was loved; I wasn't just thrown away."

"*Never* think that. You were loved—by your mother, her aunts, by me—I've never stopped loving you." Marilee rearranged a strand of Livy's hair. "And it was because of you we adopted Bryan. I love you for that too."

"Adopted Bryan? For some reason, I thought that he was your own. I just assumed."

"Oh, no. David and Carolyn were just little when we found Bryan. The daughter of some friends in Idaho Falls was pregnant and thinking about having an abortion," Jake recalled. "She wasn't ready for the kind of responsibility and the expense that a baby like Bryan would bring."

"They were heartsick about it. Naturally, we thought of my promise to little Linda. We begged the girl to let us adopt the baby. She was so relieved, and we were incredibly happy."

Guiding Livy's hand back to the picture, Marilee said, "When Bryan was little, I told him this little girl was his special angel who made sure he got to come to our family. I'd catch him looking at that picture all the time. I can't imagine how he recognized you, but he must have."

"Why didn't he tell me?"

"Hey," Jake said, "I think I have a picture of you together! There was a newspaper clipping in Bryan's stuff from New York. Why didn't I think of that before?"

He jumped up and began rummaging through a stack of papers on a bookshelf. "I stuck it in here somewhere."

Livy's heart leapt. A picture with Bryan—how often in the last few days had she wished for one? Where had Bryan found one? Had it been taken at the gala? She couldn't remember.

Someone had been knocking on the door for a few moments, and Livy finally noticed it consciously when she heard Elizabeth, Leslie, and Sarah asking to come in. Livy got up and opened the door for them.

"Mom and Dad . . . and Olivia . . . we're all ready. We're waiting for you!" Sarah cried excitedly and took Olivia's hand.

Chapter Twenty-seven

In a surprisingly short time, the Kimball family was assembled on the back porch and lined up on the steps with their eight glowing lanterns. Solemnly, the children lifted their lanterns and took the hand of a partner. Elizabeth confidently slid her white-gloved hand into Livy's. "Oh! Look how beautiful!" she whispered.

It was beautiful, indeed. The storm had lifted, leaving behind a picture-postcard winter scene. The star-filled sky was now crystal clear, a full moon shedding light on the soft blanket of sparkling new snow. Jake and Marilee clasped hands and began to sing. The children joined in, and the old melody echoed through the peaceful night.

> Oh come all ye faithful,
> Joyful and triumphant.
> Oh come ye, oh come ye to Bethlehem.

Jake and Marilee settled Livy into a cozy nest in the hay. The Kimball Players had everything ready to go in what seemed like mere moments.

The little cardboard buildings of Bethlehem appeared, and the homemade pageant began. An angel (aka Leslie) appeared in radiant white and called to Mary (Elizabeth). "Behold, you have found favor with God and shall bear a son and call his name Jesus." And little Mary, more Elizabeth than Mary, answered in her usual skeptical way, "Oh yeah? How can this be? I'm not married to a man."

And the little angel answered, "The Holy Ghost will come upon thee and the power of the Highest shall overshadow thee . . . that Holy child which shall be born of thee shall be called the Son of God." And with a touch of reproach, "With God, nothing is impossible."

It was as if Livy was hearing the Christmas story for the very first time. She had never really thought about what an inconvenient baby Jesus was. His mother was young, unmarried, and was engaged to someone who was not the father of her child. How could anyone be prepared for such a responsibility? No one could possibly understand her circumstances.

Elizabeth approached thirteen-year-old Michael, playing Joseph, and she acted out telling him of her baby and pleading with him to believe. He turned his back to her.

What that poor girl must have gone through! What Joseph must have assumed. Mary would be shunned, disgraced, and sent away from everyone and everything she knew. What faith she had, to trust and hope that God had a plan.

He did. The angel came to set Joseph straight.

Next, Joseph led little pillow-stuffed Mary through Bethlehem on a donkey, played by a Shetland pony named Old Zach who struggled and stubbornly pulled backwards, refusing to proceed as Michael directed. Finally, he irreverently bucked Mary off onto the hard ground where she bravely remained, crying softly as Joseph was turned away from every inn and the doors shut in his face. He was told they must seek shelter in a stable (a cow's stall).

Livy could only imagine Joseph's shame at only being able to provide this humble shelter for Mary at the birth of her babe—God's son.

And then again, Livy marveled that this wonderful, glorious child was not welcomed with celebration, but instead, with "no vacancy" signs. *You are not wanted here. There is no room for you.*

Then suddenly the bright-as-daylight milking lamp flashed on shining down from the loft onto shepherds and real sheep huddled fearfully below.

Sarah spoke in her beautiful African (almost British sounding) English. "For unto you, is born this day, a Savior, which is Christ, the Lord. Ye shall find the babe wrapped in swaddling clothes and lying in a manger."

Jackson, the technical director, swung the light up and over to reveal other angels in the loft singing "Glory to God in the Highest."

The "star" then led the angels and the three wise kings, who had joined in the procession, to the stall.

While the attention was focused on the shepherds, wise men, and angels, little Mary had traded her padding pillows for baby Will in the manger. The light shone down on the Holy Family, and Mary beamed at the baby with loving pride. Joseph stood watch nearby. Gradually, the worshippers arrived. "Magi Josh" tripped on Jesse's velvet robe, tossing the Frankincense into the air. Joseph made a nimble catch without ever breaking character.

Elizabeth said, "And I, Mary, pondered these things in my heart. And it was all pretty awesome!"

Livy too pondered these things in her heart, as if they were brand new. The holy child had come—inconvenient, unwelcome, and poor. *Only lowly shepherds and mysterious wise men from faraway lands rejoiced and knelt at the manger. So vehemently did King Herod want this child not to be, that he killed hundreds of babies, newly born, yet to be born, and even those up to two years old. Tiny children, innocent children!*

He knows how I feel. He understands because He's been there and beyond. He did all the wonderful things He did, and yet was still rejected by his own. His own! He was innocent and punished for the guilty. He was the Son of God and still he descended below all human things. He went through it all for us, for me . . . so He would know how I feel. And He suffered and died on the cross so He could take away my sins and my pain and bring me home.

Angel Sarah said, "This is the Christmas story. Let all the world believe."

And Livy did believe—she knew. *How could I, of all people, turn Him away? He just wants what I've wanted all along . . . room in the heart for Him to come, to be welcomed, and to be loved.*

The family concluded by singing a round that Livy had never heard. They sang these words over and over:

> We all shall raise a song of praise
> And sweet Hosannas we'll sing.
> Each knee shall bow and tongue confess
> That Jesus Christ is the King.

And as they sang of knees bending, the family knelt, one by one, forming a circle around the manger where little baby Jesus lay. Livy now felt herself almost unconsciously drawn forward. She knelt right in front of "baby Jesus" and gave him her burdens, her anger, her sins, her gratitude; she surrendered her whole heart.

And then, in his most perfect way, the little baby Jesus reached for Livy, begging her to love Him and to let Him love her. His little arms seemed to ache for her embrace as hers did for him. She gathered him up and hugged him as he pressed his little head against her heart.

In that moment, she felt other, unseen arms around her and a love she'd never experienced before in her life nourishing her, enveloping her, warming her. She would never question God's love or His awareness of her again. Nothing else mattered now. *He* was her father and she was His child.

Starting with Sarah, then Elizabeth, and then all the family members in turn, they linked arms around Livy, and she knew she was truly one of them. She was home.

Christmas morning dawned well before the sun actually rose to touch the sky. At 5 AM Michael yelled, "Let's get the party started!"

Perhaps they needed as early a start as this to tackle Christmas for nineteen! Marilee marched everyone to the kitchen for warm cinnamon rolls and cocoa before the demolition began. Livy knew she still had to do what she had come here to do—to apologize for causing Bryan's death. They didn't seem to be making the connection. But she couldn't spoil Christmas morning. There would be an appropriate time later.

After plugging in the Christmas tree lights, fiddling with the tripod and finding the perfect angle for capturing the pandemonium on video, Jake unleashed the anxious herd.

Santa had brought a mountain of previously loved and newly-polished toys, bicycles, dolls, clothes, and even a couple of massive but serviceable '80's-sized boom boxes, all of which were opened and exclaimed over with wholehearted delight. But the real fun and joy came with opening the presents the kids had found or made for each other. They had found some real treasures at the Youth Ranch Thrift Store and at the Deseret Industries. And, best of all, they had created some homemade masterpieces sure to be treasured (and laughed about) for years to come. Livy remembered Bryan's glee in watching her unwrap his simple gifts.

At last it was time for a newly-created tradition. Weeks ago, from an old hat, each had drawn a name, each to give a gift Bryan might have chosen. These, according to the new tradition, were wrapped in newsprint and distributed by the self-appointed elf, Elizabeth. They were the sweetest of all. There were lots of hugs and laughs as each child explained his gift.

"Wait. There's one more!" Elizabeth proclaimed, triumphantly waving the crudely wrapped box. "It's for Olivia!"

Livy gave Elizabeth's red hair a tousle. "You wrapped me up something? How sweet! You didn't have to do that."

Elizabeth shook her curls. "I didn't do it, honest."

Holding it where Jake and Marilee could see, Olivia ripped away the paper from the lightweight box and totally forgot to shake and guess. She lifted the lid and then stared at the contents in wonder. "How? Where did you get this?"

"I finally found it. I wanted you to have it. Okay with you, Marilee?" Jake asked.

"Sure," Marilee agreed with a smile. "We can make a copy."

Inside was a yellowed clipping from the New York Post. It was a photo taken by the publicity crew that accompanied Livy to the children's shelter event more than a year before. It showed the shelter children, an elegant and polished Livy, stacks of JTC toys, and the volunteer elf with Down syndrome. "JTC executive Olivia Thomas and one of Santa's own elves share Holiday cheer at Harlem's interim care center," read the caption.

"I told you we had one of you and Bryan together," Jake said with a smile.

"I remember this. I remember him. But where's Bryan?"

"He's right there." Jake almost laughed, pointing at the elf.

"That's Bryan?" Stunned, Livy stared at the photograph, a million thoughts bombarding her mind. Desperately she scanned the faces of Jake and Marilee, searching for an explanation. Maybe there was lingering brain damage. "No. That's not my Bryan. He wasn't . . . he was beautiful."

Jake took the clipping from Livy's trembling hand. "Well, that's our son and he was beautiful to us."

Frantically, Livy tried to explain. "I came here to tell you how sorry I was that he died in that accident . . . saving my life." She was confused to the point of dizziness and leaned back." It was my fault he died. But he's not the one."

"Are you okay, honey?" Marilee asked, trying to understand Livy's outburst. "It couldn't be your fault. Bryan didn't die in an accident in New York. He died right here in Blackfoot just days after that picture was taken. He'd just come home. It was December 3 of last year when his big old heart just gave out on him."

"Last year?" Livy practically ran from the living room and into the den, slamming the door behind her. Wildly, she pulled album after album from the shelves searching every family photo for a single one of *her* Bryan. But it was only the sweet and loving face of the elf gazing happily back at her from Disneyland, from an Easter egg hunt, from graduation day, from David's shoulders holding a lance, from all the family group shots, and from the cover of a funeral program.

She collapsed on the couch, held her head in her hands, and tried to understand. *It was real. He was real. He saved my life. He brought me home. How could this be?*

And then she heard his voice as clearly as if he stood at her side. "I told you, Livy. Some of us just take a little while longer to come into our own."

Then the room grew brighter and in the midst of the radiance stood Bryan, as his family and others had known him. But then, his blue eyes never leaving hers, he began to transform into her handsome, wise, and smiling Bryan. But he didn't stop there. His metamorphosis continued until he became a brilliant and magnificent being. Livy found herself on her way to her knees, but he shook his beautiful head of golden hair and said, "No. Save that for God." He reached for her.

Then she was with him in the light; it was like standing in a fire that warmed but didn't burn. "It's really you? Or am I losing my mind?"

"It's me. *And* you're losing your mind," he teased.

"It *is* you. But why would God send an angel to me of all people?"

"You were my angel first. I owed you one. And now, you need to be one again."

"Josie? I have to go back for Josie."

He nodded. "And other things."

"Will I see you again?"

"*See me?* Not for a long time, but I'll never be far away. I promise. I'll always be with you and always love you. It's like your Sister M said. Jesus—and I—will always know where you are."

"Can I go tell the family? They need to see you like *this.*"

He gestured to the doorway behind her, where Jake and Marilee stood mesmerized by what they saw, and he said, "That's just it, Livy. They always have."

He blew them a slow and gentle kiss of farewell and started to fade away. The light gathered around him, and he grew smaller and fainter until he was a little trail of light that disappeared into the air.

"Be not forgetful to entertain strangers: for thereby some have entertained angels unawares."
Hebrews 13:2

Epilogue

Livy returned to New York a few days after Christmas. It was now 7 PM on New Year's Eve. She checked the *Joy of Cooking* book one more time before she removed the turkey from the oven. The legs wobbled and the timer had popped. Done to perfection.

The table was beautifully set with new china and crystal. She lit the long red candles that stood in the center of a nest of pine boughs and holly berries. She had to humbly admit, the place looked and smelled heavenly.

Right at the appointed time, the buzzer sounded from downstairs. "There's a Mr. Garner here to see you, Ms. Thomas," the doorman announced.

On the way to the door, she turned down the lights, put on some low-volume Christmas music, and then checked herself in the mirror. She ditched the apron and smiled in approval. No nervous flutters. No insecure pangs of fear. But when she turned the knob and saw his handsome face again, the familiar quiver raced through her body like a small electric shock.

He carried a bouquet of red roses and wore that wonderful smile of his. She didn't notice the rest. They stood looking at each other for several seconds.

"I'm sorry," he finally said, and handed her the flowers. "These are for you."

"Thank you, Garrett. They're beautiful."

"You look great. I didn't know what to expect. Are you feeling okay?"

"Never ever better," she said. "Come in. Let me put these in water."

He followed her to the kitchen. I'm glad you got my messages—finally. But it's a bit embarrassing. I probably sounded like a frantic nutcase."

She smiled and took his hand. "That's what I liked about them."

She led him to the table and sat him down before a sumptuous-looking and delicious-smelling feast. His face communicated delight and anticipation as he breathed in the aroma.

"You made this all yourself? For me? I never thought of you as someone who spent a lot of time in the kitchen."

She sat down across from him. "I'll confess. Yesterday was a practice run. I worked out the bugs on some kids I know. No casualties so far."

When his first forkful was on the way to its destination, she stopped him and said, "Do you mind if we bless it first?"

They prayed. They ate. They laughed and talked about his kids and how he liked the New York office.

Then, clearing his throat, Garrett said, "So what about you and what's-his-name? Your doorman?"

"You mean Bryan."

"Are you seeing him? What was the deal there?"

"No, I'm not *seeing* him, but he's around." She smiled at the double meaning. "Someday I'll explain it all to you."

Finally, Garrett reached across the table to take her hand. "When Jameson told me you might not make it, I wanted to run from the hospital. After what happened with Shelly, I couldn't face losing you too. I didn't know what would have done if he'd called me with that news."

"Garrett, I'm fine. I'm really more than fine."

"I'm glad. It's so good to be here with you tonight. Thank you for calling me." Something in his eyes told Livy he really meant it.

"I invited you here to tell you I'm sorry for all the times I ran away from you, all the times I didn't trust you."

"Do you trust me now?"

"Wanna see how much?" She squeezed his hand and asked, "Cards on the table?"

He nodded.

She took a deep breath and looked only at their hands. "I love you, Garrett Garner. There. I said it." She raised her gaze to his eyes. "I always have. I just couldn't believe you would love me because I thought no one ever had and no one ever would."

"How could you ever have felt that way? Didn't I beg and plead with you to stay and marry me?"

"I thought I'd lose you like everyone else I ever cared about. It was easier to push you away first."

He came around the table and stood beside her chair. "I loved you all those years ago. I never stopped. Livy, I want to be the one to witness how wonderful you are, every day, for the rest of our lives." He pulled her slowly to her feet, took her face in his hands and gently pressed his lips to hers, igniting a tender passion that had lain dormant and waiting over seven years' time. With his warm breath tickling her ear, he whispered, "Can we try again?"

She could barely breathe. She was dizzy and felt the tingle all down her spine. "Oh, definitely. Let's try that again." She returned his kiss without holding back. Then she kissed his cheek, his closed eyes, his neck, before nestling her head on his shoulder.

He lifted her chin to look into her eyes. "Marry me, Livy. Let's not waste any more time. I never want to leave you." He held her tightly and kissed the top of her head.

It felt so right, so safe, to be wrapped in his arms. "Yes, Garrett, I will. And I promise I'll never run away again."

"I'm going to hold you to it. Now, you know I'm a package deal that includes two children. You're okay with that?"

"Of course, little Mark and Staci. That's great with me," she said, and then started to laugh.

"What's so funny?"

"It's just that I've got quite a package as well. How do you feel about the state of Idaho?"

He gave her a confused smile. "Huh?"

"You'll see." Then her expression changed and she added, "And there's one more thing. There's this little girl. Her name is Josie . . ."

Author's Note

Y ou may have begun this story with the question: who is Hannah? There are far too many painful answers. Hannah is the face of the little girl staring up from a child porn website on the Internet. Hannah is the terrorized and then raped and murdered subject of an *Amber Alert*. Hannahs' are the cries of the boy left neglected, unwashed, and unfed by a drug-addicted mother. Hannah's are the wounds of a child beaten and abused by her mother's latest temporary boyfriend. Hannah is the weapon wielded in a painful divorce to inflict the greatest pain on a now-despised ex-spouse. Hannah is the inconvenient souvenir of a forbidden affair. Hannah is the product of impulse procreation, brought into existence because someone thought it might be nice to have a baby, just as it might be nice to accessorize with matching shoes and purse. With buyer's remorse, shoes and purse go to the Goodwill; the child goes through hell or worse to a trash can, never allowed to breathe.

Hannah is everywhere. Hannahs are legion. Hannah belongs to all of us and reaches out to every heart. Hannah is our future. Hannah is our shame or she can be our opportunity and our inspiration for miracles. She is the clarion call for angels everywhere to open their hearts, their arms, and their homes to just such a child. Will we hear the call?

Resources for Helping Children

The Dave Thomas Foundation: Created by Wendy's icon, Dave Thomas, who was adopted as a young child, the organization is a non-profit public charity dedicated to increasing the adoptions of the more than 150,000 children in North America's foster care systems waiting to be adopted. The Foundation supports signature national programs and strives to simplify the adoption process and make adoption more afford-able for families. Their value statement: "Do what's best for the child."

www.davethomasfoundation.org

Alpine Academy (part of Youth Village): The Village changes the lives of troubled children and families and offers residential care in Treatment foster homes and in group homes. The Village also offers in-home help through Families First, an intensive program that teaches parents valuable skills. Other programs include Parenting For Success classes, therapy, and privately funded higher education grants for Village graduates.

One of the group homes is the Village's Alpine Academy, which provides residential treatment for teenage girls from across the country. Located in rural Tooele County, Utah, Alpine Academy provides a small, family-style environment with an emphasis on individualized treatment and academic excellence using the teaching-family model, the treatment model used in all Village programs. "Help one child, help generations to come."

http://www.youthvillage.org

Hope Meadows: Hope Meadows is a unique residential commu-nity—a five-block, small-town neighborhood where neglected and abused children who have been removed from their biological parents for their safety, find a permanent and caring home, as well as grandparents, playmates, and an entire neighborhood designed to help them grow up in a secure and nurturing environment. Hope Meadows is a place where children, adoptive parents, and surrogate grandparents develop supportive relationships capable of healing the hurts of abuse and neglect—a place where three generations care for and learn from each other.

www.generationsofhope.org

Idaho Youth Ranch: The Idaho Youth Ranch provides troubled children and families a bridge to a valued, responsible, and productive future. To this end, we help each child find the hope, vision, courage, and will to succeed. We provide stability, opportunity, and security. We encourage growth and offer a chance to develop confidence, independence, esteem, and respect. We teach values, responsibility, and self-discipline in honest, caring environments. We believe in family, work, accountability, education, and responsible behavior. We are a catalyst for change.

www.youthranch.org

Foster Care Alumni of America: FCAA successfully advocates for opportunities for people in and from foster care, working toward improvements in practice and policy in child welfare. We build the capacity of our members and the foster care system through our strength in numbers and our deep expertise gained by experience.

www.fostercarealumni.org

Discussion Questions

1. What would you say is the central theme of *Hannah's Reach*? How are dolls, turkeys, "elves," and Hannah's photo symbolic of that theme?
2. Do you think it's just poor babies who are the problem? But what does Mel show us about morality and inconvenient children for the classes?
3. What is the book saying about foster care, positive and negative? Adoption?
4. Are youth being taught how to handle the consequences of a sex life or merely how to handle a condom? "Sex is like nuclear power." How?
5. How did you feel about Bryan's symbolism after you read the ending? How is he a metaphor for God working in our lives?
6. The ending (the Idaho experience) is also meant to be symbolic of blessings that will come to children who perhaps never were loved in this life. Will God make it right in the next? Will he prepare a loving, nourishing place for those children? What symbols do you see in the Idaho experience?

About the Author

Eileen Snow is the wife of Ed Snow, a mother of three children, and a servant of three yorkshire terriers. Eileen has lived from coast to coast and currently resides in the Rocky Mountains, but her heart remains in Virginia.

She studied musical theatre at Brigham Young University and has been a professional performer, educator, music teacher, and published composer. Her love of working with children and interest in foster care and adoption issues led to her writing *Hannah's Reach*.